# Fading

## BY

## CINDY CIPRIANO

FADING
Copyright ©2018 Cindy Cipriano
All rights reserved.
Printed in the United States of America
First Edition: April 2018

WWW.CLEANTEENPUBLISHING.COM

SUMMARY: Seventeen-year-old Leath Elliott lives with her mother. After her father was killed in an accident, her best friend Victor has looked out for her. But the friendship changes when Victor starts to have deeper feelings for her. If that wasn't complicated enough, newcomer James Turner shows up...an emancipated minor with a dark past, Leath wonders if he might be the boy of her dreams—literally.

ISBN: 978-1-63422-287-7 (paperback)
ISBN:978-1-63422-286-0 (e-book)
COVER DESIGN by: Marya Heidel
TYPOGRAPHY BY: Courtney Knight
EDITING BY: Cynthia Shepp

COVER ART
© JEFUNNE / FOTOLIA

Young Adult Fiction / Romance / Paranormal
Young Adult Fiction / Fantasy / Contemporary
Young Adult Fiction / Magical Realism
Young Adult Fiction /Paranormal, Occult & Supernatural

FOR ANDREW

I wanted to touch him.

So I did.

He was light. He was air. He was gone.

The edges cracked and crumbled. The center melted, and I woke up enveloped in peace. I could still smell him, a musky, woodsy scent. I closed my eyes to see him again. Tall and strong, but gentle in the way he touched me.

He loved me. I was sure of it. I knew this even though he had never told me.

I knew this even though we had never met.

As the years passed, I was certain I had never seen the boy in my waking hours. Yet, he was there each night in my dreams, as desperate for me as I was for him. I fell asleep listening, waiting for him to call out, and when I heard his beautiful voice, I ran to him.

Maybe this time.

His hand waited for mine. I stretched my arm in anticipation. A wisp of air passed between our fingertips, and he was gone.

# 1

## *Emancipated*

THE FIRST TIME I HELD HANDS WITH VICTOR SANTANA, it wasn't romantic. Not at all. We were twelve years old, shooting hoops at his house, when the ring finger on my left hand banged tip-first into the basketball. Victor's father, Will, had been there instantly. He probed my finger, explaining it was jammed, not broken. Will instructed Victor to hold my other hand while he reset my throbbing finger.

Victor looked uncomfortable and unsure as he tenderly folded his hands around mine. The warmth of his touch soothed me. He gently stroked the back of my hand, distracting me until a sharp tug dislodged my finger, causing me to cry out in pain. In that moment, my eyes had locked with Victor's. I'll never forget how scared he looked or the worry in his warm brown eyes.

The second time Victor's hand found mine was two years later at my father's funeral.

Mom had been in near hysterics by the end of the service, and I'd been quietly checking out. Slipping away from my terrible grief, my mother, my life. Victor's strong hand cradled mine, and he became my tether to reality. Since that day, it had been nothing for him to

3

take my hand. And, really, it meant nothing.

Until last month.

Our junior year in high school was nearing the halfway mark. We were hanging out at our lockers on the Friday afternoon before Christmas break. Victor was getting the details of a history assignment he'd missed when he'd been out with the flu. I was bored and began daydreaming, as I often did, about going to college and finally leaving Woodvine, North Carolina.

Victor's hand casually slipped into mine, non-verbally asking for my patience. I reined in my restless thoughts, allowing his tether to pull me back. I looked at our hands, amazed as always by the beautiful contrast of our skin. His golden bronze against my porcelain white.

It hit me then.

Although I planned to leave Woodvine as soon as humanly possible, Victor and I hadn't talked about what *we* would do after high school. Would we go to the same college? The same city? State? A moment of panic seized me.

*What would I do without him, his gentle touch, and his calm spirit?*

My eyes found a multicolored poster on the bulletin board beside us. Stark white letters against the background grabbed my attention.

Sign up for a college cruise today!

College cruises were the campus tours the PTA scheduled for rising seniors. I'd make sure Victor and I signed up for a few together. Maybe we would find a university we both liked. We had to. I couldn't remember a time Victor wasn't in my life, couldn't even conceive of what his absence would be like. One thing was certain—I wouldn't do well on my own without him. I sighed and rested my head on his shoulder.

The effect was immediate.

Victor's body tightened, alerted by my closeness. He stood taller. As if he'd done it a thousand times before, his hand released mine and moved to my waist.

I should have seen it coming.

Right after my break up with Kevin Green, Victor had begun to look at me differently and it made me feel... what? Warm? Wanted? Truthfully, it made me feel a little self-conscious. Victor's feelings seemed to be shifting from a big-brother, best-friend type of love to something more.

When we were alone in the hallway, Victor turned to me, his arm still around my waist. "What brought that on?" he asked in his heavy Spanish accent.

"Don't know," I answered honestly. "Just felt right, I guess."

"Well, I'm not going to argue." Victor smiled then kissed the top of my head.

And with that, we were a couple.

Of sorts.

On one hand, it was a natural progression. We'd been a part of each other's lives for so long it was only logical we'd end up together. When I was younger, I'd often fantasized about dating Victor. A sappy middle-school fantasy that still haunted me. White rose petals against the green grass of a sunny day, and the image of Victor smiling, waiting for me at the altar. It was a childish daydream. Nonetheless, with every passing year, it seemed Victor and I were destined to be together.

On the other hand, our accidental couple-hood made Christmas awkward. I felt additional pressure to be with Victor—my boyfriend—instead of Victor—my friend—during most of our winter break. As hard as I tried, that I-had-to-be-with-him-or-I'd-just-die feeling wasn't there. I couldn't force it, couldn't will those feelings into existence.

Midway through break, things became stiff and disjointed between us. Before long, I surrendered to the obvious. As much as I loved Victor, I was not in love with him. At least I didn't believe I was. I'd never been in love before, so I had no idea how it felt.

Maybe if our getting together had been more organic, if we had taken the time to move from friendship to dating, but we hadn't. The ugly truth stared me in the face. I just didn't feel the way I thought a girl should feel about her boyfriend, and everything was closing in on me.

When we exchanged gifts on Christmas Eve, Victor surprised me with a silver heart on a delicate chain. I thought about the impersonal gift card I had gotten for him before deciding it was time to have *the talk*.

Victor insisted on speaking first. I waited, clutching the necklace in my hand, eager for the opportunity to return it.

"Keep it, Leath," he said, as if reading my mind. "And I hope you'll wear it. I got it for you months ago. Before we even started..."

"Dating?" I prompted.

"Is that what we're doing?" he asked with an amused expression on his face. Victor took the necklace from my hand and motioned for me to turn around. "I love you, Leath. You know that. Always have, always will."

I felt his warm fingertips graze my neck as he fastened the clasp. Drawing in a deep breath, I turned to face him. His dark eyes found mine and held me there. Victor was close, a few inches separating us from what might have been our first kiss. One I wasn't sure I wanted. I shifted away from him, but he pulled me closer. His warm lips brushed against my ear as he whispered three little words.

"I can wait."

There had been no further discussion about our status, which was fine with me. Over the next few days, things returned to normal. I was thankful the whole experiment had taken place during Christmas break because there were no witnesses to our fiasco.

I thought about all of this, waiting in line outside of the guidance office on our first day back at school. When the warning bell rang, everyone else scattered to class. I checked my watch and decided a tardy would be worth it. There was no way I was going to be stuck in Advanced Colonial Studies. Now, the only one in line, I crossed the threshold of the small office.

An enormous brown desk swallowed up most of the floor space, a wooden pew serving as a bench before it. There were no windows. Dingy white paint coated three of the four walls. Nearly every inch of the fourth wall was covered in triangular-shaped pennants from dozens of colleges and universities. A tarnished brass plate read, *New Homes of Former Students.*

I paused in the doorway, remembering the last time I'd been in this office. It was freshman year—my first day back at school after my dad had been killed. The guidance counselor was new, his inexperience evident in the way he awkwardly consoled me, handing me a tattered leaflet about grief. I quickly put the memory out of my head as I took the two steps necessary to stand in front of the desk.

"I need to change my schedule," I announced to the guidance secretary.

Mrs. Wakely was as round as the moon. Her chair groaned against the weight of her large bottom as she turned to face me. "Who doesn't?" she asked, clearly overwhelmed by the stacks of yellow schedule cards on her desk. "It's going to take me all day to sort these changes. No one will ever be able to find any of you kids." She sighed and held out her hand. "Okay. Let's see it."

"I don't know why I was assigned Advanced Colonial Studies," I said, handing my schedule card to her. "I signed up for Life Skills."

Mrs. Wakely typed something into her computer. "Leath Elliott. Yes, here you are. Well, Leath, it appears you didn't return your registration form on time. Life Skills fills up fast. You were put into Advanced Colonial Studies because it was all that was left."

"But there's got to be something else. I don't need another history credit." I smiled and tried to look deserving. Anything had to be better than Advanced Colonial Studies. *Advanced* Colonial? Was I the only one who found that ironic?

Mrs. Wakely stared at the computer screen, and a flash of recognition crossed her face. She must have remembered I was "that girl." The poor thing who'd lost her father. Almost three years later, and people still didn't know what to say to me. She looked at me sympathetically. "Well, we are looking for more office helpers."

"Perfect. Sign me up." At the last possible second, I added, "Please," and smiled again.

Mrs. Wakely pulled one of three pencils from her beauty pageant-styled hair and scribbled a note.

I speculated about what else she stored in that massive bird's nest.

"You can work with me. Give this to Ms. Babbitt. She'll take your name off her roster, and I'll see you seventh period."

"Thanks." I snagged the note, and then hurried to class.

I thought I'd learn all sorts of dark secrets as an office helper, but I was wrong. In a town this small, there just weren't any secrets to uncover. My job in guidance turned out to be a glorified study hall. There were only two good things about the arrangement. I got a head start on my homework, and I enjoyed the freedom of extended bathroom breaks.

On Tuesdays, I counted out copies of the school newspaper, *The Viking Chronicle* for every homeroom class. Although I doubted anyone actually read it. On Fridays, I was assigned the important task of putting handouts in teachers' mailboxes. I spent the rest of the week cooped up in the suffocating office with Mrs. Wakely and nothing to do.

By Valentine's Day, I had settled into a routine. I wasn't a fan of the holiday, somehow never being involved with a boy on that date. My thoughts drifted to Victor. I wondered if we'd still be a couple if I had given our relationship half a chance. As it was, all February fourteenth meant to me was there were only three more months left of school.

I was counting down the minutes to the end of the day as I walked through hallways decorated with hundreds of red paper hearts. After I entered the guidance office, I set my book bag on the floor. I slumped onto the pew, retrieving my cell from my bag. The phone was hopelessly outdated and seemed to spend more time on the charger than off. The battery life was down to seven percent. I quickly scrolled through my text messages before it died. Cell phones were taboo at school, but Mrs. Wakely always looked the other way. I thought she was glad I had a distraction. One that kept me out of her giant hair.

"Here are your handouts," Mrs. Wakely said, interrupting my reading of a backlog of texts. She let out a small groan as she leaned across her desk. Her breath smelled of sweet peppermint. Mrs. Wakely had bought a large bag of mini-candy canes on clearance at the wholesale grocery store. From the look of the bag peeking out from a low shelf, she only had about a thousand left.

I reached for the flyers, noticing the red folder on the corner of her desk. I'd been here long enough to know red folders held information about a new student. After paperwork trickled in from other schools, the contents of a red folder were placed into a purple folder. Purple for permanent. And permanent folders were kept in a locked file room. That meant I only had a couple of days to peek inside that red folder. After all, a girl had to find her secrets where she could.

There were eight hundred and fifteen students at Martin High School. On a good year, we'd get one or two students transferring in. Oddly, no one ever transferred out. This reinforced my long-held belief that Woodvine was the final stop on a one-way trip to nowhere.

The last red folder had appeared when Mrs. Wakely was away visiting a sick relative. That folder contained information for Mark Thomas Polder. I'd read Polder's file with anticipation, but was quickly disappointed. He was an average sophomore. Good grades, chess club geek, and history bowl winner. He was the kind of kid who would have been right at home in Advanced Colonial Studies.

Aside from Polder's love of history, the only other secret I'd discovered was Mrs. Wakely's. She was a smoker. She snuck out for her smoke break every day in the middle of seventh period. Right about now.

"I'll be back in a minute." Mrs. Wakely maneuvered her massive frame around the desk. She squeezed through the doorway, leaving me alone with the red folder that practically screamed at me to pick it up.

Naturally, I obliged.

I opened the folder and scanned the pupil data sheet. Name: James Turner. Age: 17. Parents: Emancipated

Minor.

The phrase conjured images of a boy in a mahogany-paneled courtroom, suing his parents for freedom. I flipped through his paperwork and found the legal documents. James *had* been in a courtroom, but not to sue his parents. After both of his parents had died, James petitioned the state to declare himself emancipated.

I glanced at the clock; Mrs. Wakely's break was almost over. I quickly looked for James's schedule card. A pink sticky note on the front of the card gave an enrollment date of the following Monday. My eyes flicked over his schedule. We had third period together and, like me, he had fourth-period lunch. The seconds raced past me as I searched for the photo card, anxious to get a look at him. I found the card, but was disappointed to see all the photos had been scraped off. I guessed that had something to do with his legal status. After I straightened the papers, I returned the folder to Mrs. Wakely's desk three heartbeats before she opened the door.

"It's nearly time for you to go." Mrs. Wakely looked at the red folder before setting her beady eyes on me in silent accusation.

I raised my eyebrows defiantly. In that moment, we both understood neither of us was in any position to tell the other's secret.

Mrs. Wakely picked up James's folder and dropped it into a tall black cabinet. She locked it away with a paperclip-sized key. "You didn't finish counting out the flyers," she noted. "That's okay. The ninth-grade helper can finish on Monday."

The bell sounded, and I grabbed my stuff. I walked out of the office wondering, but not caring, if Mrs. Wakely knew I'd read the file. I searched the hallway for Victor and found him standing by the junior lockers. He was surrounded by giggling sophomore girls who were thrusting handmade Valentine's cards into his hands. I quickly swapped my books with others in my locker, then joined Victor and his entourage.

"Hey, Leathal," he said.

No one else dared to call me that. If they did, I'd have proved them right.

Victor swept me into a bear hug. A couple of the sophomore girls glared at me as they walked away.

"That's really not very nice of you," I whispered, hugging him back.

"What do you mean, love?" he asked innocently. Victor stepped back and straightened his vintage Adidas T-shirt. It accentuated his tall, lean body nicely.

"Flirting with the young ones and then acting like we're a couple."

"We could be a couple," he said, flashing his white teeth. "I'm willing to give it another try. Anytime. Just say the word." He haphazardly shoved the Valentine's cards into his locker.

"You're so funny today, aren't you?" I asked.

While everyone else in Woodvine had no problem dating kids they'd known all their lives, it just didn't work for me. After each break up, there was the unavoidable awkwardness that came from living in a small town. Dating life in Woodvine was claustrophobic and a little incestuous. I decided to give up on it altogether until I was in college surrounded by boys who were not from Woodvine. But, if I were being honest, I'd have to admit I was touched Victor hadn't totally given up on me.

"What can I say? Do I get points for trying?" Victor grabbed a water bottle from his locker and took a sip.

"Uh, no," I said. "If we dated, really dated, we'd kill our friendship. It always happens that way." I took his bottle and pulled a long drink from it.

"It'd be different with us. Don't you think?" Victor

looked into my eyes and saw my answer. "Ah, another time." He wrapped his arm around my shoulder, and we made our way out of the building.

Victor had his own car, something my mom said we couldn't afford just yet. I loved riding to school with him, especially since we didn't have one single class together, not even lunch. I hoped to use my pull with guidance to rectify that for our senior year.

"Anamae says she's going to the Valentine's dance with you," I said as we walked to the student parking lot. Anamae Liano was my closest girlfriend. "You took a chance, didn't you? Asking her the day of the dance?"

"I didn't ask her. She asked me. So, what do you think?" He opened the passenger's side door of his white BMW and waited for me to answer.

"I think you'll have a great time."

"We always do when the three of us go out together. Why don't you come with?" He stood too close, smiling too sweetly, and I almost gave in.

"Because Anamae didn't ask me," I said pointedly. "You go ahead. You guys are perfect for each other."

I almost believed it myself as I slid into the front seat. Victor raised an eyebrow. He walked to the driver's side, climbed into the car, and quickly cranked the engine.

"We're getting a new student," I said, hoping to change the subject.

"Another Polder?" Victor's lips pinched into a smirk.

"No, this one's different. He's an emancipated minor."

"A what?"

"You know, legally on his own. No parents."

"That *is* different," he agreed.

Victor looked for an opening in the endless line of cars. He waved in thanks when Lynn Gray motioned him to go ahead of her. Just another one of his adoring crowd. He entered the line behind a red Nissan truck. I told Victor about James Turner as he inched the BMW toward the exit. He gave me a quick glance when I told him James's parents had died. Fifteen minutes later, we rolled into my driveway.

"Have fun tonight," I said, opening the car door.

"Yeah, yeah." Victor hesitated, as if debating something internally. "Want to go see a movie tomorrow?"

"Can't. I've got to write my weekly English paper." The downside of taking AP classes. Sure, I'd get lots of college credits for later, but it was butt-busting work. Still, I hated telling Victor no. Like me, he was an only child. I knew the loneliness he sometimes felt. "We'll do something next weekend. I promise." Hoisting my bag to my lap, I heaved out of his car. "See you Monday." I slammed the car door shut with a swing of my hip.

Victor gave me a quick wave and drove off.

I got the mail and walked up the hill to our storybook house. Some people thought the steep roofline made the house look haunted, but I loved it. Although the wrought iron trestle did look a bit scary in its current state.

Twisted tangles of blackened vines led the way up to my second-story bedroom, a path Victor had taken many times. Ever since I could remember, he favored using the trellis over the front door. We had sleepovers nearly every weekend when we were younger. But the last time he spent the night in my room clearly signaled the end of our slumber parties.

Victor had come by to check on me after my dad's funeral. When he came into my room, I clung to him as if my life depended on it. And maybe it did. We stood together, my head resting on his shoulder, my arms wrapped around his waist. Victor was patient, holding me there as long as I needed.

"When will it stop hurting?" I'd asked, my voice hitching between sobs.

"I don't know, Leath," Victor had said. "In time, you'll wake up one day to find it hurts a little less than it did the day before. And after more time passes, it won't hurt as much." Victor lifted my face to look at him. "I think there will always be a hole in your heart, but I promise I'll be right here. I'll help you learn how to live around that hole."

I begged Victor not to leave until I fell asleep. He sat on my bed, his back against the headboard, and held my hand until sleep finally found me. This quickly became our nighttime ritual, my falling asleep next to Victor. The warmth of his body gave a silent promise that no matter how I felt, I was not alone in the world.

One night, after I drifted off, Victor accidentally fell asleep beside me. The look on my mother's face the next morning when she opened the door and found us curled up on the bed was one of shock. We were in a mess of trouble. Victor told me later his father had explained to him, under no uncertain terms, that Victor and I were too old to have sleepovers. Over the next few weeks, we had lots of chaperoned time together, but eventually things settled down. Victor and I were once again allowed in each other's bedroom, but we had to go home well before it was time to go to bed.

I knew it was selfish, but I missed those days of having him next to me, my room filled with the smell of him. I missed the peaceful sleep that came so easily to me when I was beside Victor. Peace that almost never came when I was alone. I reconsidered going to the movies with him, but the weight of my book bag nagged me, convincing me I'd be better off doing my homework than possibly leading Victor on.

I unlocked the front door and dropped my bag in the foyer just as our black lab Sam crashed into my legs. He practically broke himself in two, wagging his tail. Sam was a big-hearted, goofy dog, forever stuck in puppyhood. I bent to stroke his head. He licked my cheek before sprinting down the hall to announce my arrival.

I put my key in an alabaster bowl on top of the antique chest Mom had inherited. Most of our furniture shared those two qualities. Antique and inherited. Not one matching piece in the entire house. Somehow, Mom made it work. Right down to the mismatched dining room chairs surrounding the oak table that had once been my great-grandmother's.

"Leath? That you?"

"Yeah." I sighed. *Of course it's me.*

I followed the aroma of simmering onions and peppers into the kitchen. Last year, Mom updated all the appliances to black stainless-steel models, although I didn't know why. She hated cooking, probably because she wasn't very good at it, at least not in the traditional sense. But Friday night meant steak and cheese, and her hoagies were better than any I'd had at the sub shop in Asheville. She'd already prepared the beef slices, so I grabbed some buns from the pantry to put them in the oven to toast.

As soon as I sat down at the kitchen counter, I knew something was up. My suspicion was confirmed when Mom looked at me without a trace of sorrow in her expression. She always said I was my father's daughter. I had his jade-green eyes, full lips, and easy smile. I didn't even get my mother's yellow-blonde hair. Mine was the exact shade of Dad's, a rusty copper color. I knew how hard it was for Mom to look at my face and not see his. But today, only happiness showed in her blue eyes.

"I got a call from an old high school friend. Beth. You remember her, don't you?" Mom asked.

"Sure," I lied. "How is she?"

"Well, she just got divorced, actually. Turns out, he was a real jerk. Anyway, Beth's on the high school reunion committee. She called me about our twenty-fifth reunion." Mom tucked her hair behind her ear before glancing at me hesitantly. "I thought I might go. It's in South Carolina the second weekend in April."

The whole reunion thing was something I couldn't understand. I was itching to graduate and shake off my small town. I wouldn't dream of coming back here for a reunion, or anything else.

"You should go, Mom. You never go anywhere."

"You think?" She looked at me, unsure.

"Definitely. You'll have a good time."

Mom seemed to ponder this as she stirred the vegetables, making swirly patterns in the pan. After a long moment, she said, "It would be nice to see everyone again." Using a slotted spoon, she transferred the onions and peppers to a paper towel to absorb the grease. She pulled the buns out of the oven and artfully made the subs.

I added chips to our plates and carried them to the table. Mom joined me there with glasses of iced tea. I could tell something was troubling her. We ate in silence until my curiosity got the better of me.

"What's wrong?" I asked.

"I'm not sure I want to leave you here while I go to an out-of-state reunion," she said, taking a bite of her sub.

"I can stay here by myself. I do it all the time," I said, polishing off my own sub.

"Still, I'd feel better if you stayed at Anamae's that weekend."

"If I do, will you promise to go to the reunion?"

Mom gave me one of her rare smiles, and I was happy to see it. This was just what she needed, a break from her stressful and sometimes depressing job. Mom was the last nurse hired at Peacehaven Retirement Center. Her non-seniority status guaranteed horrible hours on the graveyard shift. She hated my calling it that, only because it was true. Many of her patients chose the middle of the night to depart this world. It would be good if Mom did something besides go to work. An idea came to me.

"Hey, Mom? It's fine with me if you want to, you know, start dating."

She looked at me, her eyes misting. And there it was. The grief that would not allow my mother to move forward. She had been unable to commit to anyone since Dad's death. Because she couldn't get a grip on anything, her life was slipping through her fingers.

And sometimes, so was I.

"Thanks, honey. I'm just not ready yet." She avoided my gaze as she gathered her purse and keys.

"Well, I want you to know, when you are, that it's all right."

"Okay, okay, I hear you." She bent to give me a kiss. "Take care of Bessie."

"I will." I rolled my eyes.

Mom had taken to calling our alarm system Bessie after a bitter argument in which I accused her of using the alarm as a babysitter. The hurt look on her face made me immediately regret those words. The alarm wasn't my babysitter; it was peace of mind to a single mother. Bessie was my grandmother's name, but this Bessie had been upgraded. It was set to automatically text Mom whenever the alarm was turned on or off.

"Goodnight, I love you," Mom said, going through the door.

"I love you, too."

Mom always worried about leaving me alone when she was at work, but I didn't mind. Nothing ever went bump in the night in Woodvine. Her footsteps slowed outside the front door as she rummaged through her bag. I recognized her stall tactic and dutifully tapped numbers into the alarm system. The confirmation sounded. Satisfied I was locked in for the night, Mom continued down the brick walkway to her car.

"Come on, Sam," I said.

The dog pulled his nose out of the blinds covering the front window and padded down the hallway, following me upstairs to my bedroom. My furniture, like everything else, was a mixture of hand-me-downs. Every piece was whitewashed, giving the room a peculiar glow in the moonlight filtering through my windows.

Sam lay at my feet, watching me intently as I struggled through my pre-calc homework. An hour later, I reluctantly pulled up my teacher's video explaining what she'd taught earlier that day. The video helped, but it cut into my free time. By the time I finally finished my homework, it was well past ten. Sam's head popped up when I stood and stretched, my legs stiff from sitting so long at my desk.

"Okay, boy," I said. "Time to go out." Sam was on his feet, tail wagging in seconds. He raced me to the door, running circles around me. "All right, all right."

I turned off the alarm and Sam forced his nose in the crack of the door, opening it wider as the rest of his body followed. While Sam was outside, I loaded the dinner dishes into the dishwasher and started the cycle. The hum of the dishwasher was interrupted by Sam scratching the door to be let back inside. After giving Sam a dog biscuit, I reset the alarm and turned off all the lights before heading back to my bedroom.

Sam jumped onto my bed, staking his claim to the side by the door. I brushed my teeth, and then climbed in bed beside the already-snoring dog.

As always, my last thoughts before drifting to sleep

were of the boy who came to me in my dreams. He'd played with me in the park when we were four, and made clay pots with me when we were seven. When we were thirteen, a goofy selfie forever captured our awkwardness at my eighth-grade dance. We had done all these things and more as we grew up together in my dreams.

The dreams of this boy brought with them a feeling so pure and powerful. A sense that with him, I was home. I used to dream about him several times a week, but it had been years since I'd last dreamt of him, and the details were getting fuzzy.

An indescribable yearning consumed me. My heart ached to return to that time when everything was so much easier. When Victor and I were just two best friends. When Dad was still alive. When Mom didn't have to work long hours in the middle of the night. Back to the time when nightly dreams of a boy, whose face I'd never seen, protected me from all that was dark in the daylight. Snuggling close to Sam, I fell asleep in the cold February night, wishing the dream would return and bring the boy back to me.

# 2

## James

ANAMAE WAS IN THE FRONT SEAT, *MY* SEAT, OF VICTOR'S car on Monday morning. *Their date must have gone well.* This thought irritated me, but I quickly shrugged it off as morning grumpiness.

"Hey, Groover," Anamae said as I climbed in behind Victor. Her thick brown hair spilled down the seat back in fluid spirals. It retreated like a herd of snakes when she turned to face me. Anamae was beautiful, even this early in the morning. Her dark lashes naturally lined her almond-shaped eyes. A peach gloss graced her flawless lips. She smiled as she hiked her leather bag higher on her shoulder. Anamae's entire outfit reeked of money.

Most kids assumed Anamae was snobby because she was rich, but she was just the opposite. I was the only one who knew that because I was the only one brave enough to talk to her when we started kindergarten.

"My car's in the shop. Big Bear offered me a ride to school. Wasn't that sweet of him?" Anamae had called him that since kindergarten. Victor had always been bigger than her tiny frame and protective of us both.

"Yes, he's quite the gentleman." I looked into the rearview mirror and saw a wide grin spread across

21

Victor's face.

"I hear we're getting a new kid," Anamae said. Her brown eyes flitted over me. "Drundled."

Anamae has this aggravating hobby of inventing words. Drundled was a new one. I had no clue what it meant.

"Messed up," she explained. "Is that what you're wearing?"

I glanced down at last year's jeans and my pale pink hoodie. "Apparently."

"You won't stand out dressed like that," she said.

When Victor turned around to back the car out of my driveway, he winked at me.

"Why do I need to stand out?" I asked.

"Well, since you've sworn off Woodvine boys, I thought you might want to make a good impression on the new guy," Anamae said.

"You've sworn off Woodvine boys, too," I reminded her. This was, of course, pointless on her part. Anamae had already dated most of them. In fairness, it was a short list.

"Nah, I just saved the best for last." She gave Victor's shoulder a squeeze. "But maybe the new guy's the one for you."

Victor quickly glanced at me in the mirror, his grin now absent.

We arrived at school and walked into the main building. Victor and Anamae left together for marine biology. My class, pre-calc, was one building over. I walked through the crowded hallway toward the rear exit. It bothered me that Victor had given Anamae a ride to school, and I didn't know why. Three days ago, I'd said they were perfect for each other. Today, I wasn't so sure.

I reached the exit and pushed against the door. It didn't budge. Stupid ancient building. I shoved harder.

This time, the door flew wide open, throwing me off balance. I didn't look up as I lost my balance and stumbled right into a brick wall. Only it wasn't a wall.

"I don't usually get this close to a girl unless I'm going to kiss her," the boy said, giving me a playful smile.

My mother had a moonstone I'd lost for her when I was nine. It was a beautiful, silvery-gray color, and I never thought I'd see it again. Now, I saw it twice as I looked into gray eyes that bore through me.

"Whoa," I answered intelligently.

"Hey, are you all right? Here, sit down." He guided me to a nearby bench. "Sorry about that. I wasn't paying attention. I'm trying to find my physics class."

I glanced briefly into his exquisite eyes, but they were just the appetizer. A straight nose led to perfect lips. I stared, wondering brazenly what it would be like to kiss them.

"Are you okay?" he asked awkwardly.

*Wake up, moron.*

"What? Yeah. I'm fine. You're new. Right?" I tried to shake the cloudiness from my brain.

"Yeah. I'm James. James Turner."

"Leath Elliott."

"Good to know you, Leath." He glanced at his watch. "Look, if you're okay, I'd better get going. Don't want to be late on my first day."

"Yeah, sure. Physics is in there." I pointed to the main building.

"Thanks. Maybe I'll see ya later?"

"Yeah, later."

*Definitely.*

James smiled, turned, and walked away toward the main building. He was, without a doubt, the best-looking boy in Woodvine. Maybe in the whole of North Carolina. I couldn't get those gray eyes out of my head. And though

I'd never seen him before, there was something familiar about James.

His scent.

Victor and Anamae always teased that I had a superpower, something to do with noticing people's scents. It was weird, but everyone close to me had a unique fragrance, a natural perfume of sorts. Some were tied to a memory, others to a personality trait. My mom had the essence of a first snowfall; My dad had the muted tones of sawdust that stayed in his hair after a day spent working in his woodshop.. Victor's was kind of like relajo, the mix of fiery spices his mother used in so many of their meals. His scent mostly resembled spicy cumin. Anamae's reflected her personality, or maybe it was a link to when we first met. Anamae's natural perfume was exactly like Play-Doh.

But James?

This was a first. I didn't know him at all, but there was something about his fragrance that tugged at me. It was subtly familiar, as if designed only for me. I breathed deeply, trying to draw in what I could from the surrounding air. The warning bell brought me to my senses. I didn't have time to go to my locker, but if I hurried, I wouldn't be late for class. I grabbed my book bag, and then headed toward the math building.

Talia Morris was in the same pre-calc class, and she veered in to walk alongside me. "What a weirdo," she said, flipping her inky-black hair over her shoulder.

"Who?" I asked.

"The new guy. He was sitting over there, reading one of the campus maps. You know the blue ones they gave out at open house?"

I nodded, half-paying attention.

"Anyway," she continued. "I sat down next to him and asked if he needed help finding his classes. I mean, he's new, right? Only he acted like he didn't see me, or even hear me. He just jumped up and ran to the main building. He held the door shut with his foot and shoved the map into his back pocket. Then he moved away from the door, and you ran into him. Like he did it on purpose somehow. What's up with that?"

"Who knows?" I asked. I regretted being short with her, but I was annoyed with Talia for breaking my focus on James. I also didn't like that her observations made James seem a little off. New kids were always a little off, but no need to bring notice to it.

My first two classes crept by like an inchworm scaling a skyscraper. When it was time for third period, I walked into English and dropped my paper onto Mrs. Green's desk. She glared at me in response. I was used to her dirty looks. Mrs. Green was Kevin's mom, and she had not forgiven me for breaking his heart. Apparently, it took longer for mothers to get over these things than it did their sons. Kevin, however, was dating another girl two weeks after we broke up.

I made a beeline to a desk at the back of the classroom and waited. My stomach knotted even though I wasn't the slightest bit hungry.

I stared at James when he entered the room. He was at least six feet tall. His wavy brown hair held glimmers of golden highlights. He wore loose-fitting jeans and a brown leather jacket over a tight T-shirt. James swung his book bag off his shoulder and his shirt rose, briefly exposing his flat stomach. He handed his schedule card to Mrs. Green. A moment later, she returned it, along with a copy of the course syllabus.

Now I was in trouble.

I'd stared long enough to call attention to myself, yet I still couldn't look away. As James sauntered down the aisle, every girl watched him until he chose the desk beside mine. I hoped I'd remembered to wear deodorant that morning.

"Leath, right?" he asked, sitting down. He smiled one of those smiles that made me wonder if he was being friendly, or was up to no good. Either way was fine with me.

"Yeah." I stared stupidly into his gorgeous eyes. Geez, he was going to think I was a nut case. "How's it going?" I blurted. Several heads turned in our direction at my outburst.

James smiled kindly. "It's good. Everyone seems nice."

*I'm sure everyone does.*

I flashed back on the crowd of sophomore girls at Victor's locker the Friday before and wondered if they'd spotted James yet.

"But I'm not used to eating this late." He patted his stomach. "I've got lunch next. Do you?"

"Yeah. I can show you where the cafeteria is if you want." I bit my lip, waiting for the brush-off.

"Only if you sit with me," he said, grinning.

Before I could answer, Mrs. Green started her lecture on the second chapter of *East of Eden*. It was a good thing because at that same moment, I lost the ability to speak. I was thrilled James had asked me to go to lunch with him, but I realized I'd have nothing to talk about once there. What was there to say about this boring town? Anyone who had been here for five minutes had heard it all. I spent the rest of the class period pretending to listen to Mrs. Green while stealing glimpses of James. It was obvious whenever I turned to look at him, but he smiled back each time, probably secretly regretting his lunch invitation. Amazingly, he stood and waited for me at the end of class as I packed my bag.

*Say something.* To my horror, my stomach roared

loudly.

"Yeah, me too," James said with a grin.

"This way," I croaked.

James held the door for me as we exited the building. "How long have you been in Woodvine?"

*How long have I been in Woodvine?*

*What?*

*Wait. I know this one.*

"All my life," I said.

"Seems like a nice town, but it's much smaller than where I used to live."

Since he didn't ask a question, I didn't know how, or if, I should respond. I had the feeling if I said the wrong thing, did the wrong thing, I'd scare him off. We walked along in awkward silence.

"I moved here from Charlotte," James said. "Have you ever been there?"

"Once. My class visited Discovery Place when I was in the eighth grade." I thought about the field trip, one of many I'd gone on with Victor. That day, he had convinced me to leave the group and sneak into the reptile room. I smiled as I remembered Victor trying to get two box turtles to race down the hallway.

James and I reached the cafeteria, where he held the door for me. As I stepped past him, his scent muddled my brain. It was musky with a hint of something sweet. Beautiful and strangely familiar.

I followed James through the serving line. He bravely chose the salisbury steak and potatoes. I settled for the safer choice of cheese pizza. After we paid, we made our way to a corner table and sat near two panels of cloudy industrial windows. They were too marred to see through, and I liked the way they kept us hidden from the outside world. I tried not to stare at James as we ate in silence. With food in my belly, I began to relax.

"Where do your parents work?" he asked, pushing his tray away.

"My mom's a nurse." I paused. Telling someone about my dad wasn't easy and almost always a conversation ender. "My dad died in a car accident when I was fourteen." I waited for the usual "Sorry to hear that," but his response surprised me.

"That sucks," he said.

"Yeah, it does." I finished my lunch as the minutes dragged on.

"This is when you're supposed to ask me about *my* parents. Although, I get the feeling you already know." He smiled a friendly smile, but his eyes were piercing, studying me for a reaction.

A chill shot up my spine. I felt exposed, as if he somehow knew I'd snooped in his file. That was impossible, of course, but the hundreds of conversations around us suddenly became deafening.

"It's okay," he said. "This is my third high school this year. My reputation always precedes me. And yes, it's true. Both of my parents are dead."

I was an awful actor, so pretending I didn't already know about his parents wasn't an option. Still, asking him about his parent's death, about how they died, seemed a little forward. A freshman girl walked past us, carrying a silver binder in front of her like a shield. This distracted James and saved me from having to give any response at all.

"What's the deal with all those dates marked through on the backs of binders?" he asked, jerking his thumb in her direction.

"It's stupid," I said, feeling like a freshman myself. "They're called scratch-offs. The date was the day she started dating her boyfriend. When they broke up, she scratched through it."

"So that means she's single?"

"Yeah." It bugged me when he watched her leave. An unreasonable jealousy gripped me until his eyes returned to mine.

"And what about you? Do you have a date or a scratch-off on that binder of yours?"

I laughed a little too loudly. Our conversation stalled for a few seconds until, mercifully, the bell rang. We dropped our Styrofoam trays into the trash before walking out of the cafeteria.

"Thanks for sitting with me, Leath."

The sound of my name on his lips was magical. It was as if he was calling to me, not just saying my name. I could get used to that.

"I'm sure your regular lunch group missed you," he said.

I doubted it. I used to eat lunch with Kevin. After we broke up, I began a self-imposed exile, choosing to sit alone in a corner of the cafeteria. That way, I couldn't feel Kevin's new girlfriend's eyes stabbing into my back like daggers.

"My friends don't have the same lunch period as I do. I usually just read a book while I'm eating."

*Desperate, anyone?*

"Well, if you want, we could sit together." He smiled. I was sure that smile could make me do just about anything. "See you in English tomorrow."

"Yeah, see ya." I watched James walk away, headed toward the gym.

*Follow me.*

A few seconds passed before I realized I was doing just that. It was odd I subconsciously followed this boy, but more alarming was a feeling that I would follow him anywhere. It seemed I was meant to go with James. Latching on to someone so quickly could prove to be stupid, or worse. I turned and backtracked my way to the main building.

I spent the next couple of hours stressing over my brief and embarrassing attempt at lunch conversation with James. He probably thought I was a loser with no friends. While I wasn't the most popular girl in school, I did have plenty of friends with whom I managed to have lucid conversations. By the time the last bell rang, I was quite perturbed with myself. I'd spent too much time obsessing over James. It was crazy. Who was he to me, anyway? The next time I saw him, I'd show him the fully functioning and intelligent girl I was. If there *was* a next time. And if there wasn't, it was his loss.

*Right.*

Ugh. Did I really want to get into anything with James, anyway? He was an unknown quantity, and I didn't need any complications. Not now. Not when escape from Woodvine was within my reach.

Victor wasn't at his locker, so I headed to the student parking lot. I was anxious to see him. My self-esteem needed a boost. Victor was already waiting beside his BMW. I was glad to see Anamae hadn't shown up.

"Hey, babe," he said. Victor hugged me his usual hello, and I responded with a hearty hug back. Victor pulled me closer. "Well, hi there. Long day?" he whispered.

"You have no idea." In his arms, my worries about what I'd said or didn't say to James slid off me, pooling around my feet.

Victor opened my door. I climbed inside and then leaned back against the leather seat. This day was finally over. I wouldn't have to answer any more tough questions like, "How long have you been in Woodvine?" How did James expect me to answer him, looking at me the way he did?

"Hello, Leathal. Are you there?"

"What? Oh, sorry."

"May I?" Victor stretched his right arm and cradled the base of my head in his warm hand. He gently massaged the muscles in my neck. "Better?"

"Much," I murmured. I was surprised by my reaction to his touch. This was bliss. My earlier embarrassment forgotten, I lost track of time as we sat in his car. This felt right. Being with Victor was easy because I could be myself around him. I considered what he'd said about being a couple, and for one moment, I could see us dating.

I knew what I was getting into with Victor. He was loyal. He was safe. Victor would never break my heart. But would I break his? I closed my eyes, relaxing further against his hand as he continued massaging my neck. Victor's free hand reached for mine, cradling it on my lap. Yes, it would be effortless to slip into a relationship with Victor. This time, I would really try.

*Bang, bang, bang.* A fist knocked hard on the window.

My eyes flew open, and I instinctively sat straight up. I looked out the window as Anamae peered inside. Her eyes darted from Victor to me before she jerked the back door open. I felt her knee hit the back of my seat as she slid in, slamming the door.

"Hey, Anamae," I said brightly. When she didn't respond, I turned around to face her. She had earbuds in both ears. As she scrolled through a playlist, I looked at Victor, who rolled his eyes. I creased my eyebrows questioningly. Victor shrugged in response.

The ride home was silent. When Victor stopped in my driveway, Anamae grabbed her bag, climbed out, and slammed the door. She stood by the car, waiting to take my place in the front seat.

"What's up with her?" I asked.

"Who knows? You know how emotional she is," Victor said.

I gathered my things and joined Anamae outside. To my surprise, she shut the car door and waved goodbye to Victor. He drove off, looking back at us with a puzzled expression.

"We need to talk," Anamae said. She turned, marching up my driveway.

I unlocked the door and led Anamae inside. After I turned off the alarm, we walked to the family room. She slung her bag on the floor, kicked off her shoes, and sat cross-legged on the couch.

I joined her. "What's up?"

Anamae burst into tears.

"Whoa, what's going on? What happened?" I reached for a box of tissues and passed them to her.

"Victor happened." She roughly wiped the tears from her cheeks.

"You guys didn't..." I held my breath, anxious for her answer. This feeling was quickly followed by confusion. Why was I suddenly concerned about what might have gone on between them? I swallowed hard. "What happened at the dance, or after the dance?"

"Nothing, really. Oh, Leath, no. Not that," she said.

I let out a silent breath of relief.

"The dance was great. I mean, I always have fun with Victor, but Friday night was different. He really is a gentleman. He opened the car door for me, and then held my arm when we walked up the steps. He even gave me a corsage. That night, I saw him for the first time as a guy, not just a guy friend."

"Then, what's the problem?"

"I think you're the problem, Leath."

I flinched.

"That didn't come out right. I mean, I think Victor's

confused about you. Now I'm confused about him. And I have to know. Are you interested in Victor?" she blurted.

"What? No. He's my best friend. One of my best friends," I clarified. "Don't worry. I'm not going to date him."

"That's not what I asked you."

It had been two months since Victor and I had ended the shortest romance known to mankind, or more accurately, known to no one. But I wasn't about to go into all that with Anamae, especially not now. Some things really were better left unsaid.

"Seriously, I'm not interested in Victor. He's like a big brother." That part seemed like a lie, even to me, but I pushed forward. "You have my blessing. Is that better?"

"Yes. If you're sure."

"Of course I'm sure." Only I didn't feel sure about anything. My heart betrayed me by fluttering when I thought about those few minutes with Victor after school. Maybe I was making a mistake by not giving him a real chance. Then again, I might have just missed my opportunity. "A little advice?"

She nodded, dabbing her eyes with another tissue.

"Go easy on Victor."

"I will," Anamae said, blowing her nose. "I'll call him tonight and apologize. And I really am sorry for how I acted earlier."

"No problem."

She balled the tissue into her hand. "Hey, did you see the new guy today?" A grin formed on her lips.

I nodded, hoping she'd let it go. She didn't.

"Well, did you happen to notice how absolutely beautiful he is? Or are you still starry-eyed over Mr. Midnight?"

Anamae was the only person on the planet I had told about the boy in my dreams. Mr. Midnight was the nickname she had given him. Sensing there was no discouraging her desire to talk about James, I gave in.

"I noticed. He's in my English class, and we had lunch together."

"So what would you give?"

Ugh. The What-Would-You-Give game. It was something Anamae and I made up years ago, a way for us to convey how important or unimportant something was. At the moment, I'd give just about anything to end this conversation.

"Too soon to tell," I said.

"Well, tell me what he's like then."

I spent the next twenty minutes describing my lunch with James. Upon reflection, my former awkwardness seemed minor. I chalked up my nervousness to being around a boy with such a beautiful face and muscled body. But there was more to James than good looks. There was something in his eyes that drew me in, as if he spoke only to me..

Anticipation grew inside me at the thought of seeing James again, and I felt a curious mix of hopefulness and longing. My thoughts about this new boy collided with my uncertainty about Victor. If I thought I was confused before, I realized I no longer knew up from down now.

# 3

## Date by Default

VICTOR WAS ALONE THE NEXT MORNING WHEN HE picked me up for school. I was relieved Anamae wasn't riding with us. I wasn't looking forward to spending time with my two best friends as they waded through dating drama.

"So how do you feel about Anamae and me?" Victor asked as if reading my mind. It was uncanny the way he always seemed to know what I was thinking. If I ever felt low, or needed him close to me, Victor would appear, materializing at the perfect moment. Ours was a tight and strange connection.

"I guess Anamae called you last night."

He nodded.

"If you two want to date, go for it. I just hope you guys are still friends when it's over."

Actually, a small part of me hoped they wouldn't make it as a couple. And I felt bad about that. I'd had my chance. What claim did I have on Victor now?

"Wow. You're quite the optimist." He said the last word slowly, emphasizing each syllable with his Spanish accent.

"I prefer the term realist," I said, shooting him a look.

Victor spent the rest of the ride to school focusing on the road. The drive seemed to take longer than normal, probably due to our unusual silence. Things were tense between us by the time we pulled into the student lot.

Anamae waited outside of the main building. She actually skipped over to Victor as we approached. Locking her arm in Victor's, she gave him a huge smile.

"I'll see you guys later," I said, suddenly nauseous. I bolted before Victor had the chance to give me his usual goodbye hug, if he even planned to do so. Thoughts about the two of them bounced around my head like popping popcorn as I walked to class.

When I spotted James in the crowd ahead of me, a grin spread across my face. I waved, but I guessed he didn't see me. I wanted to catch up to him even though I was nervous about what I'd say if I did. Faltering, I decided I'd wait until English to see if he approached me. I barely paid attention in my first two classes as my mind drifted from thoughts of Victor and Anamae to possible topics of conversation with James.

In third period, Mrs. Green expressed her disappointment with the quality of the papers handed in last week. She banished the entire class to the library for a remedial course in citing references, taught by the lead media specialist, Mr. Perkins. His enthusiasm for the proper citing of work wasn't catching. After his excessively dull lecture, Mrs. Green added to the torment by forcing us to create a bibliography. Old school. Print media only. She stressed the independent nature of our work by assigning us to various sections in the media center, effectively killing any opportunity for side conversations.

I dragged an encyclopedia off the wooden bookshelf and plopped onto an outdated armchair to finish my last entry. Dust escaped the volume as I snapped it shut, causing me to sneeze and break the tomb-like silence of the media center.

Mr. Perkins gave me a curt, "Bless you."

Blushing, I dug through my bag for something, anything. I looked up briefly to see everyone had returned to their work. Thankful I was no longer the center of attention I settled into the armchair and waited for class to end.

I reflected on my conversation with Anamae, unsure of how honest I'd been with her or even myself. The idea of her dating Victor disturbed me, which made me question my feelings about him. Maybe I did have feelings for Victor, other than friend-type ones.

I pulled a piece of paper from my binder and began doodling, drawing a large text bubble. Inside, I wrote *Victor* and made a list of things I knew about him. *Best friend. Love him. Loves me. I want him to be happy.* But there were other things, questions I had, so I added them to the list too. *Does Victor really like Anamae? Why does that bother me? Will Victor and Anamae stay together? Am I okay with that?* I underlined the last question. And, because I was trying to be totally honest, I wrote one more. *What would it be like to kiss him?*

I glanced at the clock, wondering when this class would finally end, and spied a glimpse of James. He sat a few seats away, reading a tattered copy of *Watership Down*. I added another text bubble and titled it *James*. I scribbled down things I knew about him. *Good looking. Smells delicious. Feels like I already know him.*

*What happened to his parents?*

It seemed unlikely they both would have died at the same time from natural causes. That left one other possibility. They were killed. Either by some accident or by someone.

I thought I heard my name. Looking up, I scanned

the room. Everyone was still agonizing over the bibliography assignment. Everyone except James. He stared at me with a curious expression. I felt my face warm and dropped my gaze. A small piece of fuzz on the armchair suddenly became an object of deep fascination. I stared at it for a few minutes before risking another glance at James, who had resumed his reading.

I returned to my paper and added a question under the James column. *What do I want to know about him?* To which I supplied the answer. I wrote one word. *Everything.*

The bell rang, waking me from my daydreams. I crumpled the piece of paper and tucked it into my binder. I'd throw it away at home. No way I wanted my doodles to be found at school. I gathered the rest of my books and stood. Turning swiftly to leave, I barged right into James and his mile-wide shoulders.

"Nice bumping into you again," he said, grinning.

"Sorry," I mumbled, embarrassed to feel heat rising on my cheeks.

"No problem. You ready to get some lunch? I'm starved."

He smiled at me, and my insides melted. Not trusting my voice, I merely nodded before following him out of the library. Instead of heading to the cafeteria, James led me to the student parking lot.

"Did you forget something in your car?" I asked.

"No," he said. "*I* have a good memory."

My breath caught in my throat. I experienced the same icy chill I'd felt yesterday when I thought he knew about my snooping in his file. I guessed I deserved it then, but this time, I'd done nothing wrong. I stopped walking, my intuition demanding attention. A warning crept out from some corner of my mind, but I quickly squashed it when James turned back to me and smiled.

"It's too noisy in the cafeteria," he said. "I thought we'd go off-campus. Or don't you guys do that here?"

"Yeah. We go to Burger Mike's all the time," I lied, not wanting to broadcast my small-town experience. I hadn't even thought about eating lunch off-campus because only seniors had that privilege. And they had to have written approval from their parents. What was I doing? I hardly knew this boy, yet here I was, happily following him down the road to detention.

James stopped beside a black Range Rover and opened the passenger side door.

I stared at the expensive SUV, amazed he could afford it.

"My parents had an obscene amount of life insurance," he said, answering my unspoken question.

I climbed into the black Rover like a nervous bird as a sense of dread settled on my shoulders. But that was more of an outside feeling. On the inside, I was overjoyed to be going somewhere, anywhere, with this handsome boy.

James got in, and then eased the Rover out of the lot. I rested my elbow on the console, noticing how close his arm was to mine. My thoughts were jumbled by being alone with him in this confined space. His heavenly scent was everywhere, invading my mind, compelling my imagination. We drove in silence, which was fine with me. I needed the quiet to switch my focus to something besides the fantasies filling my head.

I ran my fingernails along the outside seam of my jeans as I weighed the likelihood of a suspension for leaving campus without permission. Although I was worried I would get into trouble when we got back, breaking the rules with James was exhilarating. This was just what I needed—an adventure. A distraction from my life in Woodvine if only for an hour.

*Fading*

I became concerned when James drove past Burger Mike's. I had mentioned that restaurant on purpose, knowing we would have time to get there and back before the end of the lunch period. If he drove any further away from the school, we would definitely be late. The worried feeling was winning over. Who was I kidding? I was no rule breaker.

It seemed as if James was lost. He slowed down at several intersections as if he were deciding which way he should go, where he should take me. I was about to offer a suggestion when it seemed he'd finally reached a decision, and he drove with more confidence. A few minutes later, we turned into Claire's Diner, a small café built from old railroad sleeper cars. James parked. I pulled on the door handle only to find I was trapped inside the car. I glanced at him curiously.

"Think I could go in with you?" I asked.

"Sorry about that," he said. "The child-safety button is in a weird place. I'm always accidentally turning it on." He pushed a button on his door. "Try again."

This time, the door opened. We climbed out of the car, shut the doors, and then walked inside Claire's. The diner was empty except for one other couple finishing their meal in the main part of the restaurant. James led me through two narrow doorways to one of the compartments in the last railroad car. He slid the pocket door open, and we sat at a red vinyl booth. I wondered, not so idly, if the sleeper beds had been removed from the compartment.

"I hope you don't mind," he said. "They serve breakfast here twenty-four-seven. I'm in the mood for eggs."

"Works for me." I was grateful he had suggested it. Breakfast didn't take long to cook, and we were short on time.

"Hey, Leath. How y'all doing today?" asked a blue-eyed blonde in tight jeans and a hot pink T-shirt.

I could never get away with anything. I sighed. Why did I have to live in such a small town?

"I'm fine, Becky. How's college?"

"Oh, girl, you know, whiskey and wine. But, it's so much fun. Just you wait and see," she said, flipping open a small pad of paper.

"One check," James said.

"You don't have to do that," I said, embarrassed.

"I do. I invited you to lunch, so it's my treat."

"I'll buy next time." *What was I thinking? Next time?*

"Agreed," James said, smirking at my presumption.

Becky took our orders and left, returning moments later with two large glasses of orange juice. She put them down, giving me a wink before leaving again. I hoped she wouldn't tell anyone about seeing me off-campus. In a town this size, it would take all of ten minutes for it to get back to my mother.

"Okay, I give up," James said. "Whiskey and wine?"

"One of those quaint mountain sayings," I said.

"Which means what exactly?" he asked.

"Woodvine was founded by 'shiners."

James looked at me with a puzzled expression.

"Moonshiners," I explained. "A few of them were good people, but most were corrupt. It was pretty bad back then. When the town was cleaned up, all the 'shiners decided to go legit and switched to wine making. The town's name is a play on words, wood for the oak barrels that used to make moonshine, and vine for the grapes that now make wine."

"So, whiskey and wine?"

"Whiskey and wine means having some tough times with the good."

Becky reappeared, setting our plates in front of us.

Our meal arrived so quickly I believed we might get back to school on time. James's omelet looked delicious, and I regretted ordering the sausage casserole. We ate quietly, me hurrying a little to ensure a timely return to campus, but when we finished, James ordered coffee as if it were a lazy Sunday morning.

He clasped his hands on top of the table. Leaning forward, James stared at me with his penetrating eyes. "You didn't answer my question yesterday."

"What question was that?" I struggled to remember, which was difficult with him looking at me like that.

"Whether you have a date or a scratch-off on your binder."

"A scratch-off," I admitted sheepishly.

"That's good to know." There was that hint of coolness in his tone again.

Becky brought the coffees and the bill, telling James to pay on the way out. She disappeared back into the kitchen.

James leaned out of the booth and slid the compartment door shut, cutting us off from the rest of the world. "Tell me about your family," he said, easing back into his seat.

"Don't you think we should be heading out?" I pointedly looked at my watch.

"We've got plenty of time. Trust me."

And so help me, I did trust him. Enough that I told him all about Mom and her working nights at the retirement home. Then common sense returned like a Fourth of July parade. I could not believe I'd just told a stranger I was alone most nights. It worried me how easily I'd shared that information with him. Feeling completely exposed, I added, "Mom's home on the weekends. Friday and Saturday nights." I tried to change the subject. "What about your family?" I asked without thinking. Seeing his hardened expression, I quickly regretted my inquiry.

"Just me. No brothers, no sisters, and as you already know, no parents." His eyebrows knit together in a pained expression.

"I'm sorry," I stammered.

"It's okay." He smiled at me. "Of all the people I've met, you're probably the only one who understands how it feels to lose a parent."

"It sucks," I said, repeating his response from yesterday.

James nodded.

"For me, it's like my dad's being kept away from me. Even in my dreams, I can't get close to him." I stopped talking, acutely aware I had said too much.

"Like they're somehow still with you, just out of reach," he said.

That was the best description of how it felt when I lost my dad. I was taken by the fact that out of all the people I knew, James, who was two days ago a stranger to me, seemed to be the only one to understand, or remotely comprehend, my loss.

"Do you have any cousins, or other family?" I was desperate for any information about him.

"Both of my parents were only children. My grandparents passed away when I was little. So no family at all, but I have a lot of friends. You know, at my old school in Charlotte. A few might come up over spring break. I thought I'd throw a party if you'd like to come."

"That sounds fun, but if we don't get back to school, I'll be grounded until spring break's over."

James rolled his eyes at my sense of urgency. He looked at the check. Ignoring Becky's instructions about paying up front, he put a twenty on top of the check and left both on the table. James led me through the diner and then outside to the Range Rover. He drove back to campus at a snail's pace. I believed he did that on purpose, just to watch me squirm. I tried to look cool, but I was sure he saw right through me. When he finally parked in the student lot, I jumped out like a five-year-old at a water park. I walked briskly toward the main building, putting distance between us.

James caught up to me, saw my panicked expression, and chuckled lightly. "It's okay, Leath. Everyone's in the assembly," he said, flashing a wicked grin.

I felt like an idiot. I'd totally forgotten about the purple flyers I'd put in the teachers' mailboxes two weeks ago. Spirit Week started yesterday with Twin Day. Today, we had a guest speaker. He was a former Martin High School student, who was now in the NBA.

We entered the main gym, creeping into seats on the edge of a bleacher. Every creak of the wooden stands echoed in my ears, but all eyes were focused on the basketball player. I sighed in relief.

We had gotten away with it.

I glanced around the room. Hardly anyone, including myself, had dressed in our school colors of red, white, and black. Apparently, day two of Spirit Week was Apathy.

Just as my heart rate returned to normal, James's leg brushed against mine, setting my pulse racing again. I looked at him and saw he was watching me, more like studying me. It seemed he was testing me in some way, as if he were measuring my reaction to his fleeting touch.

The guest speaker finished his talk, and the crowd erupted into riotous applause that continued longer than necessary, an obvious ploy to delay returning to class. As we slowly filed out of the gym, I realized I'd heard nothing of the speaker's presentation. Although he was the most famous person I'd ever seen, I didn't even remember his name.

My life fell into a beautiful pattern over the next couple of days. James usually sought me out before school, sat next to me in English class, and ate lunch with me in the cafeteria. Whenever we were together at lunch, or even just walking across campus, it was as if we were in our own world. A world closed to outsiders.

While Victor seemed to attract a never-ending supply of girls, James was always alone. I found it hard to believe he wouldn't spark the same, if not higher, level of interest amongst my female classmates than Victor did. James was the new kid. A drop-dead gorgeous one at that. Yes, he had a quiet confidence, an aloofness that told others he preferred to be alone. But what teenage girl didn't like a challenge? James should have had loads of friends, but every time we met up on campus, he was by himself. No girls hanging around, no guys talking to him.

Upon further reflection, I realized the guys seemed to be intimidated by James. He was okay with this, happy to keep others away. But it made me feel a little sad for him, not having made any friends except for me. Did it make me a bad person that at the same time, I felt a secret joy over our sudden exclusivity?

No matter how much time I spent with James, I always craved more. I felt an unusual thirst to learn everything I could about him. James seemed equally curious about me. He continued to ask me about my exceedingly dull life. Did I have any cousins? *Yes, two.* Who were my closest friends? *Victor and Anamae.* Where did everyone go to hang out? *Asheville since Woodvine didn't even have a theater.* And while I'd answer any question just to spend time with him, it seemed as if James were fact-checking, not making small talk. But whenever I felt any doubt about him, or his motives, he flashed me a quick smile, looked into my eyes, and all my doubts were erased.

I was struck by the instant connection we seemed to have. One that grew stronger with every moment I spent with him. I became more confident, eager to share the details of my life. As we got to know each other better, I was able to see past his good looks and began to relax around him. Even with the mystery surrounding James and his parents, I felt oddly at ease when we were together. I could not believe a boy I had only known a few days had become so very important to me.

Like most of the students, I was decidedly indifferent toward the remaining days of Spirit Week. There was one exception. Thursday was Mix It Up Day and students were allowed to sign up for the lunch period of their choice. Victor and Anamae signed up for fourth period. I thought it would be fun having lunch with my two best friends, but they had ulterior motives. I didn't know which one of them was more eager to meet the new boy.

James and I sat at our usual table in the cafeteria. I waved Victor and Anamae over as they exited the serving line. When I introduced everyone, Victor shook James's hand, but Anamae was uncharacteristically shy.

"How you liking Woodvine?" Victor asked in his heavy accent.

James gave me a meaningful look while raising an eyebrow. "I like it fine."

Anamae giggled, batting her thick eyelashes at James. I wanted to kick her under the table, but my foot didn't reach.

"Leathal says you moved here from Charlotte," Victor said, obviously trying to draw James's attention away from me.

"Leathal?" James asked.

"Victor's nickname for me," I explained.

James's eyes narrowed. "I prefer Leath," he said disparagingly.

I was flattered by the fact James had an opinion, but at the same time, I wondered about the tone of his voice. He seemed a bit possessive. What worried me more was that I liked it.

"Are you from Charlotte? Originally?" Victor pressed as he casually plucked fries from my plate.

"No. Columbia, South Carolina," James said.

This caught my attention. "My grandparents used to live there."

"Oooh," Anamae said. "That sounds like destiny."

I tried to kick her again.

Victor tossed his half-eaten fry on his tray.

"My high school was called Lower Richland," James said. "Maybe you've heard of it?"

I shook my head. "I was ten the last time we were in Columbia. We haven't been back since my Grandma died and my Granddad moved to Georgia."

"Well, after my parents died, I switched to another school, AC Flora, to get a fresh start. But it didn't work out," James said.

"Why not?" Anamae asked, hanging on his every word.

"It was awkward when track season rolled around and I ran against my old relay team." James smiled. "I'd heard Charlotte was similar to Columbia. Some family friends had moved there, and they convinced me to give it a try."

"How did you end up in Woodvine?" Victor asked.

"I threw a dart at a map," James said.

Anamae burst out laughing. "I believe you. I mean, why else would anyone move here?"

"I can think of one reason," James said, glancing at me again.

I felt my face flush. When I looked away, I saw Victor's jaw clench. I could not understand his reaction to James. It was so unlike him. Victor always made friends quickly, easily talking to random people whenever we hung out in Asheville. I'd often joked he didn't seem to know any strangers.

"We should get going," Victor said, glancing at his watch.

We all rose, then threw our lunch trays into the black trash cans. Leaving the cafeteria, I embraced Victor, as was our habit. He clung to me longer than usual. I looked up to see him give James a smug smile.

Releasing me, Victor looked down and said, "Come with us to Asheville Saturday night for midnight bowling. It's been too long since the three of us have gone out together."

I was embarrassed by Victor's purposeful exclusion of James, which Anamae must have sensed. She stepped up to give me a cursory hug. "Yes, do come," she said overdramatically, then added, "James, you come, too."

"Sounds fun. I haven't made it over to Asheville yet," James answered.

Anamae reached into her designer bag and pulled out a pen. She took James's hand and wrote something on his palm. James smiled down at her. Their closeness troubled me. I glanced at Victor, but he seemed unfazed.

"That's Leath's number, give her a call when you're ready to pick her up," Anamae said. She tucked the pen back into her bag before turning to me. "See there, I got you a date." Anamae put her arm around Victor's waist and grinned at James.

I threw her a look and blushed a deep red.

"I don't think it counts as a date if someone else has to do the asking," Victor said.

"It's close enough," James said. He stepped closer to

me, keeping his eyes trained on Victor.

I didn't know what to say or think. Victor and James were playing tug of war and I was the rope. James casually draped his arm around my shoulder. At his touch, a butterfly ballet began in my stomach. An unfamiliar sensation traveled through me, a longing to stay in this moment forever with James's arm around me. We headed for the door after a quick goodbye.

I was not surprised by Victor's surly attitude after school. After a quick hello, he was quiet the rest of the ride home.

"What's up?" I asked when I could no longer stand the silence.

"Come on, Leathal. I'm sure you know."

"I have a good idea, but I thought you'd bring it up on your own. Let's see, it's about James, right?" I asked, pretending to be ignorant.

"Of course it's about James. I don't trust that guy."

"You feel that way about every boy I date. Ever think it's you and not them?"

In that moment, I realized it *was* him. Waiting in the wings with a quiet assurance that whomever I dated would not be the one for me. Victor always waited for me to reach the same conclusion.

Victor had dated several girls, but he'd never had a serious relationship. Every girl at Martin High wanted to be with Victor, but he wanted to be with me. Didn't I owe it to him to give us a chance before this thing with James, whatever it was, got started?

Before that thought took root in my head, another popped up in its place. Anamae. I had promised her I was not interested in Victor.

"There's something off about him," Victor said.

"You're being silly. He's harmless." As the words left my mouth, I wondered if they were true.

# 4

## Does Anyone Else Feel Awkward?

MOM HAD THREE DATING RULES. ANSWER MY CELL when she called. Be home before curfew. And the most important rule, well, the most important to *her*, she had to meet the boy before we could go on a date. And she meant before. Not the day of the date.

I mentioned the midnight bowling plan Thursday night as Mom left for work. She said the words I've come to dread. "We'll have dinner." Mom wasn't about to let me off on a technicality, like James not actually asking me to go anywhere.

*Great.*

I began to wonder if Mom volunteered to work the graveyard shift just so she could have every Friday and Saturday night off. Coincidentally, they were the only two nights during the school year I was allowed to go out. I had no idea how James would react to my mother's rules, but I knew there was no getting around them. I decided to suck it up and tell him all about the family dinner the next day at lunch.

"About bowling tomorrow night," I said, lightly drumming my fingers on the hard plastic table. "My mom won't let me go with you unless she meets you first." I rolled my eyes. "She invited you to come over for dinner tonight. I know it's late notice. If you can't make it, I understand."

"It's not a problem, Leath. It's not like anyone's waiting for me to come home." He smiled, placing his hand on mine, probably to cease the drumming.

My pulse quickened at his touch.

"Tell your mom thanks. I'll definitely be there."

I couldn't believe it was that easy. Once again, James's reaction surprised me. He was so different from the other boys I'd dated. They'd made such a stink about meeting Mom beforehand I thought they were going to stand me up. But James was more mature and confident than other kids our age. Of course he wouldn't be the slightest bit uncomfortable meeting Mom or anyone.

The doorbell rang at six, sending Sam into a fit, which was weird. Sam was a pitiful watchdog. He never barked, not even when the Fed-Ex guy delivered. That night with James, though, Sam was uncontrollable. Mom had to half-drag Sam by his collar and shut him in the laundry room before I could answer the door.

James held a bouquet of daisies, which wasn't for me. I wasn't sure how he knew it, but daisies were Mom's favorite flower. She was euphoric. James had scored major points before he had even gotten two words out of his mouth. Mom put the flowers into a vase, and then carried them to our oversized table in the dining room. We hardly ever used that room, except for the inquisitions.

"What's the trophy for?" James asked, pointing to the mantle over the fireplace in the living room.

"A shooting competition with my dad. He started taking me there when I was thirteen."

Of all the things Dad and I did together, shooting was the only activity that stuck with me. It was in that way I kept my father close to me as I transitioned from tomboy to girly teenager.

Mom wasn't a huge fan of guns. But after Dad died, leaving us without his protection, I think she was secretly thankful I knew how to handle a weapon. Her confidence in my shooting abilities eased her fear of someone breaking into the house and stealing me away in the middle of the night.

"I was the only girl there." I smiled, remembering the puzzled looks of all the boys and their fathers when Dad and I entered the shooting range. "Everyone was shocked when we won."

"That's cool," James said. "Maybe we could go sometime."

"You shoot?" I asked, surprised. None of my other friends did.

"Yeah, just recently," James said, running his hand through his hair. His thoughts seemed to be somewhere else.

"Then, let's go sometime," I said, happy to find someone who shared my hobby. Not sure of how involved James was in the sport, I quickly added, "You can use my .22."

He replied so quietly I barely heard him. "I have my own gun."

I was about to ask what kind when Mom called us for dinner. A large pan of lasagna, breadsticks, and a bowl of chopped spinach salad waited for us to sit down. We did and then began filling our plates.

"James, how do you like Woodvine?" Mom asked.

I remembered how James answered that question when Victor had asked it. I was suddenly nervous as I tried hard to fight off a semi-hysterical fit of giggles.

Mom looked at me as if I was nuts.

"It's great. Especially my English class," James said,

grinning.

I blushed at his words.

"Well, I'm a transplant myself. From Columbia, like you. I'm going back there for my high school reunion later this month," she said.

Mom and James continued chasing small talk while we ate. I didn't usually participate in these conversations, giving her full reign to interrogate, but Mom was different with James. Instead of bombarding him with nosy questions, she surprised me by taking James on a trip down memory lane. Mom listed off some of her old stomping grounds in Columbia. She was delighted when he said things like, "Yeah, that place is still there," or "They have the best milkshakes." Everything was going great until I nearly choked on my lasagna when Mom brought up the most delicate of subjects.

"Leath told me about your parents. I'm so sorry to hear about them. How did it happen?"

"Home invasion," James said bluntly. Either he'd practiced his answer, or he'd said it too many times before, because his voice was emotionless.

"Oh, no," Mom said, looking at him sympathetically. "Were you there? Did they catch the people who did it?"

"Mom," I chastised her.

"You're right, Leath," she said. "I'm sorry. Please forgive me, James."

"It's okay," he said, offering no other details.

I guessed he was used to adults asking him about his parents. I was used to people asking me about my dad. It probably seemed normal to him that people wondered how he came to live on his own at such an early age.

"Where are you staying?" Mom asked, her voice full of maternal concern. "Are you doing all right?"

"I found a nice house not far from here. Over on Exton Shore. It's small, but it suits me."

I made a mental note of the street, which was just around the corner from our house.

"Well, if you ever need anything, please don't hesitate to come by," Mom said.

"I will," James said. He smiled at her. "My kitchen doesn't get much use. It's really nice to have a home-cooked meal. Thanks for inviting me."

I hoped he wouldn't see the take-out cartons on the kitchen counter.

"We don't have all that many home-cooked meals either with my working five nights a week," Mom said, giving me a conspiratorial glance. "But we'll be sure to invite you over the next time we do."

If she was inviting him back, that meant James had passed her test. We could now go on our non-date with her approval.

"I'd like that." James seemed genuinely grateful for future invitations. "I have been missing one thing though."

"What's that?" Mom asked.

"A good cup of coffee," he said. "You know, like they have at Goatfeathers?"

"Goatfeathers. That brings back memories," Mom said, smiling. "No Goatfeathers here, but we do have Grinds. They have great lattes and desserts, which I seem to have forgotten tonight."

My face blushed at her none-too-subtle suggestion. *Mom*, I propelled the word silently through space, hoping she would pick up on my embarrassment.

"Want to go get some coffee then?" James asked, giving her a huge smile.

Mom burst out laughing. "Very funny. I already like you, so you can lighten up." She shook her head as she began clearing the dishes. I stood to help clear the table, but she waved me off, "You two go ahead, and have fun."

She carried the dishes to the kitchen, muttering under her breath, "Do I want to get coffee?" She chuckled lightly.

"Thanks for humoring her," I said to James.

"No problem. Your mom's cool."

I thought he was being sweet until his next comment.

"It's great how she keeps up with her responsibilities at home while working a real job, too."

"What do you mean by a *real* job?"

"You know, working outside of the house."

"Working inside the house is also a real job," I said evenly.

"Yeah, but she's supposed to take care of the house. It's not really a job."

There was the chink in his armor.

"You're kidding, right? I mean, you can't be serious."

"It's just, where I'm from, the father works and the mother stays home. You know, the way it's supposed to be."

My eyebrows rose. My face flushed, for once out of anger instead of embarrassment. "And where are you from? The Middle Ages?"

James caught on quickly. "I'm sorry. That sounds really bad. My mom was a stay-at-home-mom. And you're right. Raising me was definitely a full-time job." He smiled apologetically at me.

One look at the remorse covering his face, and I caved. It seemed impossible for me to stay angry with James. Maybe he was ignorant of such things because of the way he was brought up. My dad used to say it was okay to be ignorant. Ignorance, he had said, was temporary. Now stupid, well, stupid was just plain permanent.

"How about you? Would you like to go for a coffee?" he asked, trying to change the subject. "Please don't say no; I don't think my ego could handle two rejections in less than five minutes."

I smiled at him, doubting he'd ever experienced any true form of rejection. "Sure," I said, feeling hopeful the night wasn't ruined. I grabbed my coat and followed James to his car. He retrieved something from the backseat before climbing in beside me.

"This one's for you," he said, handing me a single rose, the bottom of the stem encased in a tiny vial of water.

"Thank you. It's so pretty," I said, trying to determine the color. It was a cross between apricot and pink. Salmon? I inhaled the aroma of the perfect flower. "Why didn't you bring it inside?"

"I wanted it to be special, just between us. I took the chance that we'd be going out after dinner," he said.

James lightly stroked my cheek before he turned and backed down the driveway. My skin warmed at his touch. I breathed in the beautiful flower again, trying to calm my thoughts.

Ten minutes later, we pulled into Grinds. It was the only coffee shop in Woodvine, and no bigger than a large shed, but I absolutely love it. The smell of roasted coffee beans greeted us, giving me a warm feeling inside. There was something about drinking restaurant coffee that made me feel like an adult. We got our coffees—mine was decaf, Mom's rule—and two slivers of chocolate cake. James placed his hand on the small of my back, gently guiding me to the only open table in a secluded corner.

When we'd finished the cake, James pushed the small plates to the side of the table. He pulled a paper from his pocket. "I got this in the mail today."

I immediately recognized the letter. It was a permission slip, giving information about this year's College Cruises. I'd forgotten the college tours were about to start up.

James moved his chair to sit beside me and placed the letter on the table between us. My thoughts raced ahead, seeking different possibilities as to what might happen next. Would he put his arm around me again like he did the other day at school? My insides rolled. If I didn't know better, I would have thought he sensed and enjoyed the sudden turmoil inside me. He pulled a pen from his pocket and gave me a sly grin.

"I was hoping you'd help me decide which colleges I should visit." He shifted even closer and bent his head over the letter. The heat of his body filled the tiny space between us.

"Er," I faltered, struggling to remember the names of the colleges on the form I'd completed so long ago with Victor and Anamae. "They're all good choices."

"Well, yeah, they are. But I was more interested in which ones *you* were going to visit."

His voice was deep and low. Something hidden called to me through the words he spoke. An invitation? No, a temptation to be with him on one of the out-of-town trips. I wondered if I was ready for something like that, but I quickly dismissed the thought. I'd probably read too much into this conversation. I suddenly felt I had something to prove to myself. Shaking off my insecurities, I moved closer to James.

There were five tours listed on the form. The first, a large university in Columbia. Anamae and I had chosen that one when we turned our forms in at the beginning of the school year. She wanted to see where I'd spent many of my summers when I used to visit my grandparents. I glanced down the list and felt a pang of guilt. The last three colleges were ones Victor and I had chosen. Given James's brief encounter with Victor, I didn't think it would be a good idea for the three of us to spend an entire weekend together.

I tapped the names of the first two dates with my finger. "These are supposed to be good schools."

"Well, I know the first one is," James said, smiling. "I visited USC many times when I lived in Columbia. Are you going to visit these two?" he asked.

*I am now.* I nodded.

James put a check beside both schools. He folded the paper and slipped it into his pocket.

I felt a thrill and a rush of excitement at the possibility of going with him on two overnight trips. Then I remembered Anamae. She'd called the trip to Columbia our, "Girls Only," weekend. Anamae was not going to be happy about this, but I decided to worry about that later. Plus, I figured she kind of owed me. What with my stepping aside and staying out of the way of her pursuit of Victor.

James sipped his coffee. I did the same, feeling pleased he hadn't moved his chair back to its original location. My free hand turned a coffee stirrer top over bottom repeatedly until he took my hand. His touch was gentle and warm. I silently willed my hand to remain sweat free.

When our cups were empty, he drove me back home. As I opened the car door, James hurried around from the driver's side. He stood at my door just as I climbed out.

"Next time, let me get that for you," he said, gently shutting the door. As we walked to the front porch, I wondered how James would say goodnight. I unlocked the door, and then expectantly turned to him.

"Thanks for having me over," he said.

"It was fun," I said.

The seconds dragged. *Come on, do something.* I thought hopefully.

"Guess I'll see you tomorrow," he said. He walked to his car, but halfway there, he turned back, grinning at me. "Thanks for your help with the college visits."

"Anytime," I said. I watched him get into his car, and then I went inside the house. I was disappointed, but at the same time, a little thankful. I was sure I had coffee breath. I didn't want our first kiss to be our last.

When James arrived for bowling on Saturday night, he offered a foot-long rawhide bone to Sam. The dog grumbled a little before sniffing the treat and quickly snatching it from James's hand. Sam bounded up to the top of the stairs where he sank down on the landing, noisily gnawing the bone, keeping his eyes trained on James.

James seemed at ease as he presented me with another salmon-colored rose.

I smiled. I'd never been one to want or expect flowers, but this sweet gesture touched me. I had to admit I'd be disappointed if he had shown up without one.

"Where do you get these?" I asked. "I've never seen one this color."

"My house has a rose garden. This color reminds me of you. It's the same as the color on your cheeks when you blush."

His words caused me to do just that.

"I'll see you later," Mom said as she met us at the door. She saw the rose and gave me a smile. Mom was on her way out to meet a friend for the annual midnight madness sale at Woodvine's only boutique. "When you live in a small town, it's quite the event," she explained to James. Hugging me, she whispered in my ear, "Have fun and be careful. Don't forget about Bessie."

This was a reminder she'd be waiting for a text from the alarm system. Just one text to let her know the motion sensor of the alarm had been set as James and I headed out. The sensor beam was high enough that Sam never accidentally tripped it. It was hard to pull one over on Mom with Bessie set up for texting. If I didn't set the alarm with the right code, Mom would know James and I were hanging around here, unsupervised. I kissed Mom's cheek before she walked out.

James moved swiftly between the door and me, locking it with one hand. "And finally, I have you all to myself."

I felt that icy feeling work its way up my back. I didn't understand how I could be so attracted to James and a little fearful at the same time. Instinct told me to run. I tried hard to ignore it as I felt my pulse quicken.

He burst out laughing. "Wow, you actually look scared."

"I don't scare that easily." My voice broke, betraying my confidence. He laughed again, and it infuriated me. I hated being teased like that, as if I were a child. "You know what? I changed my mind. Find the bowling alley on your own."

James continued laughing, and my anger pushed me to my limit.

"On second thought, maybe you should just forget about going. I don't know what your game is, but I don't have time for it. My friends are waiting." I had completely forgotten I had no transportation. I headed for the kitchen, the rose clutched in my fist. I was going to stick the rose in a vase before calling Victor to cancel. James followed closely behind.

"Game?" he asked, turning me to face him.

"Yeah. Whatever game you're playing, I'm not interested."

"So why don't you tell me what you are interested in, and we can do that instead." James smiled the smile that made me forget the world. He stepped closer, and I froze. Leaning in, he whispered in my ear, "I thought you didn't scare easily."

His warm breath traveled over me, melting the chill in my spine. I felt an overpowering desire to pull him to me. Instead, I jumped when my cell phone shrieked.

James chuckled. His eyes still on mine, he stretched his right hand to the kitchen counter and picked up my cell phone, glancing at the caller ID. "It seems Victor is tired of waiting." He handed me my cell.

"Hey," I said. Victor's voice was like a bucket of ice water, shocking me into action. "We're on the way now. See you in a bit."

I ended the call. "We need to get going, James." I pulled a bud vase from under the sink, filled it with water, and then added the blush-colored rose.

"No problem. We can finish our conversation later." His eyes made a promise to me, one that made me almost forget all about Victor and bowling.

James led the way outside to his car where he opened the door for me.

I got myself together before he climbed into the driver's seat. Aside from my telling him where to turn, the ride was silent. By the time we'd reached the halfway point on our road trip, awkwardness seemed to creep between us and settled on me like a suffocating gel.

"What the devil is that?" James asked, pointing to a house off to the right. The house was small, mostly front porch, and had a black tar roof. A large skeleton draped over the porch railing, its legs frozen in a twisted two-step.

I laughed when I saw the expression on his face. "Just some local color," I said.

"How's that?"

"We're going through what used to be called 'Crooked Dance Gorge.' Before there was a highway here, the road was curvier, twisting back on itself in some places. The story was the road jackknifed so badly, you could put one foot on the north end, the other on the south end, and dance all the way across the gorge."

He looked at me skeptically.

"I've grown up hearing all kinds of weird stories about the mountains," I said.

"Ever hear any that were true?" he asked.

"You mean they aren't?" I asked in mock disbelief.

James chuckled. "Well, you know what they say."

"What's that?"

"Every myth is based on some piece of truth."

"If that's true, there's a lot of jacked-up truth out there."

He laughed again, seemingly lost in his own thoughts.

We arrived at the bowling alley a few minutes later. James opened the door, and we walked into a tidal wave of noise. The sound of bowling balls smacking into pins was chased by shouts and loud laughter.

I spotted Victor and Anamae sitting in the alley's snack bar. Victor's face was creased with worry. Anamae looked miffed. Her finger slowly traced the rim of her cup. This was going to be a fun night.

"What took you so long?" Victor asked, standing as we approached their table.

"Yes, what?" Anamae asked, clearly disinterested in my reply.

"It was my fault. I got distracted," James, staring at me appreciatively.

Victor shot him a contemptuous look.

"It's only fifteen after," I said, hugging Victor. At first, his body felt tense, but he relaxed as we embraced.

Anamae rolled her eyes. I gave her a hug hello, which she returned stiffly. "Can we just get on with it?" She led us to the register where we picked out shoes and bowling balls.

We were assigned the last open lane. Four young

girls bowled in the alley next to us. They giggled as they stared and pointed at James and Victor. Anamae glared in response. She sat down to enter our names into the lane's computer.

I laced up my rental shoes. We hadn't even started bowling, and already I wished the night was over. James seemed oblivious to the building tension. He bowled first, getting a strike. Anamae followed with two gutter balls. Victor got a strike, and I got a spare. By the fifth frame, Victor and Anamae cheered each other on as they bowled, and the mood gradually lightened. James won the first game. Victor the second. I was relieved everything had returned to normal.

"I'm worn out," Anamae said. She sat on a hard plastic chair that at must have been considered a modern design at one time, but was no longer.

"Me, too," I said, sitting beside her.

"Lightweights," Victor teased. He sat down and loosened the laces of his rented shoes.

"How about one more game?" James asked. "Unless you'd rather leave it a tie."

Victor automatically tightened his laces. "I can do one more game, but let's make it interesting." He motioned James to the top of the lane out of earshot. They talked for a moment before shaking hands.

I looked at Anamae.

She shrugged her shoulders and yawned. "Let's turn in our shoes and get something to drink."

We sipped sodas at a small table, watching groups of people leave the bowling alley. Before long, only two games continued. I glanced at our lane and watched as Victor rolled his bowling ball down the alley. Another strike. He turned around and grinned at James.

"I wonder what that's all about," I said, pointing to the lane.

"Puh-lease," Anamae said, rolling her eyes.

I gave her a puzzled look.

"I'm sure their little bet has something to do with you."

"Why would you say that?"

"Big Bear obviously has a problem with you dating James."

"We're not dating," I said unconvincingly.

"Whatever. I just hope Victor gets over you before I get over him."

"You're being ridiculous, you know," I said.

"I don't think so. Listen, it's hard for me to say this." Anamae struggled with her words. "You know I love you, Leath, but I don't want us to double date again. I really like Victor. I want this to work out for us, but we don't stand a chance if you're always hanging around."

Tonight, the four of us together had been difficult to say the least. I was glad to have an out. "No problem. From now on, it'll just be the two of you." I smiled at her, and she returned it. It was short-lived.

"You guys ready to go home?" Victor asked.

I scanned the bowling alley for James.

"He's gone," Victor said, as if reading my mind.

"Where?" Anamae and I asked together.

"He lost the bet. By the way, he's a lousy sport," Victor replied. "You left this on the table in the lane." He passed my cell to me.

"What was the bet?" Anamae suspiciously asked.

"It's no big deal." Victor looked uncomfortable.

I knew better, and I also knew Victor was incapable of lying to me. "What did you bet?" I demanded.

"If James won, I agreed to, how did he put it? Oh, yeah, butt out," Victor said.

"And if you won?" I pressed.

"If I won, he agreed to let me drive you home," he

said.

"Are you even kidding me?" Anamae asked, sounding irritated. "Okay, what exactly is the deal with you and Leath? Tell me the truth if you don't mind."

"The deal with Leath and me is the same as the deal with you and Leath," Victor said, his tone angry. "She's our best friend. And if you would stop being jealous for just one second, you'd see James is no good for her."

"You do realize I'm standing right here?" I asked.

"Yes, you are. And completely unaware of James's intentions," Victor shot at me.

"His intentions?" I asked, my voice shrill. "Who are you? My mother?"

"He's up to something," Victor continued, unaffected by my outburst. "I can feel it, and I know you feel it, too. You're on your guard when he's around. Face it, that guy's bad news. You need to stay away from him."

I was so angry with Victor that I could choke him. "Is there anything else you think I need?"

Victor stepped away from me as if injured by my backlash.

"No? Great. Glad that's settled because right now, I can tell you that I *need* to go home." Even Anamae knew better than to say anything more about the subject.

We drove back to Woodvine in stony silence. I wasn't sure who deserved my anger more—Victor for his parental imitation, or James for leaving me at the bowling alley. Even if we weren't on an official date, it was weird, him leaving me behind without saying goodbye. But a lot of things about James were weird. Like the fact that he was leaning against his black Rover, which was parked in the driveway beside my mother's gray Honda. Victor pulled in behind James's car.

"Thanks," I said gruffly as I reached for the door handle.

"Leath, just a second." Victor looked at me in the rearview mirror. His voice was soft, pleading. "I'm sorry. I guess I was being overprotective. It won't happen again."

"It better not," I spat, immediately regretting my acidic tone.

"Terrific. Now, can this horrendous date please end?" Anamae crossed her arms over her chest, turning to stare out of her window.

As if on cue, James opened the door for me.

"Night, guys." I climbed out of the car, and James closed the door. We walked toward the house as Victor backed slowly down the driveway.

"Way to leave me stranded," I said. I should have been angry, I tried to be angry, but I couldn't do it. I was just thrilled to see him again.

"I'm good to my word," he said. "I lost the bet, fair and square, and I kept my end of the bargain. But I also told you we'd finish our conversation."

I blushed, remembering his whispers earlier in the kitchen.

"And I agree with you by the way," he said.

"About what?" I asked.

"We don't have time for games." He reached for my hand, our fingers intertwined as we walked to the front porch.

I unlocked the door, and James followed me inside. "Thanks for going with me tonight. Besides being a complete and utter disaster, I had a good time."

"Me too," he said, smiling down at me. "I'd better get going if I want to stay on your mom's good side." Instead of leaving, he pulled me into his arms.

Without meaning to, I compared this embrace to the hundreds I'd shared with Victor. Victor and I fit together smoothly, seamlessly, harmoniously. This embrace was different. It was deliberate, purposeful. As James held me, the rest of the world was shut out. In that moment, I found I no longer cared about the rest of the world. I looked into his gray eyes and waited, anticipating his lips on mine.

He leaned in and kissed my forehead.

"I'm not going to attach our first kiss to a 'complete and utter disaster.' Next time, we'll have a real date. Goodnight, Leath." He released me and then walked out the door, closing it behind him.

What he didn't realize was I considered that night at Grinds our first date. I'd never enter that place again without looking at it as such. I stood staring after James, willing him to come back and give me a proper goodnight kiss. A flash of headlights came through the front window as he backed down the driveway. I set the alarm, feeling amazingly happy.

There was going to be a next time.

# 5

## Invasion

ON SUNDAY MORNING, MOM AND I SAT ON THE DECK, enjoying what we called cartoon brunch: bagels, cream cheese, pepperoni, grapes, and apple juice. It had been years since I'd watched cartoons, but the weekend breakfast tradition stuck. It was one of those days, the kind I referred to as a hidden day. An unseasonably warm day hidden within the winter months, a promise that spring would return. I kicked off my slippers and rested my bare feet on the deck boards, soaking up the heat from the wood.

"James seems like a nice boy," Mom said.

"I think so."

She didn't miss the implication. "You think so. What do Victor and Anamae think?"

"Victor doesn't like James at all. Anamae, well, did you see James, Mom? He's gorgeous, so Anamae likes him just fine."

"Honey, Victor's been in love with you since the day you met. It's natural for him to be a little jealous. And Anamae's not going to risk your friendship over a boy." She spread a thick layer of cream cheese on a bagel and took a bite. "Are you going out with James again?"

"Last night didn't count as going out." As I explained how it all happened, Mom gave me a huge grin.

"What's so funny?"

"Nothing, honey. I just think it's sweet—James being too shy to ask you out, I mean." She gave me a quick glance, noticing the impatience on my face. "He'll find his courage."

"Do you think it'll be sometime this year?" I grumbled. Mom and I both laughed.

I spent the day on edge, waiting for James to call. My cell buzzed, but it was only the low-battery notification. I dug through my nightstand, found the charger, and then plugged in my cell.

The quiet evening gave me too much time to replay James's goodbye from the night before. And when I did, doubt barged into my memory. Maybe James didn't kiss me because he didn't feel that way about me. Maybe he was trying to let me down gently. The more I thought about it, the more I believed there wasn't going to be a next time.

I couldn't sleep that night, scrutinizing every moment of my time with James. I dissected everything I'd said, fantasizing how things might have ended differently if only I'd said this or done that. It was worse than when I'd obsessed over my first conversation with him because this time we'd been alone. I had my shot with James, and I blew it. I fell asleep out of exhaustion just before daybreak.

The next morning, I felt grumpy and out of sorts. When Victor picked me up for school, he was quiet to the point of aggravation. My lack of sleep didn't afford me any patience.

"Just spit it out," I said.

"It's nothing, really. Anamae wants to ride to school with us tomorrow. Well, every day actually."

"You mean ride with you," I corrected. Of course she did. Girls liked riding to school with their boyfriends. "Sure. Why not?" I asked. "It'll be fun." The words sounded hollow in my ears, but they seemed to satisfy him.

"Thanks, Leath." He relaxed, returning to his old self.

"So I guess you guys are going to give it a try."

"Yeah, I know. It's weird, right?"

"Not really. One of us was bound to end up with you," I said.

He parked in the crowded lot and decided to wait for Anamae to arrive. I headed to campus, eager to see James before school started. When he was nowhere to be found, I couldn't shake the feeling he was blowing me off. My feelings were erratic, as if on a spinner, stopping first on one emotion and then another. At last, it was time for English class. A wave of happiness passed through me as James walked into the room. This was quickly followed by a wave of embarrassment, while I wondered, for the hundredth time, why he hadn't called all weekend.

"Hi, Leath," he said, sitting at the desk next to mine.

I ignored him, pretending I was preoccupied with our mind-numbing literature text.

"Well, this is awkward," he said.

I didn't need to look at him to know he was smirking, which caused my emotional spinner to be stuck on anger. I felt my heart beating so hard I was sure he could have seen my shirt vibrate. "If you mean your inability to see I'm busy, then I agree," I said frostily. "It is awkward."

"Oh, someone's got her feelings hurt," he said in a teasing tone.

My spinner shifted to the next emotion. Fury. Unfortunately for James, fury was on both sides of the anger space on my emotional spinner. He didn't stand a chance.

Mrs. Green called the class to order and began telling us about an upcoming project.

"I'm sorry I didn't call yesterday. I had to go out of town," James whispered.

"You don't owe me an explanation," I hissed, burning the words of the textbook with my glare.

"You're right. I don't," he said smugly.

"Is there a problem?" asked Mrs. Green. She shot a look to the back of the room where James and I sat.

"I'm sorry, Mrs. Green. I can't hear you back here." James got up, moving to a seat at the front of the classroom. Mrs. Green gave him an approving nod and continued her lecture.

I felt stupid for running James off like that, but it was maddening the way he swayed my emotions from high ecstasy to a seething fury. And there was that eerie feeling I sometimes had when I was alone with him. It was as if James was teetering on the edge of a cliff, one he seemed determined to drag me over. There was something dangerous about him; I was certain of it. And I wasn't the only one who thought so. Victor felt it, too.

I stared at James's back. At that moment, he turned slightly, to look out the window. I studied his profile, his posture, the smile that played on his lips. Something stirred inside and my heart softened as I continued watching him. James had his rough edges, but looking at him now, all I could see was a boy who seemed out of place, lost somehow. Still, if he wasn't dangerous, he was definitely trouble. Or maybe, he was *in* trouble. I wondered if it would be better if I stayed away from him, but deep inside, I didn't believe that at all. And even if I did, I knew it would be impossible for me to do so.

I skipped lunch that day, feeling ashamed by how I'd treated James. I decided to hide out in the media center and indulge in a little self-pity. My head throbbed from a combination of sleep deprivation and hunger. Finding an unoccupied cubicle, I flung myself into the chair. I rested my cheek on the cool desktop and woke up just in time for fifth period. I debated about going to class, but in the end, I called my mother, asking her to come get me.

Mom picked me up at the front of the school. "Hi, honey." She smiled sympathetically, handing me two aspirins and a bottle of water. "Want to talk about it?"

"No. It's just a stupid headache." I swallowed the pills. The bitter taste burned all the way down my throat. I quickly chased them with gulps of water, slouched in my seat, and closed my eyes.

"A little rest will do you good." Mom patted my arm.

As soon as we got home, I climbed the steps to my room and fell onto my bed, giving way to a deep sleep. I awoke several hours later in the same awkward position. My headache had completely gone. The smell of pizza lured me downstairs, where I ate several slices under my mother's watchful eyes.

"Feeling better?" she asked.

I nodded, my thoughts returning to James. She must have picked up on it.

"Leath, you know if you ever want to talk, I'm here. Okay?"

"I know, Mom."

She'd told me that at least a thousand times before. And I knew she would continue to remind me. I'd spent hours with Dad, driving to competitions, shooting together, and practicing at the range. I'd had more opportunities to talk to him about my problems, and since time couldn't be manufactured, all those hours with Dad limited the time I had with Mom. It was an unfair trade-off, for sure. It was no wonder she never seemed to know what I needed to hear, but I loved her even more for trying so hard. I carried my plate to the kitchen. Mom followed me.

"Beth called today. She wants to come this weekend and catch up before the reunion."

"That'll be nice." I said, scrubbing one of the plates distractedly. The seconds dragged on as wild thoughts raced through my head. Where had James gone yesterday? I watched scene after scene play out in my mind, and my anger returned. Even if he had gone out of town, he still could have called. He still *should* have called.

"Looks like you're about to scrub a hole in that one," Mom said, taking the scouring pad from my hand. "I'll take care of these, sweetie." She took the plate from me, rinsed it, and loaded it into the dishwasher.

An idea formed in my head. "Mom, is it okay if I run over to Anamae's house and pick up my English homework?"

"I didn't know you and Anamae had a class together," she said, puzzled.

"We don't. Same teacher, different period."

"Well, if you're sure you're up to it," she said, casting a worried look my way.

"I'm fine," I assured her, eager my plan might just work.

"Okay. But don't stay too long," she said. "It'll be dark soon."

"Thanks." I gave her a quick hug, grabbed my wallet from my book bag, and plucked the car keys that hung from a key-shaped board near the back door. "I'll be right back," I called to her as I walked outside.

I felt a little guilty for being dishonest, and I almost changed my mind. But I knew that would only make Mom more suspicious. I decided to run by Anamae's house afterward and see if I had any homework, turning the fib into a truth. Yes, I'd go to her house right after I made one other stop, one that was quite literally on the way.

With great restraint, I slowly and carefully backed down the driveway. I drove away from our house, following the curve that led to the end of our street. When I turned right onto Exton Shore, my breathing quickened. I didn't know James's house number, but I hoped his Range Rover was parked in his driveway.

*I'm just going to drive by*, I thought. *I'm not going to stop, not unless he's outside. No, even if he is, I'm not going to stop. Maybe I'll give him a casual wave. Make him think I'm just being friendly, neighborly even.*

I spotted the Rover in front of a two-story brick house.

*Maybe I should stop*, I thought. *Surely he could spare a few minutes. I can apologize for how I'd overreacted earlier. James was mature enough to discuss this with me.*

My heart pounded as I craned my neck, scanning the grounds around his house, searching for the rose garden that produced James's never-ending supply of blush-colored roses. But the purple shadows of the advancing evening covered most of the yard, masking anything that might be there.

I pulled into the driveway and parked behind the Rover. I was impressed by my boldness, and not entirely surprised by my decision to stop. In the back of my mind, I had known I would do this very thing from the second I'd hatched this plan. No sense in pretending.

I tried to fight the excited feeling growing inside me, tried to remind myself I was angry with James. But as hard as I tried, I couldn't help being thrilled by the mere thought of seeing him again. My heart raced as I turned the keys and cut the engine.

*Take it easy*, I thought. *It's just a friendly visit.* Taking a deep breath, I climbed out of the car. I hoped he wasn't watching me. I'd rather surprise him.

Another deep breath gave me the courage to knock on the front door. I couldn't contain the grin that spread across my face as I prepared to see him. I hoped he liked surprises.

I didn't.

She was stunning, standing in the doorway, wearing what appeared to be one of James's dress shirts and nothing else. She had long legs that were not pencil thin like mine. Hers had shape. *She* had shape. The girl held a cup of yogurt in one hand, a spoon in the other, stirring and pulling the fruit to the top. Her thick blonde hair waved down, just touching the pocket of James's shirt.

The warm radiance of yellow light spilled out of the doorway, casting her in a golden glow. The light stopped abruptly at my feet, creating a boundary in the shadow between us. The girl pushed a bit of her hair away from her crystal-blue eyes, which she then used to stare at me as if I were a simpleminded child.

To lend credence to her belief, I stood staring at her in complete silence.

"Yes?" she asked impatiently.

Apparently, she'd spoken to me. I was in a state of shock, unable to answer.

"Some girl," she called back into the house. She turned to face me again, and the light caught the pendant hanging from a long chain around her neck. It was muted gold, with one initial, "J."

I stammered something unintelligible and backed away from the door. When I tripped over the last step of the front porch, I decided looking forward while walking straight ahead was a better combination. I turned around and ran to my car. After I cranked the engine, I jammed the gear in reverse and backed straight into the street without checking. Thankfully, no one else was on the road.

I drove past a few houses before I remembered I was on a neighborhood road, not a racetrack. I inched my foot from the gas pedal, allowing the car to slow to the speed limit. Bitter tears left warm trails down my cheeks. I didn't glance into my rearview mirror until I was certain the girl could no longer see me, although I doubted she was still looking.

So that was why James hadn't called.

*No. He said he'd gone out of town.* I immediately chastised myself for even thinking of being on his side, for thinking he was telling me the truth, when I'd just met the truth, standing half-naked in his doorway.

*Stupid.*

*I'm sure he did go out of town*, I thought angrily. *But he didn't go alone.*

I'd always prided myself by how quickly I learned from my mistakes. James and I were so new that I didn't even know if we were considered a "thing" yet. It was all happening too fast, and it was my fault for falling for him so quickly.

I wiped the tears from my cheeks, deciding right then to fall back into my old mindset, my fantasy of leaving Woodvine, as I made way back home. I'd stick to my original plan of waiting until I left this small town before I started dating again. I gave myself over completely to the familiar fantasy until bedtime when only a tiny piece of my mind was still concerned with James Turner and his mystery girl. I fell asleep and slept dreamlessly.

When I woke up, I knew two things right away. One, the shadows on the walls of my bedroom told me the sun had been up for some time. I'd forgotten to set my alarm last night. And two, I was absolutely exhausted. There was no way I was going to school. I pulled the covers over my head, rolled over, and fell back to sleep.

When Mom got home from work later that morning, she acted pretty upset about my ditching after having "gone to Anamae's" last night. Truth be told, I thought Mom was happy I'd stayed home. She seemed glad to have the extra time together because after she showered and slept, she drove me to Asheville for a late lunch at Bistro 162.

Afterward, Mom stopped at her favorite bookstore, Bindings. She bought the next two novels in a historical romance series she'd been reading. It was fun spending the day with her, and the best part came when she pulled into the gun club.

"Your pistol's in the back," she said as she popped the trunk.

I looked at her, surprised and stunned. Clearly, the disconnect I felt between us was more on my side than hers. A trip to the range was just what I need to clear my mind. Mom knew this before I'd even thought of it.

She registered me with the range master before retreating to the lobby with her novel. I signed and initialed the paperwork, stating I understood the rules. *No hip shooting. Hearing and eye protection must be worn on the range. Leave jammed firearms in the stall. Do not bring a jammed firearm into the lobby, etc.* Having been here many times with my dad, I knew the drill. I selected three paper targets, put on my safety glasses and earmuffs, and opened the glass door to the gun range. The familiar and pungent odor of gunpowder was comforting as I headed for the last empty stall.

I clipped my first target to the wire. Using a button on the wall beside me, I ran the target to the twenty-five-yard marker. I opened my gun case and lifted out my .22. It felt great to have the pistol in my hands again. I pointed the barrel of the gun down range, and then laid it on the bench. Next, I loaded a magazine and slid it into the pistol's grip. I edged my left foot slightly forward and picked up my pistol. After I clicked the safety off, I rested my right index finger on the side of the frame as I raised the pistol to eye level. My left hand instinctively cupped the bottom in a palm-supported grip. I took a few deep breaths while aligning my sights to the target. Slowly exhaling, I squeezed off my first shot.

It wasn't long before I'd emptied the first magazine. I brought the target back and was pleased to see my groupings were tight. Dead on. As I removed the paper target, I heard a low whistle from the stall on my right. A boy about my age smiled and gave me a thumbs-up. Normally, I'd encourage conversation with a fellow gun enthusiast, but I already had too many boys on my plate. I needed this time alone in my element. Disinterestedly, I nodded at him. I felt a little guilty for my borderline rudeness, but I figured I'd never see him again, so I shrugged it off.

I clipped a fresh target to the wire, and then sent the target back to the twenty-five-yard mark. Refocusing my attention, I loaded a second magazine. I relaxed as I fired into the target. My shots became more accurate with each round.

I turned the dial, and my last target flew backward as it raced down range. I loaded the magazine then quickly emptied it, hitting several bull's-eyes. Movement on my right caught my attention. I pulled the target back to me, removed the magazine, and set the safety. Annoyed with the boy for distracting me, I spun around to give him a private lesson on range safety. Only he wasn't there. He had joined a small group of people, all clustered around another stall.

Looking down range, I saw the only target still on a wire. I heard the shots ring out, but I couldn't make out the pattern. Then I realized each shot had struck in the exact same location. The range manager entered, surely to break up the crowd. The target zoomed back to its owner as the crowd dispersed. I stretched on my toes to get a glimpse of the shooter, but I barely caught a look at the back of his head.

*James?*

A tapping caught my attention. Mom stood behind the protective glass. She beamed with pride and pointed to my target on the line. I packed up my gear, heading out to meet her in the lobby.

"Let me see," Mom said, taking the targets.

It was embarrassing, the way she laid them on the floor, looking over each one, saying all the while how good of a shot I was. But I didn't mind, not really. At least she was showing an interest.

While she surveyed each target, I scanned the room, trying to find James. I glanced out the front windows into the parking lot, but there was no sign of his Rover.

"I said, maybe I'll give it a try next time." Mom's voice sounded a little loud, like she was repeating herself. She hooked her arm in mine, raising an eyebrow.

"Oh, sorry. That'd be great, Mom. Anytime you want to learn."

She carefully folded the targets and tucked them under her arm. Mom carried them to the car as if they were priceless portraits.

I was silent on the ride home as my mind buzzed with possibilities. James had said he owned a gun. It wouldn't be unusual for him to go to a shooting range. I shook my head. I wasn't even sure it was James. If he had been there, he would have shown himself. Maybe. Whoever the shooter was, he was an excellent shot, every bullet striking the dead center of the target.

\*\*\*

79

Victor and Anamae were in a weird happy mood when they picked me up for school the next day.

"Good morning, Leathal," they said together.

"Hey," I said, internally gagging.

"Are you feeling better?" Victor asked.

"Yeah, I was just super tired."

"How'd it go with James after we left the other night?" Anamae asked.

*Had that only been a few nights ago?* I wondered.

"Come on. Tell me all about it," she pressed.

My carefully constructed facade shattered like brittle glass. Sometimes, I wondered about Anamae's timing. I did not want to have this conversation with anyone, especially Mr. and Mrs. Bliss.

"Nothing to tell. He walked me to the door, said goodnight, and left."

"Ouch," Anamae said, wincing.

Victor subtly shook his head.

"I mean, I'm sure he'll come around," Anamae amended.

"Whatever." I stared out the window as Anamae prattled on about what she and Victor were doing on Saturday. Some couples-only event. I felt sullen about being excluded and began to feel sorry for myself again.

I was relieved to see James had returned to his regular seat beside me in English. In spite of my elation, it bugged me, too. James remained silent until class ended.

"Hey, Leath," he said as he packed up. "Want to get something to eat?"

I looked at him curiously. Was he going to explain things? Or let me down easy over a bite of lunch? I weighed my options. Go to lunch with him and learn he wasn't into me at all. Or not go, and always wonder. I knew the latter would drive me to distraction, so I swallowed hard and managed to choke out one word,

"Sure."

I walked alongside him to the cafeteria as if I were going to the gallows. Mechanically, I moved through the serving line, choosing random items. We sat at our usual table. Since I refused to say anything, we ate in silence. My dry throat made it difficult for me to swallow. I pushed my meal aside, waiting for him to say something.

James smiled. "I really did go out of town," he said.

*Great*, I thought.

"It's okay. You don't have to explain." I plastered on a fake smile, all the while hoping he would. Hoping there was a logical explanation for the gorgeous girl who was staying at his house.

"I was in South Carolina, visiting my parents. I go every month." He looked down as he said this.

My smile froze idiotically on my face. He had gone to visit his parents' graves. I reminded myself that I hadn't known about the girl when I'd first gotten upset in class yesterday. At that time, I was being petty to the point of being childish. "I'm sorry. I shouldn't have gotten angry."

"It's okay. I should have told you. I guess I've been living on my own too long. I didn't even think to mention it when we were together Saturday night."

But he wasn't exactly on his own.

We stared into each other's eyes for a long moment. My heart and brain struggled for control. I wanted so badly to believe him, but he'd have to tell me more. I had to find out about that girl.

"Look, James," I said, deciding he needed to know that I knew about her.

"I know," he said. "Ever told me you stopped by."

Oh, gosh, she'd told him. Of course she had. She probably couldn't wait to tell him all about the babbling idiot on his front porch. I tried hard for the next few minutes to melt away and fade into the faux marble patterns of the tiled floor.

"It's okay, Leath," he said in a gentle tone. "Ever's just a friend."

The image of her standing in James's shirt flashed in my mind. The words slipped out before I could stop them. "A pretty good one, from what I saw."

James laughed, causing my blood to boil. I would not be teased by him. Wordlessly, I rose to leave the table.

"Wait," James said, lightly catching my wrist. "Please, Leath. Let me explain."

I stood for a moment, debating whether a reasonable explanation existed. His eyes softened, drawing me in. I caved and returned to my seat. "Let's hear it."

"Ever really is just a friend," James said. "She's a couple of years older than me."

*Not helping,* I thought angrily.

"I met her..." He faltered, and then stopped talking.

I sighed loudly, gripping my tray to leave again.

"Wait, please," he pleaded. "I'm sorry, it's kind of personal." He took a deep breath. "I met Ever in a support group, one the police department suggested I join after my parents were killed. Ever's dad was killed in a robbery. He was in the wrong place at the wrong time. Anyway, Ever's sort of my sponsor."

It took a full minute for me to digest this information. Ever was his sponsor, part of his support group. Okay, I got that. I had Victor. James had Ever. Got it. Fine with it even. However, not fine with her wearing James's shirt like a nightgown. I raised an eyebrow. "And this Ever— she doesn't have any clothes of her own?" I asked.

"She's a klutz. She spilled coffee all over her shirt and jeans. I was washing them for her."

"You took her to Grinds?" I asked, trying hard to conceal my jealousy. It was immature I know. But I thought of Grinds as our place. I blushed at my outburst.

"No," James said. "I wouldn't do that. I wouldn't take anyone there but you." His eyes locked onto mine. "Ever dropped me off at school, and then she drove over to Asheville. She spent the day at some coffee shop. On the way back to Woodvine, she spilled coffee all over herself."

I felt relieved Grinds wasn't sullied by this girl. Relaxing a bit in my chair, I gave him the silent signal I was ready to hear more.

"I called Ever before my trip. It was really bad this time, and she met me at my parents' graves. Afterward, she was worried I was too upset to be driving. She wanted me to stay the night. When I said no, she insisted on coming home with me. She jumped into my car and refused to get out. We argued, but I finally just drove back with her in the car. Ever spent the night." His eyes burned into mine. "But she did not spend the night with me. I promise you that, Leath. There is nothing going on between Ever and me."

"What about her necklace?" I said. "It had a 'J' on it." I hoped I didn't have to ask him directly if the J was for James.

He pulled his keys from his pocket and set them on the table between us. "Like this one?" He separated keys on the key ring until a similar J-shaped pendant stood out. It was the same size and shape as Ever's, but a slightly darker shade of gold.

I nodded at the matching token.

"Everyone in our support group has one of them. Please don't ask me to tell you what it means. It's something only members know."

Sitting silently for a few minutes, I tried to absorb what he'd said. I looked for cracks or flaws in his story. There was one thing in his favor. James had never lied to me. Not that I knew about, anyway. But was he telling the truth now? I looked at him, studying his anxious face.

He seemed to be more worried about the entire matter than I was. His expression held something else—it held fear. It was as if he was afraid of losing something.

*Afraid of losing me?*

"And where is Ever now?" I asked.

Without blinking, he responded calmly. "She's gone back to Columbia. A friend of hers picked her up last night. Not long after you stopped by."

"One more thing," I said.

"What's that?"

"Were you at the gun range yesterday?"

"Yeah," he said, sounding puzzled. "How did you know that?"

"I was there," I said. "Mom brought me."

"Too bad we didn't meet up. I'd love to see you shoot." He smiled at me.

The word love tripped me up for a second, but it didn't entirely shake me. Something didn't add up. "How did you even get in without a parent's signature?"

"Buddy system," he said. "The owner's a buddy of mine. Went to college with my dad. He signs me in when I go."

*Mystery solved.*

"You're a good shot," I said.

"Let's just say I'll never lose someone I love again," he said. James exhaled before continuing. "Now I have a question for you. Would like to ride to school with me? Every day?"

*Take things slow*, I thought. *Don't read too much into this. Think before you open your mouth.* "That's kind of a good idea. My carpool is getting a little crowded." That didn't sound too bad. It sounded like something a friend would say.

"Great, I'll pick you up tomorrow morning."

The bell rang, and we parted ways, heading to our

next class. I thought about his explanation for why Ever was in his house. It seemed reasonable. I guessed. I wanted to trust James, and this want battled against the idea I should just let him go. James and Ever had been each other's support. They must have a tight bond for Ever to drop whatever she was doing and head out of state with him. Another thing they had in common was they were both stunning. They looked like more of a couple than James and I did. Even so, I believed James when he said there was nothing going on between them. I could always tell when someone was lying. The way they fidgeted in their seat and refused to make eye contact. James was definitely telling the truth about his relationship with Ever. Either that or he was the best liar I had ever met.

The rest of the week, it was one-step forward, two steps back. At first, we were all getting along. Even James and Victor were almost civil to each other. Although we spent more time together, and there had been several opportunities for James to ask me out on a real date, he didn't. I was beginning to think he only wanted to be friends. When James dropped me at home on Friday with no word of going out, the memory of being in his arms had become a fantasy to me. One that twisted cruelly into an image of Ever standing in my place.

Mom's friend Beth was already at our house for the weekend. She was the same age as Mom, but looked much younger. Losing a husband to divorce must not age people as much as losing one to death.

To my dismay, Beth had brought her eleven-year-old daughter Quinn with her. I wasn't in the mood for babysitting, but Mom so seldom did anything with her friends, I figured I owed her. After allowing myself an hour to pout, I got into the swing of things. Quinn wasn't that bad, and Beth made her day when she let her ride with me to the grocery store to pick up more soda. Quinn thought everything I did was cool. She made a big deal about both of us having a boy's name. It was kind of nice, having my own fan club.

It was a real girls' weekend. On Saturday, Mom drove us to Asheville where we shopped, well, window-shopped. The boutiques were too pricy for my budget. When we stopped at a day spa to get pedicures, Quinn copied the polish I chose, and I was okay with that. Feeling generous, I even picked up a bottle for Anamae. Afterward, we saw a chick-flick at the pavilion, and filled up on nachos and hotdogs. Mom stopped at Grinds on the way home and treated us to iced decafs. High on girl-bonding time, I barely cringed when I spotted the empty table where James and I had sat on a night that seemed ages ago.

Sunday came too quickly, and I was disappointed the weekend was over. We took separate cars to the Whitney Hotel for brunch. Mom and Beth flipped through their senior yearbooks at the table.

"It will be fun seeing everyone," Mom said.

"Everyone? Or someone?" Beth asked, grinning.

"What do you mean?" Mom asked.

Beth took Mom's yearbook and quickly turned the pages. "This someone, maybe? Desmond?" Beth prompted.

Wait, was Mom actually blushing? I read the name under the small photo. "Who's Desmond?" I asked, curious about my mother's reaction.

"Des was my boyfriend," Mom said, sounding embarrassed. "Way before your dad," she added quickly.

I knew my parents had met in college, so I wasn't concerned that this boy had somehow wronged my father.

"I dated Des all through high school," Mom said. "He

was really sweet, and so handsome." She pointed to the yearbook photo. A good-looking boy stared back at us, his blond hair brushing the top of his shirt collar. The boy's brown eyes seemed to sparkle, and the smile on his face looked sincere, not posed.

I reached for the yearbook. "He's dreamy," I said in a teasing voice. I read the inscription aloud in my most dramatic voice.

"Penny, I'll never forget your face, your smile, or your laugh. Take care of my heart while I'm away. Love, Desmond."

Snickering, I asked, "What happened with you guys?"

"Well, he went to college in California. I stayed behind in South Carolina. And that was a good thing because that's where I met your dad." She smiled wistfully. "Des got married about the same time we did. I lost touch with him after that."

"Well, maybe you can find out what he's been up to at the reunion. Besides, I'm sure he's long overdue for a visit with his heart," I gushed, fanning the center of my chest and batting my eyelashes.

Beth burst out laughing. Mom rolled her eyes and shook her head. It was then Mom connected the dots.

"Beth, Leath's dating a boy from Columbia. Can you believe it?" she asked.

"We're not dating," I protested.

"Wow, that's kind of a full-circle thing, isn't it? You moved here for your sweetheart, and Leath's sweetheart is from Columbia," Beth mused, completely ignoring my protest. "What's his name? Do we know him? Wouldn't it be funny if we went to school with his parents?"

"His name's James Turner. We don't know his parents." Mom glanced at Quinn, who took the hint and got up to refill her orange juice. "They're both dead."

Beth was stunned by this news. "That's awful."

"I know," Mom said, sounding thoughtful. "James said they died during a home invasion. Poor kid, he doesn't have any family."

Beth's fork clanged as she dropped it to her plate. "Oh my gosh. I remember that story." She hesitated, trying to use her Mom-vision to get me to leave the table. I refused to budge. No way was I going to miss what she had to say. Beth looked around the room, and I pointed to where Quinn stood talking with a gangly boy in a fresh-from-church suit and tie.

"What happened?" Mom asked.

Beth glanced at me, speaking hesitantly. "His parents were murdered. Both shot dead in the middle of the night. Both shot just once." She lowered her voice. "Straight through the heart."

My mind went numb, trying to comprehend the horror James had experienced. My throat was dry and tight. With a trembling hand, I picked up my glass and took a careful sip,

"That's horrible," Mom said.

"The kid was there," Beth continued. "But he wasn't hurt. I think he escaped by running to a neighbor's house or something like that. The police never caught who did it."

I shivered involuntarily, anxious for a second that whoever did it was still out there and maybe looking for James.

Mom mistook my reaction for fear of my own safety and cast a worried look at Beth.

"I don't think they ever suspected the boy," Beth said quickly. "I remember seeing him on the news. He was devastated. It was just heartbreaking. I always wondered what happened to him."

What happened was a young boy had suffered a

crippling loss. No wonder he didn't know how to be close to anyone. When I first lost my dad, it was the same for me, but I'd had Victor and he got me through it. James had no one.

A nasty thought crept into my mind.

No. James had Ever.

I felt ashamed for thinking so selfishly and changed my perspective. Yes, he had had Ever, and I should be grateful for it. Ever was probably responsible for getting James through the whole ordeal. If she hadn't been there, James might not be here today. But Ever was in Columbia, and James was here. I decided right then. From now on, James would have me.

Quinn trotted back to the table and told us all about the boy she'd been talking to. The rest of her conversation and our mother's responses were a dull noise to me. I kept thinking about the terrible way James had lost his parents. I couldn't fathom his fear as someone crept through his home and murdered his mother and father. More than anything, I was incredibly grateful he got out alive. The idea of him being hurt in any way was too much for me to bear.

"Leath?" Mom asked. "Did you hear me?"

"What? No. Sorry."

"Are you all right?" She put the back of her hand to my cheek. "You feel a little warm."

"I'm fine," I said. I stared at her appreciatively. So thankful I had a mom.

"It's been great seeing you guys again, but we've got to get on the road," Beth said. She stood and hugged Mom. "I'm so glad you're staying with me for the reunion, Penny. I can't wait." Beth's eyes lit up, and she gave Mom an impish smile. "You know, there are lots of details to work out. Why don't you come a day or two early? I could use a hand."

Mom looked at her hesitantly, but I could tell she was tempted.

"Come on, Penny. We could have a few days to ourselves. Besides, when was the last time you took an actual vacation?"

"It was..."

"Never," I answered for Mom.

"And it's Quinn's week to be with her dad, so I could use the company," Beth said pleadingly. "It'll be just like old times."

Mom looked at me.

"Go on. I'll be fine," I said.

"Do you think you can stay at Anamae's a few extra days?" Mom asked.

Beth squealed with delight and clapped her hands, signaling what we all knew. It was a done deal. "It's going to be so much fun." She hugged Mom and gave her a kiss on the cheek. "We'll talk more later. Come on, Quinn."

"Sounds good," Mom said. "Drive safe."

Quinn surprised me by hugging me tightly around the waist. "Text me sometime," she pleaded.

"I will," I assured her as I returned her hug. "You, too. Okay?"

Quinn beamed at me and nodded.

"Bye, guys," Mom said.

Beth waved and turned to leave the restaurant. Quinn followed, looking back to grin widely at me.

I smiled, wondering what she'd kept from us about the boy she just met. Mom wrapped her arm around my shoulder as we walked out of the restaurant.

"Are you sure you're okay with my going to the reunion early?" she asked.

"I'll be fine." I sighed, wondering if mothers ever got a break.

We walked to the car silently. Mom paused before

90

unlocking the door and turned to me, a worried expression on her face. "Leath, about James." There was a hard edge to her voice.

I sucked in a deep breath. Here it came—the "he's-too-dangerous" speech. I prepared myself for what was sure to be some decree against my seeing James again.

"I know you like James. I like him too. Just take it slow, okay?"

I wondered how much slower James and I could go. Tilting my head to the side, I looked at her for clarification of what she was trying to say.

"He's been through a gruesome experience. Although he seems to be handling everything okay, sometimes that kind of trauma... well, there could be things he's still working out. Those kinds of events tend to mark a person for the rest of their life."

Then she put on her nurse voice, turning to face me. "Post-traumatic stress is a horrible and serious problem. Sometimes after an event like that, people have a difficult time dealing with stressful situations."

"He has a grief group," I said, hoping to placate her.

"That's good." Mom seemed relieved. "If you get any idea that James is struggling, please tell me. I know people who can help if he needs it."

Her heart was in the right place. I smiled at her. "I will. Thanks."

Another weekend had passed without hearing from James, but I was glad for the time to think about what I'd learned about his parents. Obviously he didn't want me to know the details, or he would have told me. I needed to fully process this news so the next time I saw him, I wouldn't give anything away. I'd let him tell me when he was ready.

I was at the mercy of my imagination that night, and nightmares burned into my subconscious. Each one was some variation of someone breaking into our house, skulking around, searching. Looking for me.

In one nightmare, I was asleep in my bed when the security alarm sounded, waking me. As the alarm pierced the night, I remembered Mom was at work. I didn't know where Sam was, but it was odd he wasn't barking at the intruder. I jumped out of bed and ran to my closet. I found my gun safe and opened it with trembling hands. Pulling out my pistol out of its holster, I instinctively slammed a pre-loaded clip into the handle. I pointed the muzzle through the crack in the closet door and waited.

I heard someone shuffling through the hallway, opening and closing doors on their way. Breathing in slow deep breaths, I focused my thoughts as I raised my pistol to eye level.

A few seconds later, the intruder crossed into my room, the glint of a silver handgun flashing in the dark. He moved to my bed, flinging the covers wildly, before his head snapped up and he turned around. He saw me then and charged toward me. I slowly exhaled, aimed for center mass, and pulled the trigger.

And then I realized the intruder was James.

# 6

## Judaculla Rock

ALTHOUGH I'D BEEN PREOCCUPIED ALL WEEKEND, I was anxious to see James. I felt a strong desire to comfort him, to take away the heartache he must have endured over the violent loss of his parents. My anxiety faded as I watched his Rover pull into the driveway on Monday morning. I couldn't believe how much I'd missed him. It actually pained me, waiting for him to walk up the front porch steps. I fought the urge to run to him, to be in his arms and breathe in his scent. It was, of course, absurd I should continue having these feelings for him, when he hadn't expressed a similar interest in me. All the same, I was excited to be with him one more time. I flung my book bag over my shoulder and stepped outside.

As James approached, I noticed his swagger was off. He wasn't his usual easygoing self. James seemed tense, as if he were expecting a bolt from the sky. Then I saw the dark circles beneath his beautiful eyes.

"You don't look so good," I said. "Coming down with the flu?"

"No. I didn't sleep well last night. I kept having these crazy nightmares."

I reflected on my own nightmares, especially the

one about him. "I know what you mean."

"Here, let me," he said, taking my bag.

He tossed it onto the backseat of the Rover, and then joined me in the front. We sat there for a few minutes, and I wondered why he hadn't started the car.

"I haven't done this thing right," he said, turning to me. "Not at all."

"What thing?" I asked, my throat suddenly tight.

He motioned a loop between us with his right hand. "Us."

My heart fluttered at the word.

"This is going to sound weird, and I'm sure I haven't acted like it, but ever since we went bowling..." He hesitated.

*Find your courage,* I thought as I held my breath.

"Since that night, I've thought of you as my girlfriend, like you belong to me. I can't help it, but I just feel that way about you. And that isn't right, because we haven't even been on one date. I want to fix that. Will you go out with me Friday?"

I should have balked at his saying I belonged to him. I didn't belong to anyone but myself. But I'd waited so long for him to ask me out. All I could say was a barely audible, "Yes." A tingling sensation started in my chest and rose to my mouth, pulling the corners up into a broad smile.

"Great." He turned to start the engine, stopped, and then turned back to me. "You know what? Screw doing things right."

James leaned across the seat. Tenderly, he cupped the back of my neck, bringing me close. He put his lips on mine and kissed me softly. My body reacted as if it had been waiting my whole life to take charge. I surprised myself by wrapping my arms around his neck, kissing him back while pulling him closer.

James gently backed away, "I guess you feel the same way about me." He chuckled and started the car.

I blushed, embarrassed by my reaction, but I smiled that entire day. The morning was made even better when we pulled into Grinds for lattes to go. This small gesture probably meant more to me than to James, but stopping at "our place" on the way to school on the morning of our first kiss made our relationship seem real.

The next few days were a blur. I worked late every night, trying to stay on top of all my class assignments. I knew there was no way Mom would let me go out on Friday otherwise. Thankfully, by Thursday, I was actually ahead in my schoolwork.

Friday arrived, and the day passed without incident. Anamae and I had been working overtime, keeping Victor and James apart since Monday afternoon when Victor had accidentally bumped into James, knocking his books to the floor. Only it hadn't seemed like an accident. Unfortunately, keeping Victor and James apart also kept me away from Anamae and Victor. While I missed them, I knew they needed time to grow as a couple just as I needed time to get to know James. I walked with James to his car after school, my mood light ahead of our date.

"So what time are you going to pick me up?" I asked.

"I thought I'd pick you up now," he said. James swept me up into his arms, and I laughed at his joke. He spun me around once before lightly setting me back down.

"Now? Where are we going?" I asked, breathless from laughing so hard.

"It's a surprise. And we need to get moving. This trip is best made at sunset," he said, giving me a wink. He retrieved a perfect blush-colored rose from the front seat and handed it to me before closing my car door.

I raised an eyebrow, wondering how he'd gotten the rose. It wasn't in his car this morning. The rose was freshly cut. He must have ditched last period. James mimicked my expression, raising his eyebrow in response.

"Can I at least have a hint where we're going?" I asked, inhaling the sweet aroma of the rose as he pulled out of the student parking lot.

"Nope," he said, smiling. He turned on the stereo, and the car was filled with music from a satellite radio 90's grunge station.

"Just one tiny word?"

"Tell you what. I'll give you two. Judaculla Rock," he said, and then he turned up the music, effectively ending any more discussion about his surprise.

I thought about the words, Jew-duh-culla Rock. My father had mentioned the place years ago as a possible camping trip, one we never got to take. I wondered why James wanted to go there. As far as I knew, Judaculla Rock didn't even have official tent sites. Aside from a hiking trial, there was nothing else to do. I stared out of the window as we drove past Claire's Diner and headed out of Woodvine.

When the main road dissolved into a two-lane highway, houses and buildings faded into the background. For a time, there was nothing but wide-open space. Then clusters of trees trickled into view as poplars, oaks, and sugar maples introduced the beginning of a thick forest. And we drove on.

The highway twisted as we headed into the mountains. On my right, sheer rock faces tried to shrug the road off the mountainside. We arrived in the small town of Sylva a little after five. The highway cut through a row of restaurants and shops that made up the main drag of the tiny town. The windows of the last building had soap-painted advertisements, offering steaming cups of coffee. A Sylva police car was parked outside the diner.

We crossed the boundary between Sylva and

Cullowhee without even a sign to separate the two tiny towns. The only clue we'd traveled from one to the other was different names on storefronts. Not long after we passed Western Carolina University, James turned left down a gravel road that was concealed by low bushes. If I were driving, I would have gone right past it. James drove a few more miles, the Rover's tires kicking up rocks and dust clouds behind us. When he finally parked in a small paved lot, ours was the only car there. Sudden isolation closed in on me.

As much as I was falling for James, Victor had been right. I was on my guard whenever James was around. It was as if he put out a weird vibe. I thought about what Mom had said. Maybe James had been marked by the unspeakable horror he had survived, and this mark left him changed in ways I wouldn't be able to understand. The nightmare I'd had of James haunted me, and a creepy sensation rolled through me like an electric current. And there it was. I was afraid of James.

Afraid I'd lose him.

Afraid I wouldn't.

This was stupid. If I wanted to be with James, wanted to date him, I was going to have to sort this all out. Logically, I knew there was absolutely no reason for me to be frightened of him. And yet, my uneasy feeling was compounded when I glanced down at my cell and saw I had no service.

*Get it together, Leath,* I thought. *Don't invite drama.*

I slowed my breathing, purposely inhaling through my nose and exhaling through my mouth. My father had taught me this technique during our first whitewater rafting trip on the nearby Nantahala River. I was fearful of falling out of the raft, or the raft flipping over and my being caught in the current. *Keepers* was the term the raft guide had called the rough waters. Places where a body could be trapped and kept there.

"You've talked about this trip for weeks, Leath," Dad had said. "Don't ever let fear rob you of something you want. Fear is just the flip side of excitement. Exhale the fear and breathe in the excitement."

I breathed in, counting to ten before I slowly exhaled. This was what I wanted. I wanted James. Fear was not going to rob me of him.

"We're here," James said, opening my door.

I took a deep breath and stepped out of the Rover.

"We might need these." He reached past me, grabbing our jackets from the front seat. My mind blurred by his closeness, his incredible scent. I was tempted to grab him, to be bold enough to steal a kiss. But the moment raced past me.

James straightened and slipped his jacket on, then draped mine around my shoulders. I followed him to a path off the parking lot.

I glanced back one last time before the graceful branches of a loblolly pine obstructed the view. Other trees had snarls of limbs that looked as if they were reaching out to pluck me from the path. I studied them curiously, not paying attention to where I walked. I slipped on sweet-gum seedpods and nearly fell.

James steadied me, putting his arm around my waist. We walked on. "You don't get into the woods much, do you?"

The memory of my last camping trip with my dad flashed through my mind. I had enjoyed being out in the woods with him. Enjoyed learning all the names of the trees and the calls of the animals. I could do this. This forest was no different from the campgrounds Dad and I had visited. I let the familiar sights and sounds of the forest comfort me, and I began to feel at ease.

"It's been a while," I said.

"Don't worry; I take all my victims this way."

I stopped dead in my tracks.

James looked at me and smirked. "You really are too easy." He turned me toward him. His hands traveled up both of my arms, to my shoulders, and across my back until he was holding me close. "I'm not dangerous." He reached down and lifted my chin. "Well, maybe a little."

Before my brain could register what he'd said, he was kissing me. Slowly at first, and then building until I had a tough time keeping up with him. Our bodies pressed tightly together. His scent was overwhelming and erased my questions about him. I lifted my hands, grabbing the front of his shirt and pulling him closer, as if that were even possible.

"See, just a little dangerous," he murmured in my ear. He kissed me softly on my cheek before leaning away from me. "Come on, it's right over here."

Daylight was slipping away. I caught glimpses of a pink sky through the patches of lush green leaves as I followed James down a narrow path. Brown park signs reminded visitors not to sit on, or even touch, Judaculla Rock. The path led to a wooden platform with three small decks. We stopped at the largest, which was directly in front of a gray boulder the size of a small car. The stone jutted out of the earth at an unusual angle. The semicircular platform around it was a pitiful protection, one James disregarded as he continued to the edge of the last deck and jumped off.

"This is the three-thousand-year-old stone known as Judaculla Rock." His hands moved in a sweeping motion over the boulder.

I looked at the scarred rock face. The front was covered in faint white lines, circles, and a mix of indecipherable shapes and random marks. I stared more closely, trying to find patterns in the carvings. Some of the markings looked like people, spear-throwers. Others were just squiggly lines. If the stone held a story, there was no rhyme or reason to it.

"Hieroglyphics?" I asked.

"Sort of. It's a petroglyph. A rock carving."

"What do the pictures mean?"

"No one knows for sure, but there are a lot of legends. Some people think the marks are stories about an alien visitation." James smiled and raised his eyebrows questioningly.

I scrunched my eyes together, pretending to study the rock. "Yes, this does look like the place the mothership dropped me off," I said, playing along.

"I thought you'd recognize it," he teased.

But when he continued, his tone was serious. "Some people think the rock's a map to secret Cherokee hunting grounds in another world. According to Cherokee legend, a slant-eyed giant called Judaculla threw the rock here. That's his handprint." He pointed to a seven-fingered hand carved into the rock. James picked up a handful of milky-white pebbles. He shook them in his closed fist, their clatter seeming too loud in the silent clearing. James offered his other hand, and I climbed off the platform to join him. He led me around the rock, to the other side, which faced a dark forest. He carefully placed the pebbles on the edge of the boulder. There were seven of them.

I was lost in thought, intrigued by the stone and its mystery, but also by the sound of James's voice. It seemed paramount I memorize everything about this place—as if the massive boulder was somehow crucial to my existence.

"Some people think the rock itself is a portal to another world. Others think it gives special abilities."

"What do you think?"

"About what?" I asked, shaken from my thoughts.

"Do you think I can fly?" He gave a sly grin and raised an eyebrow.

I knew he was teasing me for zoning out, but for a split second, I believed he could. I believed James could do anything he wanted.

"What do you think about the stories?" he asked. "Do you think there could be other worlds? Or connections to those other worlds?"

That had been a reoccurring fantasy of mine. One of those things I'd told myself about Dad. He wasn't gone; he just wasn't here anymore. "I guess it's possible," I said.

James leaned against the boulder and placed his finger on one of the pebbles. He casually moved the milky-white stone to the supposed handprint of Judaculla, stopping just above the first finger.

"I think we're surrounded by connections," he said, sliding a second pebble above the second finger.

"What kind of connections?" I asked, mesmerized by his delicate rearrangement of the pebbles.

"Connections to other worlds and other connections we don't even realize. I think there are many kinds," he said. "For example, I think we're connected by dreams."

"How?" I asked, intrigued.

"I think the people in our dreams are real, and we have connections with them."

"Wait a minute, you think when we're dreaming, dreaming about other people, even people we don't know, we're making actual connections with them?"

"I don't think we connect with everyone in our dreams." His eyes burned into mine. "But maybe we connect with some."

The intensity of his stare made me drop my gaze. I noticed he had moved all but one of the pebbles to the fingers of the handprint. "I'd have to see some proof before I could believe that theory."

"How 'bout this? Do you believe in destiny?" he asked.

Of course I did. What girl didn't hang her hopes on the idea that the perfect boy was out there just waiting to be found? Her soul mate. "I believe there's someone for everyone. If that's destiny, yes."

"If you believe in destiny, you have to believe there are connections, or groundwork being laid, to get those two people together. I believe in destiny. That two people are meant to complete each other, or to be each other's undoing," James chuckled. He was sliding the last pebble toward the handprint when something caught my eye.

It was so quick I wasn't sure what I was seeing. There was a slight movement, a flash of something beautiful and golden in the forest on the other side of the clearing. But what? Maybe a leaf, struck by the last rays of sunshine as it drifted in the wind. Couldn't be. Leaves didn't cast a reflection. I stared harder, trying to find the shimmering light in the mesh of leaves and thick branches.

"Do you want to take a walk?" he asked, pointing to a faint trail that led into the heart of the forest, one I hadn't noticed earlier.

The sky changed, growing grayer with each passing minute, and I realized how quickly darkness was joining us. The combination of the mysterious light and James's interest in the woods left me unsettled. Had he seen the light, too? "I'm not really dressed for hiking."

"I didn't bring you here to go hiking," he said, sounding deep in thought. He raked his hand through his hair, in a somewhat desperate manner.

"Why did you bring me here?" I asked anxiously.

James was silent, staring into the forest. It seemed an internal battle raged deep within him. As if he were making one of the most difficult decisions of his life. Was it something he needed to say? Or something he needed to do? After a long moment, he threw the last pebble against the base of the boulder. It bounced once and landed in the sand at my feet.

James cleared his throat, and I braced myself.

"I brought you here because I wanted to take you somewhere you'd never been before. Someplace special. And now I regret my impatience earlier this week." He moved closer, staring into my eyes. "I wanted our first kiss to be at Judaculla."

I breathed a sigh of relief. James was trying to make a romantic gesture. Was I this inept at romance? James wasn't dangerous—he was intense, purposeful, and confident. He was all the things I wasn't.

I stepped into his arms, walking away from my fears. I trampled them under my feet, leaving them on the ground behind me. When his arms enveloped me, I knew this was where I belonged. There was no more worry, no more fear. I vowed to never let either emotion return. Nothing would rob me from what I wanted. I felt a surge of relief at releasing the doubt, casting off the heavy burden of caution. Being in James's arms made me strong, bold even.

"I liked our first kiss just fine," I said. "But this will be the place I kiss you first." I stretched onto my toes and lightly kissed his lips. He responded by crushing me to him, kissing me back deeply, urgently. I wanted to get closer, close enough to be a part of him. My pulse quickened as I wrapped my arms around his shoulders, trying to lift myself higher. He grabbed me by the waist, pulling me up until my feet lost their hold on the ground.

"I love you, Leath," he whispered. "I always have."

I didn't know how to respond. Of course his words thrilled me to no end, but it was crazy. He loved me? He barely knew me. Even crazier was the *I always have* part.

103

Always? Always as in for three weeks? It made no sense. I stared at him, unable to form a response to his words. He smiled, seeming satisfied to leave me speechless.

The night brought cooler air. James took off his jacket and wrapped it around me. I rested my head on his chest and listened to his heartbeat. It seemed it kept the same rhythm as my own, like they were perfectly matched. The heat of his body warmed me as we watched the sun slide lower. Watched as it melted on the far side of the mountains. Too soon, James pulled away. He leaned forward and gently kissed me on the forehead, just the same as he'd done the night we'd gone bowling.

"We need to head back," he said, leading me away from Judaculla Rock and onto the platform.

Moonlight guided us toward the path to the parking lot. I turned back for one last look, searching for the strange glittering in the forest. Maybe I was trying to attach something unique and unusual to Judaculla. Something sealing this as a special place, its existence a gift to be shared only between James and me. Whatever the light was, it was gone.

As we entered the path, the trees were so thick they completely trapped any light in their broad branches. Not even moonlight shone through to the pitch black of the forest floor. I thought about the light again. Maybe my eyes had been playing tricks on me, and there had never been a light. I didn't care. I would forever count Judaculla Rock as my most treasured of places. It didn't matter if the glimmering light was real or in my imagination. I had seen it. The fact I was the only one made the light more special.

We walked slowly to the car, holding hands with no words between us.

"Are you hungry?" he asked, opening my car door.

"No," I said, but my stomach made me a liar. It

growled, demanding food as I climbed into the Rover.

James laughed. "Let's get something to eat before we head back." He walked around to the driver's side, got in, and started the car. "Asheville?"

I nodded, not in the mood for a burger or the diner in Woodvine.

"Where do you want to go?"

I was suddenly famished, and thought of the perfect place. "Watanabe's?"

"Hibachi sounds good," he agreed.

The ride to Asheville was quiet. Maybe it was because we were heading back toward home, but the night seemed to be getting away from me. I wanted time to slow down, go backward even. I thought about the prematurity of James's declaration of love. Surely I'd imagined those words, just as I had imagined the glimmering light in the forest. Too soon, we pulled into the parking lot of Watanabe's and I had to put my thoughts aside.

We were early for dinner. There were no other customers waiting at the hostess stand where a tall blonde girl greeted us. We followed her through the maze of low-slung chairs and jet-black tables of the darkened bar into the main dining area. This room had better lighting. Long metal tables filled it, each separated by panels of heavy red cloth decorated by golden dragon silhouettes. I felt the heat of the stovetops as we passed.

The hostess stopped at a table where a couple sat with one young boy and four younger girls. The boy had a scowl on his face, but one of the girls beamed under a pink paper crown. I smiled at her as James and I claimed the two remaining seats at the opposite side of the table. The woman glanced at me, smiling briefly before returning her attention to the children.

A waitress wrote everyone's orders on a small gray

tablet. A server followed a few minutes later with crisp salads covered in ginger dressing and bowls of miso soup. Our chef arrived and chopped vegetables with smooth, skillful motions. The chef turned large bowls upside down, dumping piles of rice onto the steaming cooktop. My stomach growled again as the room filled with the aroma of sizzling strips of beef. As we ate, the chef cleaned the grill. Afterward, everyone at our table applauded his performance.

While I finished my meal, I watched the woman blot soy sauce from the boy's shirt. She smiled and said, "See, it's all out." He grinned, seeming happy to have her attention. She wrapped her arm around his waist and pulled him to stand next to her chair.

I glanced at James. He was studying them with a sad expression on his face. I hoped he would share some memory of his mother, but he didn't. It was obvious he missed her and I wanted to comfort him, but I didn't know how or if he would want me to. He paid for our meal and we returned to Woodvine, beating my curfew by ten minutes.

James walked me to the front porch. The light flicked on, the timing too perfect to be coincidental. I knew my mother waited on the other side of the door.

"I guess this is goodnight," he said. James smiled, pointing up at the porch light.

"I guess." I stepped closer to him.

As we faced each other, our hands intertwined at our sides. James bent and brushed his lips against mine. "I love you," he whispered. "Sweet dreams."

He turned to go, and I opened the front door. I heard Mom's quick footsteps, skipping down the hall away from the door. I put the alarm on before heading to the living room.

"Did you have a good time?" she asked.

-"Yes, Mom," I said. I yawned, hoping she'd take the hint.

She smiled, seeming to understand. "Well, you can tell me all about it tomorrow. Goodnight, sweetie."

I was thankful to have this conversation another time and hopeful it might not happen at all. After I kissed her cheek, I climbed the stairs to take a long, hot shower. An hour later, I lay awake in bed, replaying every minute of my time with James.

Kissing him was different from any other experience I'd ever had. Okay, I didn't have that much experience. But I had kissed other boys. Looking back, those kisses were childish, clumsy, and awkward. When James kissed me, it was perfection. While there was no question our kisses were fueled by desire, there was something else. Something significant.

*Love?*

I had no frame of reference for how it felt to be in love. To love a boy so much it hurt to be away from him. No experience with that emotion whatsoever, except that was exactly the way I felt whenever James and I were apart.

*Destiny?*

Yes.

I was falling in love with James, falling hard and without a care of where I'd land. It was then I decided to throw myself off that cliff and fully commit to seeing where things went with him.

My mind whirled at the notion, and I was unable to settle my thoughts. I was frustrated this perfect day had come to such a restless end. But if I didn't go to sleep, how could I start the next perfect day with James? The springs in my mattress screeched with every move I made.

"Leath?"

"Yeah," I responded, cranky from being over-tired.

Mom entered my bedroom. "I heard you tossing and turning on my way to bed. Are you okay?"

"I'm okay. Just restless, I guess."

"See if this helps." She pulled a tiny vial from the pocket of her robe. The vial was clear smooth glass, with an oddly shaped yellow crystal that served as a stopper.

"What is it?"

"A mixture of essential oils. Lavender and a few relaxation herbs. I used it when you were younger. Just a drop on your wrist or pillowcase and you would go straight to sleep. I found it in the cabinet when I was looking for the Tylenol earlier." She put the bottle on my nightstand. "Let me know if you need anything. Goodnight, honey."

"Goodnight," I said as she closed my door.

I looked at the vial skeptically.

I remembered a trip Mom and I had made to the day spa in Asheville. What was the name of the place? Oh yeah... *Suggestions*. Mom had surprised me with a mother/daughter package on my sixteenth birthday. Part of our package included a visit to their aromatherapy room. There were all kinds of elixirs, some to brighten a mood, others to spark creativity, and some to relax the mind.

*Why not?* I thought.

I picked up the bottle, lifted the stopper, and dabbed a bit on the inside of my wrist. Laying down, I breathed in the musky fragrance and froze. This aroma was similar to what I'd come to know as James's. No. Not similar. It was exactly the same fragrance. I searched the bottle for a label. There was nothing. Nothing etched into the glass either.

Strange.

I returned the bottle to my nightstand then laid

back, one of my wrists directly under my nose. Breathing deeply, I enjoyed the wonderful aroma. And because my room was filled with the scent of him, I fell asleep, thinking of how it beautiful it was to be in James's arms.

That night, the dream of the boy returned to me. We held hands as we strolled along a riverfront I remembered from a visit to my grandparents in South Carolina. There was a gentle breeze. The air was cool, and we both wore hooded sweatshirts with an ice cream-cone logo on the bottom of the sleeves. One I didn't recognize. Our flip-flops made thumping noises as we walked on the boardwalk. The boy was taller than I was. I looked up at his face, but it was hidden by the hood of his sweatshirt. The desire to see him was irresistible. Even in my slumber, I knew it had been years since I'd last dreamt of him. I couldn't risk not getting another opportunity to finally see his face. I grasped the edge of his hood and gasped, simultaneously jolting myself awake.

# 7

## Of All the Luck

JAMES AND I WERE INSEPARABLE AT SCHOOL OVER THE next few days, and time moved in illogical ways. When James and I were together, it seemed as if only minutes had passed. When we were apart, it seemed as if all of eternity passed before I saw him again. James and I had developed what seemed to be an unbreakable hold on each other, one that grew stronger each day as our relationship deepened.

Daydreaming about what the upcoming weekend held for us as we walked together after school to the parking lot on Friday, I noticed Victor's car parked right beside the black Rover. Victor leaned casually against his car alongside Anamae, almost as if they'd been lying in wait for us.

James stiffened when Victor hugged me hello.

"Just checking to see what time you're coming tomorrow," Victor said.

I had no idea what he was talking about.

"Where's your head, Leathal?" Victor asked, rolling his eyes. He spoke slowly. "Every year at my house? Everybody wears green? The little leprechauns come out? We're doing it early this year because the seventeenth is on a Monday."

"Your St. Patrick's Day party," I said. I had completely forgotten about the annual tradition. I looked at James for his reaction.

"Yes, bring your ball and chain with you," Victor reluctantly said.

James glared at him. "Leath is free to do as she pleases."

"Well, that's mighty big of you," Victor smugly said.

James moved closer to him, but Anamae stepped between them.

"Victor's mom wants to meet you, James," she said, trying to smooth things over.

James tore his eyes away from Victor to smile at Anamae. "Why not? Sounds fun."

"Terrific." Victor sounded less than enthused. "See you then." He walked around his car and held the passenger side door open for Anamae. She shrugged a goodbye and smiled before getting into the car.

James and I left campus and headed to Grinds. "Sorry about that," I said as we sat at our regular table. "My family has gone to Victor's party for as long as I can remember."

"It's okay, Leath," he said, pulling me close. "We need to be a part of each other's traditions. I have my own family traditions I want to continue, traditions that have passed down for generations. Ones I would like to share with you, even if they seem outdated. I want to go to Victor's party with you. We'll have a good time." He kissed me lightly on my lips, and I decided to believe him.

Mom left early the next day to help Victor's parents set up for the party. I dressed in green lace tights, a short black skirt, and a button-up green sweater. I was just putting on thick strands of green beads when the doorbell rang. It was James, and he wasn't wearing one speck of green.

He sat on the couch, amused by my frantic digging through our box of random decorations. Thankfully, I found a dented green bowler hat. It was one my dad had worn to an earlier Kavanagh party. James balked at first, but when I explained that everyone would be in full-on green, he grudgingly wore the hat. By the time that was settled, we were running late.

Victor's stepfather Will Kavanagh greeted us at the door. He was a tall man with coal-black eyes that contrasted with his pale white skin. Will looked quite different from his usual self, a partner in the most successful medical practice in Asheville. His normally neat red hair stuck out in odd angles at the bottom of his green bowler hat. It was then I remembered he and Dad had matching ones.

"Come in, come in," Will said, kissing my cheek. "This must be James." He shook James's hand and then led us to the living room. It was packed with small groups of people, many of the adults clutching glasses of frothy green beer.

"Make yourselves at home while I go find Marisol. She's been waiting for you." Will smiled before vanishing down a short hallway.

I took James by the hand, pulling him further into the room.

"I was wondering when you'd get here," Anamae said, rising from a blood-orange couch. Her high heels clicked across the hardwood floors as she made her way through the crowd. She wore a curly green wig and a dark green jumpsuit that showed off her long legs and perfect figure. She hugged me and then turned to James. She hesitated briefly, and then said, "Why not?" before hugging him, too.

Their embrace made me a little uncomfortable. James seemed to sense this. After Anamae stepped away from him, he slipped his arm around my waist.

"Hey, Leathal," Victor said, joining us. He swept me up in a great hug, breaking James's hold on me. Victor picked me up and swung me around. "You look amazing." He set me down, smoothly transitioning into an impromptu waltz. I felt his hands move to my hips.

"Thanks. You... look... interesting." I giggled and tugged his leprechaun-style coat.

James cleared his throat.

I broke away from Victor, suddenly remembering we were not alone.

"Glad you could come, James," Victor said, his insincerity thinly disguised behind a false smile.

"I wouldn't have missed it." James's tone was dark.

"Leath," Victor's mother called. "There you are."

Marisol Kavanagh was a petite powerhouse of a woman. She barged through the crowd. Taking my hands, she pulled me into her arms. "It's been too long since your last visit. I have missed you," she exclaimed, her Spanish accent thick with punctuation.

I loved Marisol. When I'd first met her, she'd ignored my extended hand and pulled me into a tight embrace. "My Victor tells me all about you," she had murmured. She'd stepped away from me then, sizing me up with her chocolate eyes. "Yes, you will be good for my Victor."

From that moment on, I'd tried to live up to her expectations. I *had* been good for Victor, and he had been good for me. Everything was fine between us until Victor noticed I was a girl and James moved to Woodvine.

It felt good being back in the Kavanagh house, hugging Marisol. It was like going home after being away at summer camp.

"I've missed you, too," I said.

Glancing over Marisol's shoulders, I saw a tacky, multicolored lump of plastic on top of their antique phonograph. I pulled away and smiled at her. "I can't believe you kept that thing."

"The Blarney Stone?" Marisol asked. "Of course I did. It's Kavanagh tradition. It really does bring good luck. For example, it was lucky you and Victor didn't burn the house down when you melted all that plastic to make it."

I smiled, thinking of Marisol's many superstitions. She always threw salt over her left shoulder if she spilled any while cooking. I remembered the time Marisol had broken a mirror. Victor had complained that instead of seven years of bad luck, it had been seven years of listening to Marisol tell them bad luck was on the way.

Marisol released me and looked at James. As I made the introductions, Marisol and James shook hands. At his touch, her color paled. She quickly withdrew her hand from his grasp. I'd only seen Marisol react that way one time before. A long-ago trip to the library in Asheville when a politician shook Marisol's hand after his speech on education reform. When I'd asked about her reaction to the man, she'd said, "Shaking hands with him was like shaking hands with a snake."

"It's nice to meet you," James said, sounding apprehensive.

"And you," Marisol replied, looking like she meant quite the opposite. She turned to Victor. "Why don't you take your friends outside? The fire pit is already going. I've got to finish getting dinner ready." Marisol walked away briskly, heading toward the kitchen. She glanced back at James once as if she were making some kind of judgment or decision about him.

"That was fun." Anamae stormed off in a huff through the living room toward the back patio.

Victor rolled his eyes and mouthed the words,

"Drama Queen." He followed Anamae, leaving me and James alone in an ocean of silence.

"I hope you're hungry," I said, trying to break the tension. "Marisol's probably making a huge pot of her famous green arroz con pollo. Do you want to get a drink while we wait?"

"I'll tell you what I want," James said icily.

"What?" I asked, surprised by his tone.

"I want to know what's going on with you and Victor."

I shouldn't have, but I laughed. "Are you serious?"

"Dead serious."

I felt chills travel up my spine at his words.

"It's obvious he cares about you by the way he acts whenever he sees you, and his parents seem to love you as well," he said in a chastising tone. "But I don't care about any of that. I want to know how you feel about him. How you really feel."

"Victor is one of my best friends," I said, each word bitter on my tongue.

"I don't know why I bothered to ask. You won't give me a straight answer because it's clear you don't know yourself." He glared at me. "I thought you didn't have time for games, but it seems you've changed your mind. That's okay with me. I'm ready to play."

I struggled to keep my composure, to pull in the fury that built up inside me. How dare he question my relationship with Victor? Didn't I blindly accept his relationship with Ever? When I opened my mouth to respond, James turned his back on me. He headed to the patio, leaving me without a target for my anger.

"I thought he'd never leave," Victor said, coming up behind me. "That guy's a real tool."

Target acquired.

"What? He is," Victor said defensively. "And I can't bear it when he touches you."

I turned to him, prepared to unleash my full wrath. Instead, I burst out laughing. He must have caught up to Anamae because he now wore her curly green wig. "Why is it that I can never stay angry with you?"

"There's no point in it," Victor said, sliding the wig off his head. "Come on, sit with me."

He took my hand and led me in the opposite direction James had gone. We walked outside onto the wraparound porch and sat on the old wooden swing. The temperature must have been in the upper fifties. Victor put his arm around my shoulders and pulled me close. He was so warm. Instinctively, I put my head on his chest. I'd missed this. The closeness I'd once had with Victor. I couldn't remember the last time we'd been alone or he had casually taken my hand like he used to do.

We rocked for several minutes in comfortable silence. It was easy being with Victor. It was natural. As natural as waking up in the morning. Even though we no longer spent as much time together, I didn't know if I'd even want to get up each morning if Victor were truly out of my life. My mind cleared. Free of all tension, I looked up at him.

He turned to me and smiled the smile that said, "See, everything's fine."

I'd seen that look a thousand times, and it always calmed me.

Victor leaned closer. Before I could stop him—and in that moment, I wasn't sure I wanted to—his lips melted onto mine.

I was confused, but I didn't pull away from him.

"Just go with it, Leath," Victor murmured before his lips returned to mine.

Something fluttered deep inside, a feeling like wings beating against a cage. A yearning to burst out, trapped by too many years of just being friends. I could feel it rising, moving toward the doors I'd shut on Victor a long time ago. For a few seconds, I wavered, giving in to the unexpected desire building inside me. What would be the harm? I parted my lips.

"I told you," Anamae said sulkily. "If you ever need to find Leath, just look for Victor."

I pulled away from Victor, scared to raise my eyes. Praying I was wrong, but knowing it was impossible, I looked up to see who was with Anamae.

Of course it was James.

He stood beside her, silently judging me. My heart split into painful shards as I stuttered, trying to explain.

Victor, on the other hand, made no effort to explain or even move. He kept his arm wrapped around my shoulder as he narrowed his eyes. "Anamae, that was not very kind of you," he said, clearly pleased by the turn of events.

"Spare me," Anamae said, taking James's hand in hers. "Let's get out of here."

"James." I stood and searched his face, desperate to read him.

"Don't," he said, holding up one finger. "You're not who I thought you were."

The words slashed through me, sharp and unforgiving.

"Yeah, Leath. You can't call dibs on them both," Anamae said. She snuggled close to James.

James cut me with eyes that sought to rip out my soul before turning away with Anamae. As they walked down the driveway, she pulled him even closer.

I slumped back onto the swing. Although a tremendous loss wore on my heart, no tears came. My pain was too profound to be expressed in such a simple manner. It was then I realized the intensity of my feelings for James.

I truly loved him.

I loved James from the greatest depths of the ocean to the infinite measure of space. Because I loved him so intensely, he had the absolute power to anger me to almost the same degree.

Almost.

Five minutes ago, I'd been furious with James. Now, I'd give anything to have him sitting here beside me. I wished we'd never come to this party. Wished I hadn't been so careless with James's feelings. Watching the Rover drive away with Anamae inside was devastating.

*Anamae.*

She was supposed to be my best friend. I couldn't believe she'd made a play for my boyfriend. Then I acknowledged my hypocrisy. What was I doing out here snuggled up beside Victor, anyway? What was I thinking kissing him? For one second, my grief changed to white-hot anger—at myself. I had done this. I had ruined things with James. At the same time, I had been utterly cruel toward Victor. Cruel because I'd kissed him, giving him some hope that we might be together. I sat in shock, contemplating the damage one kiss had caused. The minutes passed, and all feeling floated away from me, but if I couldn't have James, I didn't care if I ever felt anything again.

"Are you all right?" Victor asked. His voice was miles away.

Shock finally gave way to emotion. "No," I said quietly. Great tears rolled from my eyes. That kiss had cost me dearly.

Gently, Victor turned my face toward his.

I didn't want to see him, so I closed my eyes.

"Leath," he said. "Please, look at me."

I did, unwillingly.

"I'm not going to say I'm sorry because I'm not. I've

wanted to kiss you for a long time, and I don't regret it."

Unable to speak, I shook my head. Tears flooded my cheeks, spilling down the front of my sweater.

Victor cradled me in his arms, and then the sobs came. "Shh, it's all right, love," he said soothingly.

"No, it isn't. Nothing is all right," I argued. "Not you and me, James, Anamae. Everything is all wrong. It won't ever be right again."

"That's just for now. Everything will be all right. Wait and see. Until it does, you shouldn't worry about Anamae."

I didn't ask why, but he answered me anyway.

"Because I'm not worried about Anamae. She wasn't really into me. Did you know she gave her number to a guy she met at the bowling alley that night we all went? She tried to cover when he called earlier this evening."

I shook my head, puzzled by this news.

"Yeah, I thought you would've told me if you'd known about him. Listen, everything will work out the way it's supposed to. It always does." Victor stroked my hair and lightly tucked a bit of it behind my ear.

"But James hates me."

"Well, I hate him, so I guess we're even."

I flinched, hurt by Victor's words.

"I'm sorry. I didn't mean that. Well, maybe I did. A little." He smiled. "What I mean is it doesn't matter what James thinks because he doesn't matter. The only thing that matters is what I know for sure. We belong together."

That word again. Belong. I had a feeling I didn't belong anywhere. I pulled away from Victor. I had to explain things to him. Try to undo what I'd done. I had to clear this up before Victor felt the same crushing sadness I did.

"We don't belong together," I said hoarsely, trying to find my voice.

"We do. You don't see that now. But you will."

"There you are," Mom said, joining us on the porch. She was followed by Marisol, both giggling as outlandish shamrock antennae jiggled from the tops of their heads. I quickly wiped my face, thankful for the cover of darkness the night gave me.

Unfortunately, my mom didn't need to see my face to know I was upset. She sat down on my other side and took my hand.

"Did you and James have a fight?" she asked softly.

I nodded. My tears returned, and I allowed her to cradle me in her arms.

"Hush now," Marisol said. "Mijo, give Penny and me a little girl time with Leath, yes?"

Victor stood and Marisol sat in his place, patting my back. I heard Victor open the front door and go inside. I waited for Marisol's comforting words. She had none for me.

"Look here, Leath," she said firmly.

I turned away from my mom, wiped my face again, and looked into Marisol's brown eyes, surprised by her tone.

"Even if you do not choose my Victor, you must not be with James. There's something about him that's not right."

At her words, my intuition did an, "I told you so," dance in my head. I knew Marisol was skilled in picking out what she called, "the bad apples," and it concerned me to think she and James would be at odds.

"I've gotten to know James. He seems really nice," Mom said. It was the second time she had defended him to one of her friends.

"That boy has a secret," Marisol said. "He's trying to keep it inside, keep it hidden. But secrets do not stay quiet. His secret will tell on him. When it does, you do not want to be around to hear it."

"Marisol, he's just a kid. Trust me. He's had a rough time, but he's all right." Mom turned to me, "Come on, honey. You'll feel better after you have something to eat," she said, coaxing me off the swing.

I followed in a stupor as Mom and Marisol led me back inside the house. It was too bright, and the party was too loud. My eyes burned, tired from crying. Victor waited for us in the kitchen. He thrust a warm bowl into my hands. The delicious and familiar smell of paprika, garlic, and onion triggered hunger pangs. I sat with him at the round table and devoured Marisol's arroz con pollo.

He refilled my bowl and handed me a soda. "Feeling better?" he asked.

"Yeah, thanks." I pulled a few sips from my drink before starting on my second bowl. This time, I ate slowly, tasting each bite of the food. When I finished, I was overwhelmed by fatigue. "I'm sorry. I'm just not in a party mood."

"No problem. I'll take you home. Let me go tell The Moms."

I smiled at his use of the nickname we'd given our mothers years ago.

A few minutes later, we were on the road. As I stared out the window, Marisol's voice rang through my head. She was right. James had a secret. But she was also wrong. When James's secret told on him, I was going to be there to hear it. If he still wanted me around.

Victor insisted on staying with me when we got to my house. I let Sam outside, and then joined Victor on the couch. We watched a ten-year-old movie series that had been on TV all weekend. It was a marathon of comforting nostalgia. An hour into the movie, I yawned loudly.

"I can take a hint," Victor said. He rose and helped me to my feet. "Walk me out so you can set the alarm." He hugged me goodbye at the front door. "It may be the worst timing ever, but I'm glad it happened. I love you, Leath."

Mentally exhausted, I didn't want to talk or even think about any of this. "Goodnight, Victor," I said. Knowing me as well as he did, he let it go. Victor walked outside without another word. I closed the door behind him and punched the code to set the alarm. I made it halfway back to the family room when a loud scratching noise caused my heart to skip a beat. My throat went dry, but then I remembered I'd left Sam outside. I retraced my steps, turned off the alarm, and opened the front door. Sam came in, giving me a look as he bounded past.

I shut the door, but it was caught on something. Panic overtook me when I looked down to see a man's boot, jamming the door open. His fingers curled around the edge of the door, easing it open. My ears buzzed loudly as I vaguely wondered why Sam wasn't barking at the intruder. It was my worst nightmare come to life. Only this time, I was nowhere near my pistol.

"Mind if I come in?" James asked, slipping through the doorway. For once, my pulse slowed when I saw it was him.

"You scared me," I said, closing the door behind him.

"I usually do."

His words made me flash with anger. He would tease me now? I wondered what he and Anamae had been doing. Then I remembered why he'd left me in the first place.

"I'm sorry about what happened," I said in a low voice.

He made no attempt to leave the foyer. Not a good sign. This would be a brief visit.

"It didn't just happen, Leath. You didn't accidentally kiss Victor."

I felt like a scolded child and reacted as such. "I didn't kiss him. He kissed me," I blurted, but the excuse sounded flimsy, even to me. "What do you want me to say?" I asked.

"There are many things you could tell me, but there's only one thing I need to hear," he said warily. "How did it make you feel?"

"How did it make me feel?" I asked, exasperated. Honestly, I hadn't allowed myself to think about that. I paused, considering it now. Hadn't I wondered what it would be like to kiss Victor? Hadn't I kissed him back? "It felt weird and just plain wrong. Look, Victor's confused." I tried to sound convincing.

"What about you? Are you confused about him?"

"No. I don't feel that way about Victor. I've known him for years, and I don't think of him in that way."

"Sometimes you can know someone for years, for your whole life even, and still not know them at all," James said distractedly.

"Maybe you're right," I said. "But I know Victor's not the one for me."

"I could have told you that." James stepped closer to me, a tender expression on his face.

It was the only encouragement I needed. I fell into his arms, crying again as I buried my face into his chest. I wondered how many tears a person could cry in one night.

"What happened with Anamae?" I asked, afraid to hear his answer.

He pulled away from me. "You're the one who made the first move."

"You're right. It's none of my business." Images of James and Anamae making out in the backseat of his

Rover spun inside my head, sickening me.

"Nothing happened," he said, sensing my distress. "Anamae asked me to take her home, and she cried all the way there. I don't know why when it seems neither is really interested in the other. I stayed with Anamae until she calmed down."

I sighed in relief, silently thanking Anamae for behaving like a true friend.

James gently stroked my cheek.

I looked up, meeting his gaze.

"Leath, the feelings I have for you are new to me. I've never been in a serious relationship before. But I'm not sure if it's new for you." James tilted his head, waiting for my reaction.

I blushed deeply. "I have dated before," I said uncomfortably. "Nothing serious, though."

"So maybe we should take things slow and see if we can get this right. You are far too important to me, too precious. One day, I hope to show you just how much." His fingers trailed down my cheek. "But I have to know that I'm your only temptation."

"You are," I promised, my face growing even redder at the word temptation.

James pulled me into his arms and gently kissed the top of my head.

As I wrapped my arms around him, I knew he was right. I definitely needed to slow down before I lost everything that was precious to me.

# 8

## Fallout

THE FIRST THING I HAD TO DO WAS TALK TO VICTOR. IT would be the hardest conversation we'd ever have, but I had to get the point across to him. We would never be a couple. I was deep in thought the next morning, trying to find the right words, when I was shaken from my contemplation by my cell phone. I read the caller ID. Anamae. I'd known I'd have to talk to her, too. I hadn't looked forward to this chat either, but maybe things would come easier with Victor if I talked to Anamae first.

"Hey, Anamae," I said hesitantly.

"Hey," she said back. "Got a second?"

"Sure." I breathed slowly, waiting for her justified outrage. I had, after all, done the unthinkable, had broken the girlfriend's code. I had kissed my best friend's boyfriend. I opened my mouth to apologize just as Anamae spoke.

"So I was stupid last night," she said. "I'm sorry I wrecked things with you and James. He's really a nice guy."

I was stunned. It took several seconds for me to find my voice. "You didn't wreck anything. I did. And I'm sorry for kissing Victor."

To my surprise, she burst out laughing.

"I take it you and Victor broke up?" I asked.

"Of course we did. Even without you in the picture, we wouldn't have made it. You were right. I think I was bored. Before you get angry with me about that, let me tell you I think Victor was bored, too. Just passing time with me. Or maybe he was trying to get you to pay attention. Don't get me wrong. Victor's wonderful and all, but it just didn't feel right kissing him, you know?"

Not wanting to compare kisses, I didn't respond to her question, hoping she'd move on.

"What about James?" she asked. "Think you guys will work things out?"

"I think we already did," I said.

"Hold that thought," she interrupted. "How do you feel about an unover?"

It was what Anamae called an early morning visit, without the sleepover part. A morning spent lounging in pajamas, talking, doing our nails, or otherwise stalling our start to weekend homework.

"Come on over," I said, smiling.

"I'm already here." She giggled and clicked off her cell.

Anamae bounded up the stairs a few minutes later with two strawberry smoothies. She set them on my dresser, quickly unzipping her pants and throwing off her shirt, revealing her PJ's underneath. She handed me one of the smoothies, and then climbed into bed beside me.

"Tell me. Tell me," she squealed. "Tell me all about it. And don't spinge on the details."

I rolled my eyes at her invented word for skimp. "All about what?" I asked, pretending not to notice she was dying for information about James.

"Well, let's start with your date the other night," she

blurted.

I took a sip of my smoothie, torturing her just a little more, before I told her everything. She gave me a huge grin when I finished. "How *are* you going to bear it next weekend?" she asked with excessive drama. Then she talked animatedly about random things, how much she loved the new polka dot scarf she just bought, how she hoped it would not rain this weekend.

This time, I didn't have to pretend. I truly had no idea what she was talking about.

Seeing the blank look on my face, she rolled her eyes. "The College Cruise?"

Oh, gosh. The first campus visit was this Saturday. The trip to Columbia. I had completely forgotten about it. I had also forgotten to tell Anamae that James was coming along. She sensed the change in my mood.

"Please don't tell me you're not going to come," she said sullenly. "I'm sure James will survive one weekend without you."

"We'll never know for sure," I said.

"Why not?" She eyed me suspiciously.

"He's coming with," I said, waiting for her reaction.

"Oh, Leath, no. Nooo," she said mournfully, as if I'd just dropped her cell phone into a running garbage disposal.

"I'm sorry, Anamae. It just sorta happened. James was asking me about the tours. He wanted to know which ones I was going on."

Anamae looked at me in full pout mode. "We're only going together on that one trip. Why didn't you pick one of the other schools to visit with James?"

"I did. He's also going with me on the second one. I'd already signed up to go on the other three trips with Victor."

Anamae burst out laughing. "Dang, girl. Which one

of them do you think is going to be angrier?" She finished her smoothie, setting the empty cup on the bedside table.

I laughed with her, avoiding her question. But suddenly, my smoothie didn't seem to sit well on my stomach. I really hadn't thought this thing through.

"I don't know. I haven't told them," I confessed.

"What?" Anamae asked. "I think you'd better, and soon. Victor will definitely notice when you're not home this weekend." She looked at me with a sympathetic expression. "Seriously, you need to decide, or be careful juggling those two. Juggling boys is like juggling shards of glass, you're bound to get cut," she said. "Just promise me one thing. Save one of the nights this weekend for me? I heard about a party at one of the houses on campus. Come with me and be sure you bring something garnet and black to wear. We'll be in Gamecock country."

"Okay, okay," I said, shaking my head. I wondered how James would feel about my ditching him to go to a party with Anamae. *I'll just have him meet us there*, I thought. "Wait, how did you find out about the party?" I asked.

Anamae giggled. "So don't be mad, but I met this guy at the bowling alley that night we were all there."

"Yes, I remember that night. Weren't you there on a date with someone named Victor?" I asked innocently.

Anamae rolled her eyes before launching into the story Victor had told me last night. As she rattled on, I wondered how the two of us had remained friends for so long. We were nothing alike. Anamae was a girly girl from birth. She seemed quite content not having a committed relationship and had no problem blurring the lines with her male friends. Even more remarkable, she remained friends with her exes long after they broke up.

Me, on the other hand.

I was never able to stay friends with a boy I'd dated.

Now I was wondering if I'd be able to stay friends with one I wouldn't date.

Knowing Victor as well as I did, I knew he was giving me time to think about what he'd said and think about that kiss. I didn't need the time. I tried hard to catch up with Victor the following week, but it proved an impossible task. We didn't have any classes together. Since I rode to and from school with James, Victor and I no longer had carpool time together either. I finally got lucky during a fire drill right before last period on Thursday afternoon when Victor and I happened to evacuate the main building at the same time.

"Where's your keeper, Leathal?" The words were playful, but I could tell he wasn't joking. "I can't believe he allowed you to stray outside on your own."

"Well, believe this. I'm not straying," I said. I turned away, no longer interested in talking to him, and pushed through the hundreds of students streaming from the building.

"Whoa, wait, Leath," Victor's voice called over the crowd. He reached me as my feet touched the grass of the south lawn. He caught my arm and spun me around. "Leath, wait."

"Leave me alone, Victor," I said, seething.

He released me, staring as though I'd scalded him. His expression changed from anger to confusion. "How did we get here?" Victor asked, a pained look on his face.

I sighed and stared into his brown eyes. "I honestly don't know," I said wearily.

"Take a walk with me?" he asked, holding out his hand.

I took his hand in mine and walked away from the crowd, away from the rest of the world. We continued walking far past the designated fire drill waiting area. We sat at one of the picnic tables of an outdoor classroom

129

abandoned long ago. In the next few minutes, it seemed like old times as we talked about everything. What classes we'd registered for senior year. I'd decided against manipulating our schedules as I'd planned, but amazingly, we learned we were in the same English class. Victor reminded me of the cruise his family had invited me to join them on over the summer. I guessed that wasn't going to happen now.

Victor squeezed my hand, and I realized how much I'd missed him. For a few moments, we were silent, just enjoying being together. Then it hit me. I loved them both, but in different ways. To one boy, I'd gladly give my heart. To the other, my life. One boy I'd loved forever it seemed. The other was someone I'd waited for forever. When I was with Victor, I felt safe. With James, I felt alive. I wondered how long a person could live like this, so completely torn in half.

As much as I hated ending this peace between us, I realized I wouldn't get another chance to tell Victor. The charter bus for the first College Cruise left right after school the next day. I couldn't put it off any longer.

"Tell me what's going on," Victor said, reading my thoughts as he often did.

He waited patiently while I ran a dozen scenarios through my mind. I tried to get the words out, but they wouldn't come. I stared down at our intertwined fingers, wishing this moment was over. I wished I'd already said what I needed to say, and this was the moment after I delivered the news. The minutes slipped by.

"I know there's something on your mind besides holding my hand. Not that I mind." He enunciated each word with his beautiful accent. How I'd missed the sound of his voice. "Just say what you need to say."

I took a deep breath. "It was great seeing you last weekend. I've missed you these past few weeks."

"I have missed you, too." He smiled at me.

"But after we kissed," I stopped and stared at our fingers again.

"Go ahead," he prodded.

"I knew we shouldn't have. That kind of relationship isn't right for us."

Victor released my hand, stood, and then walked a few steps away. He turned around. For the first time ever, he was angry with me.

"You can only think it's not right for you. You can't decide whether it's right for us because us implies you *and* me. And it *is* right for me."

I wanted to go to him and ease the pain hidden behind his anger, but he raised his hand to stop me.

"Do you know what's wrong with you? You're stuck. The newness of James hasn't worn off yet. Let me help you with that. Do you remember my cousin Sergio?"

Of course, I did. He was almost a clone of Victor. Athletic, funny, and devastatingly handsome. A wave of embarrassment passed through me.

"Yes, my cousin who you had a crush on," he said, once again reading my thoughts.

"I remember him," I blurted out, proving I could speak for myself.

"Do you remember where he lives?" His tone was calm, gentle as he asked the question.

"Yeah. Columbia, why?"

"He runs track for AC Flora. He's on the relay team, Leath."

Something pushed to the front of my memory. Relay team. James was on the relay team at his old high school in Columbia. "I get it. You checked up on James. Let's hear it, then. Give me all the dirt," I said angrily.

"Okay, I deserve that. You're right. I was hoping Sergio would tell me something I could use to turn you away from James. There's just one problem. Sergio said he'd never heard of him."

"So what?"

"Come on, Leathal. James lied to you."

"All that proves is James and Sergio never met."

"Really, Leath? Think about it. Two strangers on the same relay team?"

The truth stared me right in the face and slapped me hard. I considered myself easygoing, someone who didn't hold grudges, and someone who wasn't quick to anger. I could let some things slide, many things, actually. Pretty much anything, except for lying. Honesty was everything to me in a relationship. Without honesty, there was no trust. And for me, without trust, there was no relationship.

"Maybe your cousin got him mixed up with someone else." As I said this, I knew it was impossible.

"Come on, Leath. Deep inside, you know something isn't right with James."

I studied Victor's face for a long moment, acutely aware of how well he knew me. I thought about the times I'd questioned James's behavior, or some of the odd things he'd said. I'd told myself his strange ways were because of what he'd gone through when his parents were killed. I could excuse those things. I could not excuse dishonesty. Still, even if what Sergio had said was true, and James had lied to me, I had no intention of discussing this with Victor.

"Okay. I'm not going to push you. You'll get there in your own time. Just promise me you'll be careful around James. Think about what I said, okay?"

I doubted I'd be able to think of anything else.

The announcement came over the PA system. "All clear, please report back to class."

Victor kissed my cheek, and then turned to leave.

I grabbed his arm and turned him to face me. My eyes searched his, seeking a way to lessen his pain. "You know I will always love you," I said.

"Yes, I do," Victor said. He hugged me briefly and then headed back to class. I lingered, watching him walk away carrying a piece of my heart with him. I lagged, unsure of what else I could do about this whole mess. Crowds of students walked between us as we filed back into the main building. I slowed my pace, giving Victor time to get inside before I joined in the lengthy line of students marching back to class. Within minutes, Victor and I were separated by a distance that seemed insurmountable.

It was time to report to my job in the guidance office. I walked along slowly, knowing Mrs. Wakely wouldn't care or question if I were late. She probably used the fire drill to sneak off and have an extended smoke break. I'd still beat her to the office.

When I entered the building, I saw clusters of students forming a semi-circle around two boys.

Oh. No.

Victor grabbed the front of James's shirt and shoved him against a bank of lockers. I rushed toward them, hoping to stop Victor and James before the scuffle became a full-fledged fight. I had to reach them before one of the teachers noticed.

Anamae intercepted me. "I'm sorry, Leath. I didn't know Victor was behind us."

I looked at her, confused.

"James and I were talking about this weekend. Victor must have overheard. For some reason, he thought James and I were going together then James corrected him." Anamae took quick steps to keep up with me as I hurried toward Victor and James. I silently cursed her carelessness and poor timing as I sprinted down the hall.

"Cut it out," I said, putting a hand on each of their shoulders. "You're going to get suspended." Victor and James glared at one another as if I wasn't even there.

"What did you say?" Victor asked, his face just inches from James.

"I think you heard me," James said calmly. "Leath and I are going to Columbia tomorrow."

Why on earth did James tell him about the trip? The tortured expression on Victor's face stabbed straight through me, causing me to ache once more over his anguish. Worse was the realization that although James had said it, I had caused it. I was responsible for the pain in Victor's eyes.

"So, stay away from Leath," James said.

The words snapped Victor out of his thoughts. "Or what?"

"You don't want to know," James retorted.

Victor smirked and gave James a final shove against the lockers before releasing him. "Have a good weekend, Leath," Victor said without looking at me. He turned away and walked out of the building.

"What were you thinking?" I demanded.

"What was I thinking?" James asked. "What were you thinking? I saw you two," he said coldly. "Outside just now. Holding hands as if the two of you were dating. I thought we'd already had that conversation."

"I thought we'd already had a lot of conversations," I hissed.

The warning bell rang, and I stalked off to the guidance office, James following my every step. I turned back to him. "Just go to class, James."

Before he could respond, I slammed the door in his face. Mrs. Wakely looked up, startled by my entrance. She looked like she was in the middle of alphabetizing every document the school owned.

"Sorry," I mumbled.

Mrs. Wakely pinched her lips together as if she had just sucked twenty seeds from a lemon.

I put my book bag on the floor and noticed a light flashing on my cell. It was a text from James. I stuck my cell in my back pocket. "Is it okay if I go to the bathroom? I was on my way there when we had the fire drill."

Mrs. Wakely nodded and returned to her paperwork.

I read the text as soon as I closed the office door, this time much more quietly.

I'm sorry

*You should be*, I thought. I was so angry with him, for the way he had hurt Victor. It had been so unnecessary. My hand closed around my cell like a vice as fury consumed me. *How could James have done that?*

My cell buzzed, giving me a mini heart attack. Another text from James.

Meet me at the Rock

He was referring to Martin High's spirit rock, a small boulder near the home bleachers in the stadium. The rock was frequently covered in school slogans, sometimes inappropriate ones. But those didn't last long before a new coat of white paint erased them.

I read the text again.

Meet me at the rock

This seemed more of a demand than a request, which made me even angrier.

A battle raged inside me. Lies, secrets, and worry swirled around my head. *Oh, I'll meet you all right*, I thought as I texted back.

After school

I jammed my cell back into my pocket and returned to the guidance office. Mrs. Wakely barely noticed when I sat down on the pew. I was glad she was absorbed in her task. It gave me time to think.

I should have been the one to tell Victor, not James. How would I fix this? Could I ever fix it? Victor and I had always been completely honest with each other. I'd ruined that now. I had lied to him. It was a lie of omission, but a lie just the same.

I thought about what Victor had said about James and the relay team. Why had James lied to me about something so insignificant? I remembered something my mother had told me when I was young. Little lies.

"Little lies," she'd said, "are kindling to a great big pants fire."

More than angry, I was crushed. I had trusted James, believed everything he told me. If he was capable of lying about being on some relay team, he was certainly capable of lying about other things. Had he lied when he said he loved me? Had he lied about Ever?

There was no way I would date a liar. My next step was clear. The bell rang, and I headed outside to the spirit rock. James was waiting for me, pacing back and forth in front of the rock like a caged tiger.

"You lied to me," I accused, stopping two feet away from him.

"What?" James asked, perplexed. "What are you talking about?"

"Victor told me about your old relay team. You know the one you weren't on?"

A sad smile formed on his lips. "I'm sure he did."

"Don't even think about turning this around on Victor," I said, seething. "He was only looking out for me." I steadied myself, prepared for the volley of excuses sure to follow, wondering which lie he would try next.

James leaned against the spirit rock and ran his fingers through his hair. "Okay. It's true. I wasn't on a relay team."

He knocked the wind out of my sails. The truth. I

hadn't expected that.

"I'm sorry I lied." He stared across the football field, lost in thought.

"That's all you have to say?" I asked, irritated. "Don't you think you owe me an explanation?"

"It's embarrassing. Besides, I doubt you'll believe me."

"I think you'd better try if you expect me to have anything more to do with you."

He recoiled at my words. "You're breaking up with me?"

His disbelief refueled my anger. "Of course I am. I don't make it a habit to go out with guys I can't trust."

The pain I'd seen earlier in Victor's eyes seemed inconsequential compared to what now showed in James's expression. "Please don't say that," he said. "It's all so stupid. I was stupid." He took the fact I hadn't walked away as a signal for him to continue. "I'll explain, but I doubt it will make any sense to you."

I felt the heat rising on my chest, neck, and face. Was he stalling, buying time, while inventing a new story? I crossed my arms and glared at him.

James was motivated by my impatience. His next words came quickly. "It's true, Columbia was my home, but the last memory I have of Columbia is of losing my parents. I couldn't stop replaying the scene in my head. So, I made up the story about the relay team. It was an alternate reality, a place for me to divert my thoughts whenever my mind drifted to what happened in Columbia. Over time, I added details, embellishing the lie, writing a story of sorts. One I could tell myself whenever things got too difficult. The lie gave me something to focus on, instead of what happened to my parents. I never meant to tell you or anyone about it. But when I met Victor, it seemed like he was digging, questioning me like an interrogator. It came out accidentally. Once I'd said it, there was no way I could take it back. Not without exposing myself."

It was my turn to pace. I thought about his story, measuring it for reasonableness. He was telling the truth, and I was in the unique position to know why. I sighed, leaning against the rock beside him, staring across the length of the football field. I remembered right after my dad had died. How lost I was. How every single good memory was tarnished by his death. How I couldn't even sit in his recliner without remembering how he used to watch football from that chair, how he'd cheered and cursed his team while they played, oblivious to his own loud shouting. I had to think of something to rock me out of my memories or be swallowed up by them in my grief. And so, I invented a new reality.

"When my dad died, I made up lots of stories about why he wasn't at home. He was on a business trip, he was visiting his parents, even a story where he had a whole other family, and he'd chosen them over us. So you're wrong. I do understand about making alternatives when real life is too hard to bear. But I was a child. I'm not a child now. I thought what we had was serious."

"It is, Leath. I love you," he said.

Surely he hadn't lied about his feelings for me. There had to be one truth. He couldn't be so selfish as to kiss me without honesty. My one truth was I wanted him in my life. Although I was desperate for James, I wasn't desperate. If we were going to move forward, I had to trust him. And I wasn't sure I could. I looked at him with tears in my eyes. "How can I believe that? How can I believe anything you say?"

He stroked my cheek and stared into my eyes. "You can believe it because you feel it. You know I love you. Just as I know you love me. It's written all over your face."

He was right. Even though I'd never said it to him, it was true. I did love James. I wiped my tears away with the back of my hand. "If you have anything else you need to confess, now would be the time."

"There is one other thing," he said. "When I told you I'd never been in a serious relationship with a girl, that wasn't the whole truth."

I cringed. Here it came, something about Ever.

"The whole truth is that before you, I'd never even kissed a girl. I didn't want to tell you that because I didn't know what you'd think of me."

My head was spinning. He'd never kissed another girl? All I could think about was how special that made me. How special I was to him.

"And I am sorry about what I said to Victor," he said. "It's just… watching the two of you hold hands, walking off like that. I know it was low, but I wanted to hurt him, the way seeing you two together had hurt me. I know you and Victor are close, and I believe you when you say there's nothing between you. But you have to know this. I won't share you."

I laughed lightly. "You don't share me with anyone."

He looked at me, a relieved expression on his face, and smiled. "That's all I need to hear."

"Well, maybe a little bit this weekend with Anamae," I added.

"How's that?" James asked, puzzled.

I explained I had already committed to going with Anamae on the College Cruise. Then a new concern popped into my mind. I wondered if the trip would be a good one for James. If thoughts of his hometown were so painful to him, painful enough he'd made up stories about his time in Columbia, how would he be able to return? "Are you sure you'll be okay going back to Columbia?"

His expression was serious. "I think it's time I dealt with that. I can't go on inventing memories to replace the bad ones. I'd like to make new memories. I think a trip with you to Columbia is just what I need."

"There's something I need as well," I said, matching his serious tone. "I need to know you will be honest with me. About everything."

"I promise," he said, crossing his heart like a kid on a playground. "Going forward, nothing but the plain old ugly truth."

I looked at him, wondering if I could believe his promise. James pulled me to him and kissed me tenderly. When his lips touched mine, I forgot all about what I should do. All I could think about was what I wanted to do. I allowed his kisses to mend the hurt he'd caused me and seal us together again.

# 9

## Cruising

I WAS PRETTY SURE THE COUNSELOR WASN'T TRYING to be funny, but I couldn't stop giggling due to Anamae's incessant monologue.

Mr. Miller stood before us as we sat on the bleachers in the main gym. He was tall, well built, and looked too young to be working in a high school. He looked like he should still be in college, not leading field trips to one.

"Your schedule is pretty tight," Mr. Miller said.

"Just like you," whispered Anamae.

"We want you to have fun, but be responsible."

"Well, which is it?" Anamae asked. "Are we supposed to have fun or be responsible?"

I snickered.

"Stay with your group and don't wander away," Mr. Miller said.

"Oh, but that's where I do my best wandering," Anamae said. "Away."

"Your curfew is midnight," Mr. Miller continued.

"Like Cinderella," Anamae said.

Mr. Miller trained his eyes on Anamae. "Exactly like Cinderella. But unlike her fairy godmother, we'll be around to check that you are in for the night. We'll also give you a personal wake-up call." He raised an eyebrow, and then stared at her a few more seconds before turning to a boy a few rows over.

"How exactly are they going to do that?" I whispered.

Anamae lowered her voice, not wanting to call more attention to herself. "They tape us in."

"What?" I asked, confused.

"They go around to each room and put a piece of tape on the top of the door. We can't go out until they come by in the morning and check to see the tape is still in one piece."

"How do you know?" I asked, impressed.

"Becky told me. She said they did the same thing when she went on her college tours." Anamae nudged me. "She also told me how to get around it."

I thought about Becky, telling me how much fun college would be that day James and I had lunch off campus. I was absolutely sure Becky knew all about having fun.

"Of course she did," I said. "But I'd really rather not get kicked off the other trips I signed up for."

"What are we getting kicked out for?" James asked as he joined us. He took my hand.

"Me and my errant ways." Anamae grinned.

"All right, it's time to go." Mr. Miller motioned us to the exits. "The busses are waiting.".

My heart soared. This was the first trip I'd taken without my parents. As I walked down the narrow aisle, I felt as if I were leaving the kid in me behind for my adult version. Anamae, on the other hand, expressed immediate disappointment.

"Only two seats per row?" she groaned. "I wanted to sit beside you, Leath. Since you seem to be attached to James, well, how can I?"

She gave her patented Anamae pout, but her attitude

quickly changed when she spotted an empty seat toward the back of the bus beside Matt Brooks. I remembered Matt. I'd had a crush on him in middle school just like all the other girls. Matt had grown quite tall and was well built due to the years he'd spent on the basketball team. His dark eyes looked like warm cinnamon against his tanned skin.

"Old flame, anyone?" Anamae asked, stepping past me.

I shook my head and smiled.

"You can't blame me. Look at him. He's a real cause for concern." Anamae moved to join Matt, and I answered James's unspoken question.

"That's her way of saying she thinks he's hot."

"I am equal parts confused and impressed by your secret language," James said. He paused in the aisle, waiting for me to take the seat by the window.

"It's all Anamae." I laughed.

It was strange, going on this trip with Anamae and James, when just a few months ago my threesome was Anamae, Victor, and me.

I wondered if Victor still planned to go on any of the other college tours with me. As tense as things were between us, I hadn't given up on him. I still hoped we'd wind up on the same college campus after graduation even though I knew James would probably be going with me no matter which college I chose. Although I felt terrible for the pain my trip with James had caused Victor, I really needed him to come to terms with our relationship. Victor and I were only, and would only ever be, just friends. Good friends for sure, but that was all.

James raised the armrest between us, and I leaned my head on his chest as the bus pulled away from Martin High School. I listened to his heartbeat. It was a comforting sound, calm and steady and so perfectly matched to James's persona. I liked that I was the only one who could hear this and felt it was beautiful music written only for me, just as I knew my heart would only ever belong to him. This peaceful feeling, combined with the rocking motion of the bus, sent me to sleep just outside of Hendersonville.

I woke up two hours later when we rolled into Columbia. James's arm was still wrapped around my waist. I snuck a peek at him as the bus slowed on the busy streets. His head rested against the stuffed fabric of a built-in pillow. His eyelids were closed and his forehead free of all creases. I'd never had the opportunity to just observe him, stare at him as long as I wanted. He was beautiful, angelic, especially in sleep. I raised my hand and lightly traced his strong jaw.

James moaned in a low voice before his eyes fluttered open. He pulled my hand to his mouth where he kissed my fingertips. "Best alarm clock ever," he said.

I blushed and pulled my fingers away from his lips, still holding his hand in mine.

Mr. Miller picked up the microphone from the bus driver's dashboard. "Grab your bags and then check into your rooms." He looked at his watch. "Lunch and the afternoon are on your own, but don't forget, we're meeting at Gibbes Court at six for dinner. Remember to wear your visitor badges so you can ride the university's shuttle. See you at six." The microphone screeched feedback as Mr. Miller replaced it on the dash. He walked off the bus and into the hotel lobby.

James looked at me, a big grin on his face.

"What's that all about?" I asked.

"Just happy to have you here for the whole weekend. All to myself," he said. He pulled me close and gave me a quick kiss.

"Geesh, save that stuff for later," Anamae said as she

walked past us.

"Almost all to myself," James corrected.

I laughed, my heart lighter than it had been in months. I was eager to get the trip started, anxious to begin two full days with no parental supervision. And no worries about having to be careful around Victor, careful not to hurt his feelings.

"Come on, let's get checked in." I squeezed past James and followed our classmates.

James waited for our bags to be unloaded from underneath the bus. I joined Anamae, who was busy making late-night plans with Matt. James caught up to us, and we all walked into the lobby.

The hotel was stunning. The walls were lined with dark wood and heavy curtains framed long ornate windows. The hardwood floors were bare, except for one large rug that separated two leather couches. A table had been set up for our group where three hotel employees worked quickly to pass out our badges and room keys. Anamae and I were sharing a room on the "girls' floor," and the boys were one floor below.

"Who's your roomie?" I James asked.

"No one," he said.

"Good planning," Anamae said, giving me a wink.

I responded by blushing three shades of red.

Matt grabbed his bag and waved to Anamae before disappearing down a long corridor. James, Anamae, and I piled into the elevator.

James gave my hand a squeeze as the elevator stopped on the second floor. "Take your time," he said. "I'll wait for you in the lobby."

I smiled, staring after him until the doors creaked shut.

"Man, you got it bad," Anamae said, giggling.

"Shut up," I said with a grin.

Our room was small, but it had two queen beds. I threw my suitcase on one of the beds then quickly texted Mom to let her know we'd arrived safely. I splashed cool water on my face, blotting away the excess with a thick white towel. I debated about a complete makeup do over, but I was anxious to return to James. At the last second, I applied a coat of mascara and touched up my lipstick.

"See ya later," I said to Anamae as I headed for the door.

"Yep, you got it baaaad," Anamae said, carrying her toiletry bag to the bathroom.

"Yeah, yeah. See you at dinner," I called, leaving her to freshen up.

I took the stairway, too impatient for the elevator, and arrived in the lobby. My eyes searched the room for James.

"I'm right here," he said, taking my hand. He gave me a kiss on the cheek, and I could almost feel the judgment spears being thrown by one of the chaperones who stood a few feet away.

"Let's get some lunch," I said, eager to be free from everyone else.

"I know just the place," he said.

We headed toward the main entrance, and I stopped walking. "Oops, forgot my bag," I said, holding up my cell.

"I'll carry it for you." He took the cell and slipped it into his shirt pocket. James held open the door of a cab that had just dropped its passengers.

"Where to?" the driver casually asked.

James grinned. "Goatfeathers."

I smiled, remembering his conversation with my mom about the coffee bar and restaurant. She'd get a kick out of our going there. James held my hand as the cabbie drove down short back streets.

146

It was early for lunch, but the restaurant filled up right after we placed our order. We split a White Pie, which was the best pizza I'd ever had, and followed the meal with two cups of Goatfeathers House Blend. I felt like a traitor admitting it, but this coffee was much better than Grinds.

The waitress was refilling our cups when a beautiful girl approached our table. I thought she was walking past us to join someone else, but when she paused beside James, I recognized her.

*Ever.*

"Well, hey, James," she said, draping her arm around his shoulders. "Why didn't you tell me you were in town?"

James didn't smile but spoke cordially. "Just got here, Ever. Besides, we're not really on a vacation sort of trip."

"We're visiting USC with our school," I said, trying to insinuate myself into their too-cozy reunion.

Ever turned her cool blue eyes on me as if just noticing I was there. She smiled a smile so tight it seemed likely to crack her face. Her lips parted, and she showed her perfectly white teeth.

I wished I'd taken more time with my makeup.

"You must be Leath," she said.

"I must be," I said. I returned her smile. I was determined to win the smiling contest, and the prize.

"Well, it's so nice to meet you," Ever said. Her tone was a mix of sarcasm and insincerity. "James has told me all about you, of course."

"And you," I lied. At the time, I knew I was being unfair, rude even, but I was predisposed to dislike Ever because of the way I'd found out about her. Plus, she was stunning, even in jeans and a simple cranberry sweater. She could have any boy in the restaurant. Why was she falling all over mine?

James chuckled.

"I envy you," Ever said condescendingly. "It's always nice getting a break from school, or life back home. But every distraction leads back to where we're supposed to be. We all have to go home eventually." She glanced at her expensive watch. "And my diversion is over. I need to get back to campus. I was just grabbing lunch, you know, like we used to do, James?" She patted his shoulder. "Give me a call if you want to catch up later."

"Sorry, but it won't be this trip," James said. "We're on a very tight schedule."

"Maybe next time then. Have a good visit, y'all."

Every boy within a three-table radius turned to watch the beautiful blonde as she gracefully exited the restaurant. Every boy except James. He was watching me, studying me for a reaction.

I raised one eyebrow.

"Yeah, that's Ever," he said, shaking his head.

His non-reaction to Ever spoke volumes. The most amazing thing happened then. I felt completely secure about my relationship with James. He was not interested in Ever at all. Somehow, I knew he'd never been interested in her. I beamed at him.

"What's going on in that head of yours?" he asked, looking bemused.

"Just happy."

"Me, too," he said, stretching his hand across the table to take mine.

It was cool being in Goatfeathers, at possibly the same table where my parents had once eaten a similar meal. I wanted to see more of this campus through their eyes.

We had some time to kill before dinner, and I thought it was the perfect opportunity to get a souvenir for Mom. Her old Gamecock sweatshirt was in desperate need of replacement. "Let's go for a walk," I said.

James rose, tossing a twenty and a ten on the table. "Lead on," he said.

We made our way to the campus bookstore a few streets down. James waited patiently while I waded through mounds of campus wear until I found a sweatshirt similar to Mom's old one. As I waited in line, an idea came to me. "Can I show you something?"

"I'd say that depends on what you want to show me, but honestly, the answer will always be yes." He grinned at me, and I blushed, hoping the clerk wasn't listening to our conversation. I quickly paid for the shirt before taking James's hand.

"Come on," I said, trying not to grin back.

There were no cabs on the street, so we walked to campus. It took longer than I expected, but James didn't complain. He walked alongside me, holding my hand, looking more relaxed than I'd ever seen him.

Once we reached the edge of campus, we cut through the grounds and parking lots to the back of the Horseshoe. I hadn't been there in years, but I still recognized the landmark. Two rows of buildings bordered by double brick walkways that ended at the McKissick Museum.

I led James down the path on the left, and then paused in front of Rutledge Chapel. "This is where my parents got married," I explained. "Mind if I take a look?"

James smiled and held the door open for me.

The chapel was exactly as I remembered from countless photos of my parents' wedding. There wasn't a center aisle. Mom had explained she'd walked up the right aisle, and then back down the left. I took my mother's path as I walked toward the altar under the soft glow of a single chandelier. I stood at the bottom of three short steps and imagined my parents, standing at the front of the chapel saying their vows, just five years older than I was now.

"Are you okay?" James asked.

I hadn't realized he'd come inside. He stood near the entrance, watching me.

"Yeah," I said. "I am."

I gave one last look at the pulpit, and then took the aisle my parents had used decades before, leaving the chapel to begin their lives together. James waited for me. He pulled me into his arms and kissed me tenderly. For the first time since we'd started dating, I allowed myself to believe we had a future together. Secure in the present, I wondered what the night would bring. I smiled as I took his outstretched hand, and we rejoined the sunlight on the grounds of the Horseshoe.

The chapel bells sounded as we strolled back across campus. It was six o'clock, and we were late. There was no sign of a shuttle stop, so we walked to Gibbes Court. It was a larger version of our own café at Martin High. Except instead of two serving lines, there were seven pods with different types of food available in each location.

Still feeling my share of the enormous pizza at lunch, I decided on a chopped salad. Always by my side, James got the same, and we made our way over to where Anamae sat at an elevated booth.

"I was beginning to wonder if you'd show up," she said, looking agitated.

"Sorry about that," James said. "Lost track of time."

"So what have you been up to?" She answered her own question before I could respond, "Oh, never mind, I probably don't want to hear the details." She leaned closer to me and whispered, "Not now, anyway."

I nudged her in the ribs.

I picked at the lettuce, and then as if powered by a switch, my hunger returned. After I devoured the salad,

I returned to the pods for a bowl of chili and grabbed a dessert on the way back to the table. By the time I finished the huge piece of chocolate cake, I was feeling full and drowsy. We left Gibbes Court together and headed back to the hotel. The cool night air revived me as we waited for the shuttle. A crowd of boys burst through the front door of a nearby fraternity house and joined us at the shuttle stop. They sang a loud and off-key song about a drinking game, one they appeared to have lost.

Anamae gave one of the boys an inviting smile.

"Are you serious?" I asked. "They're all drunk."

"I'm just being friendly. Besides, I wasn't looking at them. I was trying to get a better look at the letters on their house," Anamae said. "That's not where the party is."

This caught James's attention. "Party?" he asked.

"Yeah, I was going to tell you about it." I looked at Anamae for a little help.

Anamae rolled her eyes. She leaned forward to explain to James. "It's a fraternity party tomorrow night. I asked Leath to come with."

I felt James tense beside me.

When the shuttle arrived, James, Anamae, and I squeezed into a single seat. James seemed leery of the frat boys. When they all exited the shuttle a few stops down, he finally relaxed his hold on me.

Back at the hotel, our classmates dominated the lobby, enjoying complimentary drinks, which for us meant sodas. Anamae caught up to Matt at a cozy table toward the back. James grabbed a couple of bottles of water before joining me on one of the many loveseats scattered throughout the room.

I didn't want the night to end, but I didn't know how much longer I could delay my return to my room. I was tired, and we had an early start the next morning.

Tomorrow would be filled with "official" tours of the campus, dorms, and classrooms. I glanced at Anamae, who was getting up from the table with Matt. She looked at me and raised her eyebrows as if to ask, "Come with?"

I shook my head and gave what I hoped to be a believable yawn.

"Am I keeping you up?" James asked, teasing.

Embarrassed, I quickly explained. "No, it's not that. I think Anamae wanted us to go out with her and Matt. I was just letting her know I'm not up for it. She's safe with Matt. His dad's one of Woodvine's finest." I yawned again, this time for real.

"It seems like you could use some downtime," he said. "Want to call it a night?"

I nodded reluctantly.

We took the elevator up, and then James walked me to my room.

"I'll see you downstairs for breakfast," he said. He leaned in and kissed my forehead. "Call me later if you want." He waited until I was inside my room. I watched him through the peephole as he returned to the elevators.

Yeah, I had it bad.

As I kicked off my shoes, I noticed a single blush-colored rose in the center of the bed. I picked up the rose, inhaling its beautiful fragrance, wondering how James had pulled this off.

I put the rose into one of the cups on the dresser and filled it with water from the bathroom sink. As I placed the rose on the dresser, I caught the reflection of the bed in the mirror, I debated whether I should just collapse onto it or take a shower. I groaned, grabbed my pajamas from my suitcase, and trudged back to the bathroom.

Twenty minutes later, I felt like a new person. I climbed into bed, restlessly flipping through channels on the TV. Refreshed, I no longer felt sleepy. No wonder.

The display on the bedside clock read 9:15. I couldn't remember the last time I'd gone to bed so early. What was I doing? I was out of town, completely free for the first time in my life, and here I was, going to bed before ten. I sure knew how to live.

I wondered if James was still up. I didn't want to wake him by calling, but I thought a text would be all right. If he replied, maybe we'd go out for a coffee. We still had over two hours before curfew. If he didn't, I'd see him in the morning. Then I remembered James had my cell. I could call him on the hotel phone, but that would certainly wake him if he were asleep. In the end, I dragged a brush through my damp hair, got dressed, and walked to James's room. I stood outside, listening for signs of life. I heard a commercial from his TV and sensed he was still awake. I knocked softly on the door.

James opened the door, surprised to see me.

I was surprised to see the muscles of his exposed belly and chest.

"Sorry about that," I said. "I hope I didn't wake you."

James laughed. "No. I don't usually go to bed before ten."

I felt awkward, standing in the doorway, as if it were taboo. After all, this was a hotel room, not the front door of my house, or even his. The disaster of my visit to his house flashed through my mind, and I felt even more self-conscious.

"I just came for my cell," I blurted, wishing I had stayed in my room.

"Oh, yeah," he said. "Come in, I'll get it for you."

I followed him inside, and the door closed automatically behind me. I was certain the muted click alerted everyone on the floor, "Leath's in a boy's room!" I waited by the door, looking everywhere but at the bed.

"Well, come in."

*Fading*

I laughed nervously, following him further into the room. James grabbed his shirt from the back of a chair, fished out my cell, and handed it to me. A light flashed, alerting me to a text from my mother. Thankfully, it had been sent within the last five minutes. Not long enough for her to call the authorities or launch a two-state manhunt.

I sat on the bed and quickly tapped a response. "Yes, it's been fun. Turning in early for the night. Wiped out. Love you."

My cell buzzed. "Love you, too."

"Everything all right?" James asked. He sat beside me, taking my hand in his. My heart raced, and I felt his through the steady pulse in his fingertips. The easy rhythm skipped from him to me through our touch, calming my mind and leaving me with a strong desire to rest my head against his chest and listen to his heartbeat.

"Yeah, it's just my mom. Good thing I came down here to get this."

"I agree. It is a good thing you came down here." He lifted my chin and kissed me. My cell slipped through my fingers, thudding to the carpet as I pulled him closer. James effortlessly lifted me onto the bed before bringing his mouth back to mine.

As his scent washed over me, I parted my lips, eager for his taste. His kisses were demanding, yet tender at the same time. I didn't know if my face flushed, but other parts of me did. A warm feeling settled in my core where it changed to something deeper. In that second, all my desires combined into just one. The need to be closer to him. His lips left mine to trail across my cheek, to my ear, and down my neck, before returning more urgently to kiss me again. My breath came in gasps as his warmth consumed me. One of my arms slid instinctively around his waist, holding him tightly. If there was any gap between us, any bubble of air, our bodies quickly found it and filled the space in our desire to be closer still.

"I love you, Leath. I love you," he murmured in a low, husky voice.

I stroked the back of his neck with my fingertips, coaxing him to kiss me more deeply. My hand drifted from his neck, down the length of his back. His muscles tightened at my touch. My entire body came alive with a flash of fire that burned across my skin. Everything seemed to be happening quickly and all at once.

Seconds later, there was a change in our rhythm. James stopped kissing me and rolled onto his back. He curled an arm around my shoulders and pulled me across his chest. We lay that way until our breathing calmed. The small fires throughout my body diminished to embers. I didn't understand the abrupt change in him. Had I done something wrong?

"I'm sorry, Leath." His fingers lightly stroked my arm, raising goose bumps with his touch. "This isn't the way I pictured it would happen."

"Tell me then. How did you picture it?" I was desperate to know his expectations, his desires.

James propped himself up on his elbow. He tilted my chin to look into my eyes. His gray eyes were so intense the fires threatened to ignite again. His fingertips followed the line of my jaw to my neck. His hand came to rest lightly on my stomach.

"Tell me," I repeated.

"Let's just say I was raised differently." His expression turned hard as he leaned back against the headboard. I moved closer to him and rested my head on his chest. He slid his arm around me. "I just want to do things right," he said.

What was he talking about? Marriage? A delicious shudder passed through me as I visualized us in a chapel similar to the one we'd visited that day. My cheeks felt hot, and I was glad he couldn't see my face as I blushed.

I wasn't sure how much time passed as we lay in each other's arms. Before long, I heard James's slow deep breaths. I glanced up to see his eyes were closed. I snuggled closer to him. Listening to his heartbeat, I drifted into a blissful sleep.

The hotel phone screamed like a siren piercing the night. James bolted up at the noise, looking around the room, disoriented and anxious. "What the?" he asked.

I laughed and reached for the phone. "Hello?"

"Get your butt up here!" Anamae demanded.

I looked at the clock on the nightstand. Less than ten minutes before curfew. "Crap," I said and hung up the phone, Anamae's voice still loudly calling my name.

James was already at the foot of the bed, retrieving my cell and grabbing his shirt. He led me outside to the elevator, buttoning his shirt as the elevator lurched to a stop. James walked me to my room, the door opening just as I was about to slide my key card.

"Hi, James. Bye, James," Anamae said, pulling me inside.

"Goodnight," I called as she slammed the door. I hoped he made it back to his room before he was taped in.

I breathed a sigh of relief moments later when my cell buzzed.

"Goodnight, Leath."

"Night," I texted back.

"Thanks, Anamae," I said.

"Who would have thought I'd be keeping you out of trouble?" she asked. "Isn't it usually the other way around?"

I laughed as I shrugged out of my clothes and back into my pajamas. I climbed onto my bed, hoping she'd take the hint.

"Oh, no you don't," Anamae said, plopping down next to me.

"You know you have a perfectly good bed all for yourself two feet away?" I asked, yawning.

"Yeah, but I can't poke you from over there when you cocoon up." She gave me a poke in the arm to prove her point. "Come on, let's hear it."

I sat up and propped all four of the pillows behind me. She sighed, grabbed a few pillows off her own bed, and then returned to mine. Man, she was stubborn, and apparently nocturnal. It was two in the morning before Anamae decided she'd heard enough and finally allowed me to drift off to sleep.

That night, I dreamed once more of the boy in the hoodie. This time, we were about six years old. We played in a sandbox, one I recognized from Cascade Park. I felt the grains of sand run through my fingers like water. We left the sandbox, and I climbed onto a nearby swing. The boy's feet dug into loose gravel as he gently pushed me toward the cloudless sky.

"Higher," I yelled, feeling safe in his hands. I soared so high I thought I'd leave the park. Even in my dream, I knew it was impossible, but the swing's chain snapped. I sailed through the air, no longer connected to this world. I woke up, drenched in sweat, five minutes before my alarm was set to ring.

# 10

## Dreams of Nightmares

I'D HAD THE DREAM ONCE BEFORE, A LONG TIME AGO. I remembered the fun I'd had running and playing with the boy. But last night's ending was different. I tried to understand why it had changed. The dreams of the boy had always been my safe haven, but this dream seemed to twist into a warning. An oversized pillow smacked into my back, reminding me I was not alone.

"Good morning, Anamae," I said, yawning.

"Speak for yourself," she grunted. "No, don't. You've been speaking all night."

"What?" I asked. As far as I knew, I'd never talked in my sleep.

"James. James. Over and over. Ugh."

My cheeks flushed. "Sorry about that."

"Yeah, yeah. I get it. True love and all." Anamae stretched. "Anyway, dream time is over. We need to shake a leg." She rose from her bed and padded into the bathroom.

Fifteen minutes later, we were in the lobby, looking for breakfast. The buffet had been set up in the White Room. My stomach growled as I inhaled the aroma of bacon and waffles. James waved us over to his table. He looked gorgeous as usual. He rose and kissed my cheek, "You look beautiful."

I blushed.

Anamae rolled her eyes, "Oh, for heaven's sake. I'll catch up to the two of you later." She walked away to sit with Matt at the next table.

I smiled at James, happy to be alone with him once again. Well, as alone as one can be in a room crowded with chatty teenagers.

"Shall we?" he asked. He led the way through the buffet line and back to our table where two glasses of juice had been added. "I ordered for you."

"Thanks," I said, wondering how he knew I preferred grapefruit.

The morning was perfect, and I was eager to start our day together. All was good until Mr. Miller announced we would be traveling in groups. These groups had been created based on our interest in majors. James joined the rest of those interested in a psychology major while I was directed to join the group of kids who were undecided. I looked for Anamae, but it appeared she had vanished on the spot with Matt. I envied her for thinking on her feet.

James gave me a quick wave. "See you at lunch."

*Great. Just like at school.*

I spent the morning touring every square inch of the campus. Each tree seemed significant to our tour guide, who was fully immersed in being a Gamecock. It took forever to cross the Horseshoe. A few times, I had to stop myself from interrupting to give my own tour and speed things along. I had forgotten just how humid Columbia was in the spring. I found myself hanging back, trying to be the last one exiting any building just to enjoy the air conditioning a few seconds longer. Three hours later, I was done. I was tired, hot, and frustrated. Especially when we were late returning to the hotel. James's group had already come and gone. They were well on their way to the afternoon portion of their tour by the time my tired feet shuffled into the White Room for lunch. For a few minutes, all I could do was sit there, appreciating every sore muscle in my legs. At that moment, I just wanted a cool shower and a nap.

I felt better after lunch and was relieved to hear our afternoon tour would only last two hours. This part was more interesting, mostly because it was indoors. We toured the Student Union, theater, and the massive library. It seemed we were the first group back to the hotel. I took the opportunity to take a long shower, washing away the sweat that clung to my skin. I dressed in white capris, sandals, and a periwinkle-blue tank. I'd given up on Anamae, who was obviously running her own schedule. I headed downstairs, wondering how long it would be before James returned.

He was already waiting for me.

"You got some sun today," he said, motioning to my pink nose. "Looks good on you."

I blushed. "So did you learn anything to help you make your decision in choosing a college?" I asked.

"I did," he said. "I learned I can't stand being apart from you, so I decided to never allow it to happen again. So, I choose..." He pretended to be deep in thought. "Whatever college you do."

I wondered if any campus would be large enough for James, Victor, and me.

James leaned in close and brushed his lips against my cheek. "I'm hoping to make up for lost time today after dinner."

I fought the urge to pull him closer.

"There you are," Anamae said, exasperated. "Can you cut the lovey-dovey-act for five minutes?"

She sat down, oblivious to the lack of an invitation. I

glanced at James, expecting to see disappointment in his expression, but he just stared at her in amusement.

"What's got your crank turned?" I asked.

"Well, when Matt and I accidentally missed our group's departure," she grinned, "we thought we'd take a little tour of our own. Unfortunately, one of the chaperones found us and obliged us instead. It seems he'd gone to school here sometime in the 1800s."

I laughed. "Where's Matt?"

"Apparently, he's smarter than I am. He faked an upset stomach after lunch and was excused to his room. I, on the other hand, well, let's just say I know more about USC and Columbia than both of you combined."

She cast a glance around the room, and then lowered her voice. "I did find out one handy thing though."

"What's that?" I asked.

"I know exactly where that party is." She raised an eyebrow. "Are you coming?"

My eyes flitted to James.

"Geesh, Leath. This was supposed to be a girls' trip," Anamae grumbled.

While I'd rather be with James than go to a frat party, I felt I owed her. "Anamae did save my butt last night." I said, looking at James. "Compromise?"

"What do you have in mind?" he asked.

"I'll go with Anamae." She squealed and bounced up and down in her seat. "Let me finish," I said. "I'll go with you for one hour. Just to make sure you're okay. Then I'm coming back here."

Anamae seemed to consider my offer. "Honey, if I'm not good within one hour, I'll come back with you." At that moment, she spotted Matt. "Oh, he's not getting off that easy." She left our table and finished her meal with him.

"I wish you hadn't done that," James said

reproachfully.

"Done what?" I asked.

"Said you'd go with Anamae. I don't like it."

I looked into his eyes, trying to decide if he was serious and saw that he was. Maybe I'd had too much sun today, spent too much time outside in the heat, but sometimes his possessiveness bothered me. "I didn't think I needed to ask your permission to hang out with my best friend."

"You don't. Of course not," he said apologetically. "I'm just worried about you, the two of you, being in that kind of environment. College guys are older and only interested in one thing. I don't think it is a good idea for you, or Anamae, to go to that party alone."

"We won't be alone; we'll be together."

He took my hand, looking into my eyes with such intensity it seemed we were the only two people in the room. "I just couldn't handle it if something happened to you."

My irritation disappeared with his words. "We'll be fine." I reassured him. "There will be loads of people there. Besides, some of the kids are only a year older than I am." I gave him an encouraging smile.

Mr. Miller called the group to order, reminding us once again of our midnight curfew. He then gave our instructions for check out. "Be packed and outside to load the bus by nine," he said. "I know some of you are itching to explore on your last night but remember, you reflect our school. Inappropriate behavior will not be tolerated. Any rule breaking will definitely cost you the opportunity of another trip. Otherwise, enjoy your evening."

Mr. Miller and the rest of the chaperones retreated to the hotel bar, evidently eager to enjoy their last evening as well.

"Let's get at it," Anamae said as she approached our table.

"I'll see you in an hour." I leaned in to kiss James lightly on his lips. When I stood up, he grabbed me by the hand and pulled me back to him.

"Be careful," he whispered. "And call me if anything goes wrong. Okay?"

"I will."

James stared at me for a long moment. "So much for not being apart again."

"I'll be back before you have a chance to miss me." I said.

"I already do."

I followed Anamae to the main entrance and turned back to wave at James. He stared after me as if we were saying a final goodbye.

"That boy likes to lay it on thick, doesn't he?" Anamae asked.

"What do you mean?" I asked.

"Come *on*, Leath. He nearly guilted you into changing your mind."

"He's just worried, that's all. About both of us. And I think you should leave when I do. I don't think it's safe for you to stay there, or for either of us to be walking back alone in the dark."

"I won't be alone," Anamae said. "Matt's going to meet us there."

"What?" I asked. "I thought you were bent on us having some girl time."

"I am and we will," Anamae said. "Matt's coming in an hour. Right when you want to leave. So, don't worry about me. Now that's settled, try to relax and have some fun. You remember what that's like, don't you? Having fun?"

I rolled my eyes and walked with her a few blocks

away from the hotel. The air was full of vibrations from thumping music that streamed from the open doors of a two-story brick house. Greek letters hung on the right side of the structure, and the entire lawn was filled with boys and girls carrying plastic cups. I was sure we'd get made for what we were, two high school kids crashing a college party, but no one seemed to notice us. Anamae walked up the front steps like she owned the place, and I tried to follow suit.

The music was about three times louder inside the smoke-filled house. People danced on any flat area they could find, including a low coffee table. A couple was leg-locked on one side of a couch, deeply involved in being deeply involved. A boy was passed out on the opposite end.

"I think I see Colin from Latin class last year," Anamae said. "That *Uh-Huh* sure looks yummy."

"I didn't know he went to USC," I said. I didn't know much at all about Colin other than his being an Uh-Huh, a good-looking boy. He had been a late transfer, only attending Martin High for the last part of his senior year.

"I'm gonna say hello. Be right back," Anamae said. She skipped away before I could decide if I wanted to tag along. I wondered how long I'd have to stay here before Matt showed up. Sighing, I plopped down on an unoccupied love seat.

"How's it going?" asked a boy, joining me.

"It's going," I said.

"Want to get a drink?" he asked.

"I don't drink," I said.

"Not ever? No fluids at all? You're a walking miracle," he said.

I laughed.

"I'm Toby," the boy said. "And I meant a soda. I don't drink either."

"Sorry about that," I said. "I'm Leath. Soda would be nice."

He returned a few minutes later with two cans of cola. I popped the top, and a stream of soda spurted onto the carpet. "Oops, sorry about that," I said.

Toby laughed. "No problem. Not for me anyway. It's not my house."

"Do you go to school here?" I asked, wiping the outside of the can with the hem of my sleeve.

"Yeah, just finishing my sophomore year. You?"

"No. My friend and I are uninvited guests."

"I sorta figured that out when I saw you two walk in," Toby said. "You had a real deer-in-the-headlights expression on your face. Where's your friend, anyway?" He slid a little closer to me on the already-too-small seat.

I tried to tell myself he was just making polite conversation, moving closer to be heard over the noise, but I felt uneasy about this stranger and his instant familiarity with me. I glanced at the clock on the wall. "Oh, wow," I said. "I've got to get going."

"You're going to leave your friend here, alone?" he asked. "Do you have any idea what happens at these kinds of parties?"

I pulled my arms close to my body and tried to shrink into the curve of the couch. Toby draped his arm around my shoulders and moved closer still. I held my breath, my eyes darting madly for Anamae, cursing her for leaving me while she traipsed after yet another boy.

*Matt. Wasn't Matt on the way? Where was he?*

Toby pulled me toward him and nuzzled against my neck. "There's an empty room in the back. Want to check it out?" he asked.

"No. I'd rather stay here with you," I tried to joke, but my voice cracked. At that moment, my only thought was getting off the couch and away from this boy, whose hands suddenly seemed everywhere. I stood up, but he grabbed my wrist and pulled me back down hard.

"Here's good with me if it's good with you." Tightly gripping my arm, Toby began to push me down further on the couch. "Well, for starters."

I panicked at his rough touch, briefly wondering why no one was stopping him. I struggled to get into a position to twist away and had just managed to free one of my hands to slap his face when Toby yelled out in pain. In the next instant, he was on the floor and I was yanked to my feet.

James's eyes were cold as steel. For one second, I believed he was capable of murder. "Are you all right?" he asked harshly.

Unable to speak, I merely nodded as I clutched James's hand in both of mine.

"Go find Anamae while I finish my conversation with this guy."

Toby scrambled to his feet. "Anytime."

"No," I pleaded. "Let's just go." I tugged on James's hand, but his body was rigidly locked in a defensive stance.

"Whoa, what's going on here?" Anamae asked, looking from James to Toby.

"We're leaving," James said. The tone in his voice told her not to question him.

"Sounds like a plan," Anamae said.

She linked her arm with James's, and then led us out of the house like an awkward human train as we walked back to the hotel in silence. I started breathing again when we crossed the threshold of the lobby. Even my bold, fearless Anamae looked reassured to be back inside the safety of the hotel. She caught Matt just as he was headed out. "Change in plans," she said, taking him to the hotel lounge.

"I should have never taken my eyes off you," James said, pulling me into his arms. His hand moved to my face to wipe away tears I hadn't noticed had fallen. "Are you sure you're all right?"

"I'm better now," I said. I rested my head on his chest. We stood like that for a few moments until a chaperone's fake cough caught our attention.

I didn't remember asking James to take me to my room but minutes later, we were there. We sat at the foot of the bed, me still clutching his hand. I shivered when I thought about how the night might have turned out differently if James hadn't shown up at exactly the right time.

"How did you know to come?" I asked.

"Just lucky, I guess," he said, avoiding eye contact.

"I don't think anyone's that lucky," I said. "You weren't even supposed to be there. I was going to meet you here." I glanced at the clock on the nightstand, "Right about now. So, how did you know?"

"I just did, Leath. Can we leave it at that?" he asked.

His earlier possessiveness haunted me, and I felt a knot in my stomach. "Did you follow me?"

"What? No, of course not," he said. "Why can't you accept it was just good timing?"

"Because that kind of timing doesn't happen unless the moon and the stars are aligned in just the perfect way."

James raked his hand through his hair and rose from the bed.

"You do that when you're stressed, you know?" I asked, repeating his gesture by running my hand through my own hair. "So I already know something's up. Why don't you tell me what it is?"

James sighed loudly and returned to sit beside me. "There's something I've wanted to tell you about for a long time."

"Tell me then," I said, but the somber look on his face made me wonder if it was something I wanted to hear.

"Remember that day at Judaculla Rock?" he asked. "When we talked about other worlds and connections?"

I was confused how that day had anything to do with this one, but nodded anyway.

"I knew you needed me tonight because you and I are connected."

"Of course we are," I said. "I've felt that way about you since the first time I saw you." I blushed at my words, surprised I'd spoken them so freely.

James trailed a finger down my cheek, stopping to lift my chin so I stared into his gray eyes. "And you didn't think it was strange, connecting so quickly to a stranger?"

I thought back to James's first day at Martin High. After lunch when I hadn't realized I was following him to the wrong class. Even then, I was prepared to follow him wherever he might go. And the next day, when I broke school rules to go with him off-campus. These things seemed so out of character for me. But being here with him now, it all seemed quite the opposite. I had done these things and others instinctively as if being with James was like being around someone I'd known my whole life.

He took my hand. "We're connected in a way so that I will always know when you need me. That day at Judaculla Rock, you said you'd need proof. Let me prove it to you. Better yet, let me help you prove it to yourself."

James pulled me closer, and then wrapped one arm around me, tucking me to him. He took my hand in his and rested it on his thigh. "How long have you known me?" he asked softly.

I silently counted the weeks in my head. "Almost two months."

He leaned his head on top of mine, and I was alerted by his scent. I closed my eyes, breathing it in. I recounted the weeks I'd known James. Almost two months. I was sure of it. But I was equally certain I'd known him much longer. It seemed as if I'd always known James. My mind argued facts against something indefinable as I struggled to remember a time James hadn't been in my life.

"How long?" he murmured.

His beautiful scent clouded my mind. *How long?* "I don't know," I admitted.

"It's been a lot longer than a couple of months," he said. "The first memory I have of you is when we were little kids." I studied his face. His brow was furrowed deep in thought. "We were playing in a sandbox. And we swung on the swings."

I froze.

James felt the change in my posture, and he moved to sit on the floor in front of me. He took both of my hands in his, waiting patiently as I processed this information. His words echoed in my brain, bouncing around, trying to find a foothold. It didn't make sense. I hadn't told James about that dream. I hadn't told anyone about any of my dreams of the boy, except for Anamae.

"How did you know about that dream? I never told..."

"I was there, Leath." He squeezed my hands. "You remember, don't you? When I pushed you on the swings? You were scared, but you kept asking me to push you higher."

"That's because every time..." I shook my head. No. It was crazy to think the unseen face of the boy in my dreams belonged to James. My mind begged for some rational explanation.

"It's okay. Go on," he said. "Why did you keep asking me to push you higher?"

"Because every time I felt your hands on my back, it

made me feel safe and brave." I blushed again. The most recent version of the dream flooded my mind. How I'd felt the swing break and my body fly into empty space, but I quickly pushed the memory away.

"And what about the dream when we were on the boardwalk in Columbia? Do you remember that?" he asked.

Closing my eyes, I tried to visualize the dream. I nodded as the scene played out in my mind. "What were we wearing?" I asked, testing him.

"Sweatshirts with little ice cream-cone designs." He motioned near his wrist, where the sleeve would touch if he were wearing long sleeves.

My mind reeled.

*How is this possible?*

"Hang on," he said. James reached into his pocket and quickly pulled out his cell. He began scrolling through images on the screen. "Here," he said triumphantly. He turned the screen to me, and my heart skipped a beat.

The photo was one of James and me, huddled together with bright lights hanging from the ceiling of a gym. I immediately recognized my dress and the decorations behind us. My eighth-grade dance. The boy in my dreams had snapped this selfie. I remembered holding my breath in the dream, thrilled I'd finally get to see his face. However, in that dream, the blinding flash of the camera had signaled my brain to wake up.

I stared at the photo James held out before me, trying to comprehend the truth that stared back at me. In my mind, this was impossible, but in my heart, I knew it had to be true. James was the boy I'd dreamed about all these years. That was why it was easy for me to connect to him so quickly.

His eyes were bright with excitement as he kissed my fingertips. "I knew you'd remember." He looked at me with a hopeful expression. "We've shared hundreds of dreams."

I closed my eyes, and they ran through my mind then like bursts of short movies. Dreams of a summer camp with a boy helping me collect tadpoles. Another dream with the same boy teaching me how to shoot pool. That movie was quickly replaced by one in which the boy, now older, walked down the sidewalk with me, calling for Sam, who had gotten out of the fence.

My eyes fluttered open, and I stared into his beautiful face. More dreams flooded my memory. Snowball fights in middle school at the end of Christmas break. Wading in the ocean, the waves knocking me down into the wet sand. And during freshman year, a boy kissing me behind the bleachers after a football game. It was staggering, the number of dreams I'd had.

And forgotten.

As the minutes ticked by, I tried frantically to find another explanation. Any other explanation. But there was none.

"But those were dreams," I said. "How is possible that you have that photo on your cell if it was a dream?"

"Because I was there," said James. "I can't explain it any other way. I was there."

It sounded ludicrous, but at the same time, it made sense, perfectly illogical sense. The reason I felt like I'd known James my whole life was because I had grown up with him in the quiet imaginings of our sleep. Was it really so far-fetched? There were billions of people on this planet, many dreaming at the same time each night. We all dreamt of strangers, who was to say those strangers weren't dreaming about us as well? Connections. James had said we were connected in our dreams. He wasn't speaking in general terms; he was talking about us. And, somehow, our dreams were reality.

"How could we have shared all of those dreams? Sharing just one dream seems impossible, let alone hundreds of them."

"Not when you have a catalyst," he said.

James and I jumped when Anamae crashed into the hotel room, shattering the intimacy of our conversation.

"Oops," she said, giggling. "I hope I'm not interrupting."

"No, I was just leaving," James said, rising but still holding my hands in his. He bent and gently kissed my cheek. "Forget this for now," he whispered.

I felt a ripple go through my body and my mind became muddled. We had been talking about something. What was it? I knew it was important, but I couldn't remember. I couldn't find it through the haze of my mind, and I became agitated. How could I have forgotten something we were just talking about? Whatever it was, it taunted me, dancing on the fringe of my memory.

"You need to get some sleep," James said. "We have to get up early if you want to have breakfast before the bus gets here."

I stared after him wordlessly as he walked to the door.

"Goodnight, Anamae," he called over his shoulder.

"Wait," I blurted. I glanced at Anamae, not sure of what to say that wouldn't alert her to my desperation to understand what had just happened.

"Too close to curfew," James said. "I'd better get going. I'll see you in the morning. Sweet dreams."

*Sweet dreams.*

Dreams. Yes, we were talking about dreams. My mind flashed to the dream I'd had about James searching for me in my room in the middle of the night. I had accidentally shot him. What had he said the next morning? He hadn't been able to sleep because of "crazy nightmares." He knew about that dream, had remembered being in it with me. The fog cleared, and the conversation back to me. Our dreams were connected. James wanted me to have sweet dreams so he would too.

"Night, James," Anamae said, ushering him to the door. She whirled to face me not two seconds after James closed the door behind him. "Did he ask you to marry him?" she half-shouted.

I realized what the scene must have looked like to her, James kneeling before me. "What? No."

"You seem disappointed," Anamae said. "Look, don't you even think about that until after we're out of college." She pointed her index finger at me. "And don't be thinking about that with James. By the time we're out of high school, you may not even be with him anymore." Anamae gathered her pajamas from her suitcase and headed for the shower.

But I knew otherwise. I knew I'd still be with James. I'd always be with him because I had always been with him.

I fell back onto the bed, confused by the few moments I'd forgotten our secret. I wondered how that had happened. Did my mind need a few minutes to absorb what James had said? Was it a delayed reaction to his fantastic claim that our dreams were connected?

*Was there anything more romantic?*

There was not a time in my entire life that didn't include James. I thought about the dreams, the peaceful feeling that greeted me every morning after a night spent with the boy in the hoodie. Every night before I fell asleep, I'd wished with all my heart I'd dream of him again.

I was eager for sleep. I wanted to return to my dreams and relive them all, this time while looking into James's beautiful face. Then I realized what waited for me in the morning would be far better than anything I could dream up. I had the real version of James, and my reality would be much better than any fantasy. I didn't have all the answers, and even if I had, I wasn't sure I'd understand. But right now, I had him. The boy of my dreams.

# 11

## *Unmasked*

IN MY DREAM, I WAS BAREFOOT WITH THE BOY ON A wide, wooden platform under the stars. We danced in the absence of music, swaying in time to the rise and fall of the ocean waves.

I pulled him closer and whispered in his ear, "Kiss me."

His lips found mine as I closed my eyes. We kissed deeply, and I wished I could stay there in his arms forever. But hard footsteps closed in on us. The boy stepped in front of me as he turned to face the interloper, and I woke up screaming.

"Are you all right?" Mom asked, breathless. "I heard you as soon as I walked in the front door." She sat on my bed and stroked my hair.

I couldn't tell her about the dream even if I wanted to. What would I say? "Hey, Mom, guess what? I've been sharing dreams my whole life with a boy I hardly know." Who would believe me when I wasn't sure I understood it myself? The worried look on her face made it clear I'd better tell her something.

I explained what happened at the frat party, leaving out some of the scarier details, and let her make the conclusion that the event had triggered my nightmare.

"Why didn't you call me?" she asked, hugging me close.

"It was nothing, really. And, James made sure I was locked in for the night when we got back to the hotel. Everything's okay, Mom." I hugged her and gave her several more reassurances I was fine, completely fine.

She must have believed me because she launched into a ten-minute lecture on topics ranging from peer pressure to underage drinking. Her footnote was a rhetorical on whether I should be allowed to go on another college tour. She answered her own question by saying, "Thank goodness James was there."

A shadow seemed to cross Mom's face. I'd seen that look before.

"What's wrong?" I asked.

"Nothing, nothing," Mom said, patting my arm. "It's just, the reunion's coming up, and I was wondering if I should still leave a few days early to visit Beth. Or if I should even go to the reunion at all."

"Wh... What?" I stuttered. "Of course you should go."

I could see the wheels spinning in her head. She was going to call Beth and cancel her trip as soon as I walked out the door for school. I couldn't allow that to happen. I needed time alone with James. Time I wouldn't get if Mom stayed in town. I frantically considering several arguments in my head, reasons to convince her to go.

"How can I leave you here by yourself with what's just happened?" Mom asked. "You could have been hurt."

"But I wasn't," I said.

Mom shook her head, "Doesn't matter. I should have been there."

"With me? At a frat party?" I asked. "Are you serious? You can't be with me every waking moment. Besides, what happened to me has nothing to do with your trip this weekend."

Then I realized it was more than her fear of my safety that caused her to reevaluate her trip. She wasn't only afraid for me. She was afraid for herself.

"Look, Mom. I know it must be hard going out again after all these years, but you've put your life on hold for me long enough. You need to live yours. Can't you see it's not fair to you or me if you don't?"

She looked at me with a hurt expression.

It was difficult, but I had to continue. "In one more year, I'll be in college. And unless there's a university being built in secrecy in Woodvine, I won't be living here. I can't go off to school, worrying about you wasting away alone in this house. It's time you lived your life again." I squeezed her in a half-hug.

"Thanks, sweetie," she said, squeezing me back. She pulled away wiping her eyes and smiled. "You're right."

I used the next few minutes to talk up the reunion, reminding her of how much fun she'd had when Beth had visited. How Beth was looking forward to her early arrival and wouldn't it be nice to see all of their high school friends again? Mom seemed to soften toward the idea. In the end, I got her with one simple question.

"What about Des? Won't it be nice to see him again?" I teased.

Mom grinned a shy smile. "As a matter of fact, yes."

"Then you absolutely have to go," I said.

Mom blushed.

"Wait. Has he contacted you?" I asked.

She nodded.

"Come on, then. Let's get going. We have to get you packed." I stood and tried to pull her from my bed.

"Okay, okay," Mom said, laughing. "I'll go. But I don't have to pack now. I'm not leaving until Wednesday morning."

177

"Then I'll help you pack tomorrow after school," I said. I tried to imitate my mother's voice as I continued, "Now, you behave yourself. No drinking and driving and make sure you have cash in case you need to get a cab. There's one more thing. If he tries anything, slap his face and call me."

"Ha-ha. Very funny," Mom said. "You know, I could say the same thing to you. Behave yourself at Anamae's house. Don't forget to come over here and take care of Sam. Don't stay out too late, and don't slap Anamae's face even if she aggravates you to death."

We laughed at Anamae's superior ability to annoy me. I pulled up the covers to make my bed. Mom walked to the other side, giving me a hand with the chore. In a rare moment of maturity, it occurred to me that my mother had once been seventeen.

"Mom, how did you know Dad was the one?"

She was surprised by my question. I thought I heard a curse escape her lips when she bent to pick up one of my throw pillows. "It's a little early in your relationship for you to be thinking along those lines with James. Or anyone for that matter. I didn't even think about marriage until I was in college, and even then, I knew I'd graduate first."

"It's not like I'm going to run off and get married." I rolled my eyes in exasperation.

"Well, that's certainly a relief. I have nothing to wear to a wedding," she teased, tossing the pillows back onto my bed.

"Really, Mom. How did you know?"

She changed her tone when she realized I was serious. She sighed loudly. "When I dated Des, I thought he was the one. I'd never felt that way about anyone before. When I met your dad, the love I felt for Des paled in comparison. Looking back, I only thought Des

178

was the one because he was my first love. First loves are always special, but they don't usually last." She looked at me sympathetically, and smiled before continuing, "When I met your dad, I knew for sure he was the one. It's an old cliché, but it's true. When it's right, you just know it."

I reflected on my brief dating history. I'd never felt anything stronger than friendship for my previous boyfriends. James was definitely my first love, but the connection we shared didn't feel temporary.

"Just promise me you won't run off and get married this week, the one time I go out of town without you."

I laughed. "Only if you make the same promise."

She pulled one of the pillows and tossed it in my direction. "Guess I'd better hop into the shower before I fall asleep on my feet. I'll see you after school, honey."

I breathed a sigh of relief that her trip was still on, my mood happy as I got ready for school.

James was late picking me up. No time to stop for coffees at Grinds and apparently no time for conversation either.

I tried anyway.

I had so many questions. When did our dream sharing start? How was it possible? Why did we share dreams? I'd asked him these and other questions in hushed whispers on the bus ride home yesterday, but he'd dodged each one.

"I should have never told you about that," he'd said.

"Why not?" I'd asked. "I probably would have figured it out."

"Maybe." He'd looked at me then. "But I still shouldn't have told you."

"But you did and you can't undo it."

He'd laughed darkly. "Apparently not."

"So tell me everything." I'd leaned against him and

was surprised when I felt his body stiffen. "What's wrong?" I'd asked, pulling away.

"We can't have that conversation here," he'd said. "Look around us, we're not exactly alone."

"Then tomorrow morning on the way to school," I'd pressed.

James had nodded and then returned to staring out of the bus window. There was nothing but silence the rest of the ride back to Woodvine, and I'd resigned myself to waiting until morning.

It was now morning.

I took a new approach on our way to school, asking about my most recent dream instead of digging through our shared past. "Were you there last night? In my dream?" I knew he had been, but I needed him to confirm it. The idea was still surreal to me.

"Of course I was," he said gruffly.

"Who was that guy?" I asked, hopeful to get more information. "You didn't seem to like him."

"That wasn't a guy."

*A girl?*

"Do you know her?" I asked.

"Not now, Leath," James snapped as he pulled into the student lot.

He had to be kidding. To spring this on me and not expect me to question him was crazy. I looked at him with a sullen expression. "Like it or not, we're going to have to talk about this at some point," I said angrily.

"Maybe not." He sighed. James rubbed his eyes as if he were exhausted.

Did he truly regret telling me about our dream sharing? Would he rather end our relationship than answer my questions? That seemed unlikely. Even if he wanted to end it, how could he? Apparently, we were connected subconsciously. I didn't know how he could sever that connection. My mind bounced from one conclusion to another as the minutes stretched before he finally spoke.

"You're right," he said flatly. "We need to talk. But this is a conversation that will take more than the snatches of time we have between home and school."

"Wednesday," I said. "Mom's leaving Wednesday. We'll have all the time we need."

"Wednesday," James relented.

I wondered why he was stalling. When he ran his fingers through his hair, I knew he was keeping something from me. And by the look on his face, it was something big.

There was nothing I wanted more than to talk about our dream connection and learn about the catalyst James had mentioned. But I had the terrible feeling James wanted to discuss another subject entirely. Things had cooled between us since yesterday. Although he held my hand when we walked from the parking lot to our morning classes, he seemed distant. He said goodbye quietly, and we parted ways for first period.

It took a monumental effort on my part not to press the issue with James over the next forty-eight hours, all the while his words echoing in my head.

*We need to talk.*

I tried to give James the space he needed, keeping our conversations superficial on the drive to and from school. Anxiety and irritation rivaled within me as James found excuses not to be with me at lunch. He was "getting tutoring in physics," and was busy when he dropped me at home after school with, "other commitments."

Thankfully, I was rewarded with a much-needed distraction when I helped Mom pack on Tuesday night. She was almost giddy as her cell blew up with texts from Des. I listened patiently while Mom shared her hopes about seeing him again. Out of habit, Mom's fingers found the long chain she wore around her neck. It was my father's wedding band. When I was much younger, I'd asked him about the gold band. Dad said it was his lucky ring, and it gave him his superpowers.

"I was wondering if I should wear this," she said, sliding the ring back and forth on the long chain.

Her statement seemed to be more for me than for her. Like she was asking my permission to take it off.

"Maybe this time..." I eased into my answer. "Maybe this time, you should leave it here."

Mom shook her head. "I just can't bear to set it aside." Her fingers curled protectively around the ring.

I understood her dilemma. To take the necklace off and leave it behind meant she was leaving Dad behind. "I think you're going to have to, if you want to move forward," I said gently. I moved to her side and rested my head on her shoulder.

She turned to me. "Would you mind wearing it?" she asked timidly.

I'd never considered asking her if I could, but somehow, it seemed right. "I'd like that, Mom."

She slid the necklace off and immediately over my head—as if she didn't want the last connection we had to my dad to be broken. I smiled at her.

In perfect timing, her cell buzzed again. "Des," she said.

"What are you waiting for?" I asked. "Text him back." It was late when I left her to pack her toiletry bag. I was too exhausted to continue dissecting the new relationship she had with Des or to even ponder the one I thought I had with James.

The next morning, I helped Mom load her car before she headed out to Columbia. "Drive safe," I said, hugging her neck.

"I will. And you call me if you need anything," she said, kissing me on the cheek. She rolled Dad's ring between her fingers and then placed the chain back against my skin. "Thanks, honey." I watched her back out of the driveway before turning toward the house.

My cell buzzed. A text from James. "Running late. Ride with Anamae?"

And with that, the last of my patience evaporated along with the dew on the grass under my feet. I stared at the text, too angry to form words. How long would he delay this? Before I could reply, he texted again, "I'll catch up later. promise."

James didn't make it to English class that day, and he was nowhere to be found at lunch. His absence gave credence to my fear that what he wanted to talk about had nothing to do with our dream sharing, and everything to do with his wanting to end it between us. My cell buzzed as I made my way out of the main building after school.

"In Columbia. Love you, Mom."

I texted back to head off any misgivings she'd have about leaving if I didn't respond. "Have fun. Love you, too."

I half-expected James to leave me stranded after school, but he was there waiting in the Rover, already in the car line for the parking lot exit. My cell chirped, the battery nearly dead. I quickly texted Anamae, letting her know James had shown up. I asked her to cover with her parents and said I'd be over later.

"Decide to take the day off?" I asked as I climbed into the car.

"Something like that."

"You could have told me you weren't coming at all," I said. I slammed the door so hard the car shook.

James gave me a smirk. "I see you left your anger at school."

"Yes, but I brought my rage."

"Well, the good news is I don't see a scratch-off." He pointed to my book bag where my binder poked through.

"And how could I have a scratch-off?" I asked sarcastically. "In order to have a scratch-off, I'd have to know when we actually started dating. Was it this year? Or many years ago? What is going on? First, you tell me we've been sharing dreams, and then you refuse to explain it. Honestly, it seems like you're hoping I'll forget all about it." I threw him a hard glance. His smirk had been replaced by a look of profound sadness. Something was horribly wrong.

"Why don't we take a few minutes before we say something we'll both regret?" His tone was troubled, and he didn't look me in the eyes.

I leaned against the headrest and took a few deep breaths. Closing my eyes, I silently counted to ten as I inhaled, then exhaled. A few moments later, I turned my head slightly to look at his profile. He was absolutely gorgeous. I cast my eyes to the backseat before I was caught staring at him. That was when I noticed there was no salmon-colored rose for me anywhere in the car.

"I'm taking you to where the roses grow," James said. He turned to me, his expression full of resignation, and then placed his right hand palm-side up on the console. Longing for his touch, I put my hand in his and intertwined our fingers. I glanced out my window. We were no longer in Woodvine. I knew where we were going. It was symmetry to a fault.

Suddenly, an explanation for our dreams seemed the least of my worries. I thought about what James would say when we reached our destination. The words he would use to end our relationship. I decided not to waste what precious little time we had together. Instead, I pretended we were on a date, on our way to see a movie. Maybe the theater had those double-sized seats, allowing me to snuggle up to him and rest my head on his chest. Or maybe we'd find one of those ancient drive-in theaters. I'd heard there was one left in Asheville.

The sound of tires crunching gravel disturbed my daydreams. We had arrived at Judaculla Rock. James parked, and, once again, we were the only visitors. He got out of the Rover, walked around to my door, and opened it. I sat staring straight ahead, not wanting the drive to be over. It would be different going home. We would be different. Our relationship would be scratch-off worthy.

"Come on, Leath," he said softly. "We need to talk."

"I'd rather you just say what you have to say right here." I ignored his outstretched hand. "I don't want to ruin my memory of our last visit to Judaculla Rock. So, just go ahead and get it over with." Warm tears threatened the corners of my eyes. I vowed not to let them fall until after he dropped me off at Anamae's house.

"Leath, please come with me," he said, his voice pleading.

I took his hand and unwillingly stepped out.

James shut the door, leaned against the side of the Rover, and then pulled me to him. He folded me into his arms. I rested my head on his chest, relishing every second. He lifted my chin and kissed me so sweetly I couldn't control my emotions.

"Shh," he said, sliding his thumbs under my eyes to wipe away the tears. He pulled me back onto his chest. We stood that way for several minutes while I composed myself.

"I don't want us to be over," I said, shocked by my boldness.

"I didn't bring you here to break up with you."

Although his words were meant to comfort me,

his voice was acidic. I ignored his tone, allowing relief to flood through me, bringing a new round of tears. I wrapped my arms around his neck, hugging him tightly. "I love you," I said for the first time ever.

James pulled my arms down gently, staring into my eyes. "You don't know how long I've wanted to hear you say that." He sighed, heavily. "But you might feel differently once you hear the rest of my story."

He moved away from the Rover and led me down the wooded path. When we reached Judaculla Rock, we sat down on the platform, our feet dangling over the side.

James squinted, staring into the fading sunlight then pulled me to him. I slipped one arm around his waist, the other I rested in his lap. He quickly scooped my hand into his. His thumb lightly traced the back of my hand. "I don't know where to start," he said. "Yeah, I guess I do. First, I need to tell you I'm sorry for shutting you out these past few days. It was selfish of me. I shouldn't have told you about our dreams. Once I did, I knew I had to tell you everything. I've been reluctant to do that because I'm pretty sure you'll leave me after I do."

I waited while bracing myself for his confession. No matter what James said, I would not change my mind about him. Or my heart.

"You're not going to believe what I have to tell you, but try to hold on to what you know to be true. I love you and I always have." He kissed the top of my head and then hesitated for a long moment. "I know this dream-sharing thing seems impossible, but lots of people do it. There are ways to bring the dreams on and ways to join other dreams once connections are made."

My mind returned to the last dream I'd shared with James. It was the first time our dream included other people. I thought about the girl who'd interrupted us as we danced under the night sky. Was she somehow connected to me? Or was she connected to him?

"When I was a baby, my mom gave me something that made me dream about the girl I would one day marry. That was the first time I dreamed about you."

*James had dreamt of me when he was a baby. In addition, his mother had orchestrated the whole thing.* Marisol's warning from long ago flashed to the front of my mind. *"That boy's got a secret. He's trying to keep it inside, keep it hidden. But secrets do not stay quiet. His secret will tell on him. When it does, you do not want to be around to hear it."*

"Are you still with me?" he asked apprehensively.

I nodded, unable to speak.

"My mother dream shared with me, and she saw your face. She searched for you, and then found your family in Woodvine."

I didn't move and barely breathed. "Why did your mother do that?"

"She didn't have a choice," he said. "None of them do."

"Them?" I asked.

He ignored my question. "My mother studied your mom's habits. Learned the places where she shopped and what she bought there. She discovered Penny liked going to street markets, so my mother set up a table at one of her favorite markets. That's how I knew your mother liked daisies, why I brought them the night she invited me to dinner."

The term stalker seemed inadequate compared to what James was suggesting. I swallowed hard, fighting the fear building in my chest. I was suddenly worried for my mother's safety.

"Mom sold herbs and herbal remedies," he said. "Over time, she and Penny became friends of sorts. When Penny mentioned you were having trouble sleeping,

Mom sold her a sleeping oil and told her to put a drop of it on your wrist at bedtime. She told Penny the mixture would lull you to sleep."

I immediately remembered the vial of lavender oil lying on my nightstand. "You're not talking about a potion, or a spell, are you?" I asked incredulously.

"My mother's not a witch," he said darkly.

I knew then that she was certainly something. Something not entirely human maybe. If so, what did that make James? "What was in the sleeping oil?" I asked.

"The catalyst," he said. "More accurately, my essence. It made your dreams susceptible to my image. You began dreaming with me the first night you used the oil. Over time, our connection grew stronger until we no longer needed the oil to meet in our dreams."

"But if our connection was so strong, why did I forget so many of the dreams?" I asked, struggling to understand.

"Because you stopped having them. And when that happened, we weren't able to add more connections."

"Why did they stop?" I asked.

He looked at me, his eyes cautious. "You left our dreams about three years ago when we were fourteen. I think you know why."

"Dad." I instinctively clutched his ring on the gold chain around my neck.

"Your father's death came out of left field. It was a tremendous blow. You compensated by withdrawing from your friends, family, from me. You closed the connection between us." The sadness in his voice was nearly tangible.

I found myself grieving the years I'd lost with James. Even if those years were only in my subconscious.

"It was hard for me without you. But I still had a life back home. It wasn't perfect, but it was what I knew."

His voice trailed off as if his mind was somewhere else.

I wondered about his life there. "Did you have friends? Did you date?" I asked.

"Friends, yes. Dates, no," he answered absentmindedly. "The years passed until I was finally old enough to leave my home and look for you. In our last dream, there were hints you might move to Columbia, so I went there first. When I couldn't find you, I was worried I'd lost you forever. I decided to try Woodvine on the chance you were still there."

"I thought you lived in Columbia. That you were from Columbia," I said, my voice rising on the last syllable.

"Yes, I did say that." He stroked my cheek with his free hand, gazing into my eyes. "I really shouldn't be telling you all this."

What he was telling me was something out of a nightmare. But for the moment, I was more petrified he would leave me with unanswered questions. My throat was tight as I managed to whisper my demand. "Tell me the rest."

"I guess it's too late not to. You already know too much," he said. "But when you know it all, there will be no going back."

*No going back. Home? To the dreams? To us?*

I steeled myself, knowing I had to hear everything.

"This next part is going to be pretty bad."

"I don't care. Tell me," I insisted, even though I wasn't sure how much more I could handle.

"I'm I'm going to have to show you rather than tell you."

James jumped off the platform. He picked up several moon-colored pebbles from the ground, just as he'd done the first time we'd come here. Bending, he began placing one pebble on the tip of each of the seven fingers of Judaculla. He gave me an apologetic look as he moved the last pebble into place.

The wind gusted around us, blowing my hair in my face. I pushed it away and saw James scrambling to remove the pebbles from the boulder. They seemed frozen or glued to the spot as he clawed at them with his fingers.

"Are you out of your mind?" hissed a voice behind me.

Ever charged out of the woods, her blonde hair flowing loose and wild in the wind. A golden shimmer danced behind her, stopping at the edge of the forest. It was the same light I saw my first night here with James. Ever bolted toward me, knocking me to the ground behind the low platform. Golden lights danced between the slats of the wooden structure and reflected in Ever's hard stare.

From where I sat, Ever seemed to be the one who'd lost her mind. I struggled to get out of her grasp.

"Cut it out," she said, roughly pinning me to the ground. "I'm not doing this to protect you. I'm trying to protect him."

*James.*

My eyes darted, frantic to find him. He was there, still trying to pull one of the pebbles from the boulder as the wind screamed in a fury around us.

"Protect him from what?" I whispered.

"From himself," she said.

James groaned, pushing one of the pebbles free from Judaculla's handprint. The wind blew, hurtling itself back into the forest, sucking the glimmering light with it. James yelled in frustration as he violently swept the remaining pebbles from the boulder. They flew off easily as if they were feathers on a slick marble slab. Ever's grip loosened, and I twisted from her hold. I rushed to James then threw my arms around him.

"What was I thinking?" he whispered. "I'm so sorry." James looked at me as if seeing me for the first time. His murmurs soft and calming as he stroked my hair, smoothing the tangles with his hands.

"You weren't thinking," said Ever. "That's the problem. That's twice now."

My last dream of James came to the front of my mind, his trying to protect me. I instinctively stepped in front of him, watching Ever closely.

She laughed in response. Her eyes were as cold as a glacier and seemed just as sharp, as if her glare could cut through the hull of a ship. "Don't bring her here again unless you plan to go through with it. I can't keep helping you kick that door shut." She shook leaves and bits of branches from her hair and clothes. With a last scathing look, she walked back to the fading golden light leading into the heart of the forest.

"What does she mean?" I asked in a quiet voice. "Go through with what?"

"Taking you to Judaculla," he said, his voice weary with defeat.

"We're already at Judaculla." I searched his eyes, desperate for a rational explanation.

"We're not." James gestured to the massive boulder. "The rock is a gateway to Judaculla. That's where I'm from, not Columbia."

I followed his gaze to the huge stone. Its deep carvings were faintly visible in the moonlight. I remembered the theories James discussed during our last visit. The possibility that the boulder was a door to another world. I shivered when a light breeze caused goose bumps to rise on my arm.

My breathing was erratic, and I was suddenly lightheaded. I tried to be strong, which was difficult when I felt my life dismantling around me. Looking into the sky, I half expected it to fall down in large chunks, just slide off like the toppings on a pizza turned on its end. I disconnected from the world, from my own life. It was as if I was a mere observer of all that was happening. I felt I could touch time itself and I imagined doing so, reaching out into the blur, steadying strands that stretched too thin as they tried to contain my reality. I slumped back onto the platform and forced my breathing to slow.

"And Ever?" I asked quietly. "She's not from Columbia either, is she?"

James raked his hand through his hair, struggling with something, as if he knew what he had to do, but could not bring himself to do it.

*That's twice now.*

I remembered our first trip here. James had done the same thing with the pebbles, only he'd thrown the last pebble to the ground. Had Ever stopped him that time as well? But that meant Ever was my protector, not James.

"This is the part where you're probably going to change your mind about me. If you haven't already," he said, sitting beside me.

*There was more?*

I stared at him in disbelief, feeling at once here and miles away from him, or even years apart.

"I'm nearly at the end, and then I'll take you home, okay?" he asked gently. "This involves more than just sharing dreams, but it started with the first one. That dream marked you... as mine."

"What?" I asked, completely bewildered. A memory flitted through my mind. Just before our first kiss, James had said I belonged to him. Was this what he had meant? I had been marked as his as if I were... his property? I let this idea sink in as the minutes passed.

"The dream sharing is how we find our mates."

"Mates?" I asked.

"My people in Judaculla. The boys," he explained. "All babies born in Judaculla are boys. When we're old enough, we travel outside of our world to find our mate. It's been that way since Judaculla Rock was put in Cullowhee. That's *why* it was put in Cullowhee. The gateway connects your world and mine. Just like generations before me, I traveled through it. I came here to find you and bring you back to Judaculla."

My tears flowed easily now. I dabbed at them uselessly with the sleeve of my shirt. Marisol had been right. Victor had been right. Had I even been right early on in feeling unsure, almost afraid to be alone with James?

I flinched when he cradled me in his arms. He continued in a low voice. "But when I finally found you, everything changed. The way I felt about you in our dreams is nothing compared to how much I love you. I didn't plan for that to happen, but it did."

I looked at James through my blurry eyes, angry with myself for opening the door for him to come into my life. Angry for loving him back. Angry I still loved him, despite all he'd said.

He rested his chin on my head and whispered, "I love you, Leath. That's why I'm going back without you."

# 12

## No More Secrets

THE WORDS DID NOT BELONG TOGETHER IN THE SAME sentence.

*Love.*

*Without.*

*You.*

"What are you even talking about?" I asked, struggling to break away from his embrace.

He looked at me with eyes that seemed a thousand years old. "I have to go back, Leath. Back to Judaculla."

"But you can't." The words sounded like a weak plea, a last effort to stop my heart from breaking completely. "I can't bear it when we're apart."

"Neither can I," James said gently and tucked my hair behind my ear.

"Then I'll go with you."

"Judaculla's not a place I want you to see."

"And what about what I want?" I asked. "I'd rather go there than have you leave me behind."

"You don't know what you're saying. You have no idea what it's like. The Elders blame the women for the curse of Judaculla. Men are brutal toward their wives." His lips formed a hard line. "The only time a woman is treated properly is when she's made pregnant."

I shuddered at the words *made pregnant*.

James continued, each of his words dripping with bitterness. "Expectant mothers are pampered, given anything they want, everything they need, to ensure a healthy baby. But once the baby is born—and trust me, it's always a boy—the new mother goes back to her subservient role. It's a vicious cycle, one that's been in place for thousands of years. If you came back with me, you'd be condemned to a life of misery." He hesitated, and then continued in a voice so quiet I had to strain my ears to hear his confession. "Today was the second time I tried to take you to Judaculla, because that's what I'm supposed to do. Find my mate and bring her back. But I can't go through with it, so please don't ask me to."

"Then you stay here," I said. "Stay here with me."

James stroked my cheek and his gray eyes found mine. "I wish it were that easy. My parents, well, my dad, he'll be waiting for me to return."

*His parents are alive?*

"I'm sorry I lied about my parents being killed in South Carolina. I had to have a good story. One you would believe, one you could relate to." He waited, allowing this news to sink in.

I felt dizzy. He had struck me at my most vulnerable, using the guise of the death of a parent to get close to me. Was everything he'd told me a lie?

"Hold on to what you know is true," he said as if reading my thoughts and already knowing my fears. "I do love you, Leath. I always have. As crazy as it all sounds, that is the truth."

His scent washed over me, and I was transported to the time before I'd met him, back to when he was just a dream. A wonderful dream. Our love had become the one constant in both worlds. Deliberately planted in my mind, our love blossomed and grew in our dreams until it could no longer be contained, spilling over into our waking hours. This constant was what bound us together forever.

Something tugged at me then, dancing around in my mind, taunting me. It was petty, but I couldn't help it. I had to know. "And where does Ever fit into this truth?"

James sighed. "Ever is you a few years ago."

That didn't help. "Ever was your first choice?" I asked, my voice cracking on her name.

"No," he said abruptly. He pulled me closer, whispering in my ear. "You are my first choice, my only choice, and you will always be my only choice. Ever was Cole's first choice. Cole was my best friend. He was a couple of years older than me. He made the same journey I did, traveling to this world when he was my age. Cole came here to find Ever and bring her back to Judaculla. Their story was similar to ours in that Cole fell in love with Ever, and she with him. Ever had no family, and so she willingly returned to Judaculla with Cole."

"If they can do it..." I started, but James interrupted.

"Cole and Ever were married right away. Three months later, Cole died. It was sudden and unexpected." He looked away, staring off as if watching a memory. One I had no right to view.

"Since then, Ever's been caught between our world and yours. She has no desire to return to her old life outside of Judaculla, and so the Elders don't consider her a threat to our secrecy. But they don't know what to do with her either."

It was evil of me. I should have felt sorry for Ever, for what she'd been through. But the way she behaved around James, crashing at his place, that day she met me at the door wearing one of his shirts, how she'd acted when we ran into her during our visit to USC... It was obvious she was interested in James, and I was irritated that he didn't seem to notice this.

"Can't she find someone else in Judaculla?" I asked, hoping he'd take the hint.

"Like me, all the men in Judaculla are spoken for," he said, taking my hand in his. "There's no way any of us would choose Ever over the girl of our dreams. She belonged to Cole, she was married to him, so no other man will marry her. Ever's accepted this. She doesn't seem interested in anyone else because she still wears Cole's token. That J she wears around her neck stands for Judaculla.. It's our version of a wedding ring."

My mind went to the matching J James had on his key ring. His wedding token. One that had always been meant for me.

"Ever's an outcast in Judaculla. She's an outcast in both worlds," James said.

Ever's actions an hour earlier began to make sense. She *was* trying to protect James. She must have known he wouldn't be able to live with himself if he brought me to Judaculla. But there was more to it than that. If she was trying to protect James, that meant she cared for him. I questioned Ever's motives, and I couldn't help but wonder if she were hoping James would return to Judaculla alone. She knew he'd never choose another girl. He would be an outcast. Maybe Ever hoped she and James could be outcasts together.

"I'm sorry for what I tried to do today. Bringing you here to trick you into going back with me was wrong," he said. James stroked my cheek, pulling me out of my thoughts and back into the cool night air. "You're freezing cold; let me get you over to Anamae's."

James helped me to my feet and took my hand as he led me back down the path away from Judaculla Rock. We crossed the lot and then climbed into the Rover.

James started the engine and switched on the heated seats. The warmth radiated through me. It had been a long and difficult day. All I wanted to do was climb into bed and fall into a deep sleep. One from which I would awaken to find this was all a dream. Maybe when I woke up, it would all disappear and be gone like the dark of night replaced by the morning sun.

I wondered vaguely what I would be doing right now if I'd never met James. Would I even have a boyfriend? Who would it be? Victor? Our short time together seemed a lifetime ago. The last time I'd seen Victor, he walked right past me as if I didn't exist, breaking that part of my heart that had been permanently reserved for him.

I wondered if I would be the same person I was now if I had never met James. My dad used to say life was made of events. The time we stayed in one event was up to us, but we had to go through all of them to end up where we were meant to be.

James had come to me when I was a baby, and our dreams shaped me into who I now was. I wondered if this connection with James, even when it was in my subconscious, was what kept me from getting serious about Victor or any boy I'd dated. Now that all the dreams had returned to me, I could not remember a time without James. Seventeen years together. The question was, could I picture the next seventeen years, or a future that didn't include him?

As for what he'd said about Judaculla, had I not witnessed the door opening to that world, I never would have believed other worlds existed, hiding in plain sight right alongside my own. The only thing separating our worlds an invisible barrier, a veil as thick as the breadth of a single strand of hair, but as impenetrable as steel. A barrier James had crossed as a helpless infant by entering my dreams. I felt ashamed for my cowardice, but thankful

James had the strength and courage to cross that barrier and find me.

I felt James take my hand as we entered Woodvine. He wanted to take me straight to Anamae's house, but I insisted on going home first. Sam hadn't been out for hours, and I needed to get my things. It was black as pitch by the time we reached my house. Sam gave me an indignant look when I opened the door. He ignored me, choosing instead to greet James. I watched as James bent to hug Sam's neck and scratch his ears before putting him outside.

I sat on the couch, waiting while Sam was outside. James joined me, and I rested my head on his chest. I was so exhausted, worn out by what I'd learned, and overwhelmed by the knowledge that the worst was yet to come. There were still so many questions, but for now, I focused on the one that mattered the most.

"How long are you going to stay in Woodvine?" I asked. I held my breath, waiting for his response.

"As long as you want me to." He rested his head on mine.

I wanted to believe him. But he'd already said he'd have to go back. His parents were in Judaculla. Surely they were waiting for him to come home. We sat in silence, and I imagined catching each minute that passed, saving them all. I wished I could trap them in a glass jar like I used to do with lightning bugs on a summer night. Even then, I had to let the bugs fly, releasing them to return to their families. I couldn't expect James to stay away from his family forever.

Could I stay away from mine?

I thought about life inside Judaculla. Did I love James enough to give up my freedom? To live with him there the way Ever had done with her husband? Did I have the strength to abandon Mom? She'd already lost

Dad. How could I do that to her? But then again, wasn't that exactly what I was asking James to do? Abandon his parents for me? The impossibility of our situation was devastating, and my heart wept at the cruelty of it all.

I was alerted by the patterns his fingertips lightly traced on my hip. Pushing all of my questions into a dark corner in my mind, I kissed him, trying desperately to bind us together forever. James cupped the back of my head, pulling my mouth to his as he returned my kisses with equal passion. Something tugged at my memory. Mom wasn't home, wouldn't be home for days. We were completely alone in the house. I climbed onto his lap, straddling him as I worked to loosen his belt. I felt his sharp intake of breath. In one quick motion, James lifted me, laying me down on the couch. His lips couldn't reach mine fast enough, and I clung to him as if my life depended on it. I wanted more of his kisses; I wanted more of everything. I began tugging at his shirt, trying to slide it up his back.

"I love you," he said, kissing me over and over.

I needed to hear more. It took all of my willpower to stop his kisses, but I turned slightly to whisper in his ear. "Promise me you will love me forever."

"Forever," he said. "Till death do us part."

"Not even in death," I pressed. "Promise you won't stop loving me, even in death."

James looked into my eyes, his next words melting straight into my heart. "Not even in death."

His lips found mine again as my arms wrapped around his shoulders, pulling him closer. He kissed me repeatedly, murmuring how much he loved me, how he never wanted us to be apart, all while leaving a trail of kisses across my throat and back to my lips. In that moment, we were alone in our own unhurried world. No one else and no other demands except for the ones our bodies made on each other. A demand to be close enough as one.

I tried to block out everything from this terrible day, to be aware of only his touch, his lips lingering on my neck. But for one brief second, a sense of finality crept into my mind. As much as I hated it, I couldn't help wonder if I were pushing this to happen because I knew I'd lose him soon. Did this mean I'd abandoned all hope of our being able to somehow fix the mess we were in?

James sensed my hesitation. He shifted away to lie beside me while still holding me in his arms.

Even though I had just questioned our timing, even though I was uncertain, wavering on whether I was ready, I was frustrated when James broke the bubble of our private world. I rose on my elbows, confronting him with my gaze. "Don't you want to be with me?"

"Of course I do." He pulled me on top of him, kissing me tenderly before gently easing me to rest on his chest. "But, not like this. Not because we think it's the end of us."

I was as much annoyed with James as I was with myself for putting the brakes on, but I was also a little relieved. He was right. This would not be our way. We would not come together out of desperation or fear. We would do this when I knew for sure we'd never be apart again. I snuggled closer, clinging to him as I breathed in his beautiful essence. My frustration gave way to blissful contentment as I wished this moment would never end.

I was awakened a short time later by Sam's scratching on the front door. My eyes flew open, remembering the time and place. I sat up quickly, waking James in my haste. I glanced at the grandfather clock. It was ten at night! Why hadn't Anamae called me? I was surprised her parents hadn't come over here looking for me... or worse, that Mom hadn't driven back when I went MIA.

I jumped up and ran to the door to let Sam in. "We

have got to get going," I said frantically.

James yawned, unfazed by my flurry of activity. "It appears we're late for something." He smiled. When I ducked under the couch looking for my shoe, he rose and gently pulled me to him. He kissed me, and my anxiety subsided. "We're a little late, big deal. Take your time. I'll be outside." He kissed my forehead before he walked out the front door.

As soon he was outside, I bolted to my room, taking the steps two at a time. I quickly packed a bag, not really paying attention to what I threw into it. I caught my reflection in my dresser mirror and was horrified to see my makeup had streaked in random areas around my eyes, giving my face a zombie-like quality. I raced to the bathroom, touched up my makeup, and brushed my teeth before returning downstairs. I hurriedly fed Sam, the extra cup of food a peace offering. After giving his fur a brief pat, I set the alarm. I grabbed my bag and ran out of the house.

Moments later, we were on the road. I was keyed up, tense over what mess I'd step into at Anamae's. Anxiety brewed inside me as I tried to think of something to say to Anamae's parents, coming home so late and on a school night. We pulled onto her street, and I was relieved to see her parents weren't home. Victor's BMW was parked in their usual spot of the driveway. James pulled in and killed the engine.

Sudden insecurity gripped me. "I have to hear it again," I said.

"Anything," he whispered, staring into my eyes.

"Tell me you'll stay in Woodvine. No, promise me," I said, the fear in my heart transferring to my voice. "Because if you go, I miss out on you, and if that happens, I'll miss out on everything."

"I promise I'll stay in Woodvine as long as you want

me to." James kissed my fingers and smiled reassuringly.

At that moment, Anamae burst through the front door of her house. She ran to my side of the car and wrenched the door open. "Where have you been?" she asked urgently. "Didn't you get my texts?"

"No. My cell's dead," I answered, puzzled by her alarm.

"That's not all that's going to be dead," she said.

As Anamae nearly dragged me from the Rover, James climbed out and opened the back door to retrieve my suitcase. He carried it, following behind us.

"What are you doing?" She groaned impatiently. "Just leave it there and go." When she turned to me, her expression changed from impatience to disbelief. "Oh my gosh, tell me that's not a hickey."

My hand flew to my neck, and I blushed. By the time I saw Victor, it was too late. James must have sensed him. He turned around, and his face met Victor's fist. The sucker punch knocked James to the ground in a heap. Victor reached down and pulled him up by the collar of his shirt. A string of profanity flowed freely from Victor's lips. His deep voice switched fluidly between English and Spanish as he punched James repeatedly. James staggered and fell against the side of the Rover.

"Fight back, jerk!" Victor shouted.

A look of pure rage crossed James's face. For a moment, I thought he might kill Victor. James charged at him, knocking Victor to the ground, but he didn't hit him. James pinned him down as Anamae and I begged them to stop. Victor struggled and his right hand broke free. He drove another punch to James's chin, putting him on the ground again. I screamed and ran toward James.

"Get up!" Victor growled, towering over him.

Anamae grabbed Victor's arm, pulling him

backward. At her touch, Victor slowly backed away, but his profanity continued. Anamae tried to soothe Victor's anger in a rush of muted words, calling him "Big Bear." She managed to move him several feet away from James before Victor turned back to him.

"You have one minute to get the hell out of here," Victor said, struggling to control his fury.

James rolled onto his stomach and pushed off the ground. I was at his side instantly. "Come on," I murmured. I put my arm around his waist, attempting to help him back to his car. He refused to budge.

"I will not leave you here with that nut job," he said thickly. "He's obviously crazy."

"You haven't even seen crazy!" roared Victor. Breaking away from Anamae, he charged at James again.

"Stop it!" I screamed, stepping between them.

"Get out of the way, Leath," Victor seethed. A flash of headlights momentarily blinded me as a car turned onto the street.

"Great. My parents are home," Anamae said. "That's it. Victor, get back inside. James, say goodnight." She put her hand on Victor's shoulder. He shrugged it off and stomped into the house.

"Please don't make me leave you here with him," James said desperately.

"He's not angry with me. I'll be fine." I pulled the sleeve of my sweater over my fingers, and used it to dab the blood from his lip, hoping to get him cleaned up before Anamae's parents parked their car. Thankfully, the car continued down the street, passing slowly by the house. "You need to go before her parents really get here. I'll sort this out. I promise."

James pulled me into his arms. "I'm coming back if I don't hear from you in fifteen minutes."

I hugged him back, and he was gone. I turned and

headed up the driveway to Anamae's house. As soon as James's car turned off her street, Victor stormed outside, slamming the door behind him.

My blood boiled. "You had absolutely no right to do that," I hissed, intercepting him before he reached his car.

"Not a good time, Leath," Victor said. He sidestepped me to open his car door.

I grabbed his arm, trying to spin him around.

"I cannot talk to you right now." Victor shook my hand from his arm and climbed into his car.

I stood beside the driver's seat, preventing him from shutting the car door. I yelled the words without thinking. "Well, if now doesn't work for you, try never."

Victor's shoulders sagged, and he glanced at me. Anguish filled his face.

I recoiled at the sight of his heartbreak, not sure of what to say. After what seemed like hours of just staring into each other's eyes, I silently backed away from his car.

Victor slammed the door, driving away without another word.

# 13

## You Never Know When Your Time is Up

I WASN'T SURE HOW LONG I STOOD ON ANAMAE'S FRONT porch, foolishly waiting for one of them to return. I couldn't get the images of Victor and James fighting out of my head, praying James wasn't seriously hurt and that Victor would forgive me for what I'd said. The ring of a phone inside the house shook me from my thoughts.

Anamae joined me outside a few seconds later. "That was my mom. She called earlier to check on us, and I told her you fell asleep when you went home to get your things. She was just calling to see if you'd gotten here."

I didn't care.

"Hello, Leath?" She sighed when I didn't respond. "Look, you don't have to talk if you don't want to. But you do have to come with me. I'm starved."

She jangled her keys, and I awoke from my stupor. I stared at her blankly.

"Everything's going to be all right," she said.

Then my tears came.

"Boys are idiots." She put her arm around my shoulders. "You'll feel better after you eat. Pan bottoms, anyone?"

I gave a wry smile at her crazy name for pancakes. "Wait. Can I borrow your cell?" Anamae handed it to

206

me. I quickly texted James. Victor's gone. Everything's fine. See you tomorrow? Leath. A few seconds later, he responded.

Definitely.

This small promise made me feel better, and I realized how hungry I was. There wasn't a restaurant open past ten in Woodvine, but it didn't take us long to drive to Asheville at that time of the night. We pulled into a twenty-four hour pancake house. It was packed with students from UNC Asheville. Their blue attire clashed with the lime green walls of the restaurant. I felt several eyes on me as we followed the waitress across the cracked vinyl floor to a small booth against the wall. One of the college students called out for more napkins. The waitress sighed wearily before taking our order. She returned moments later with two cups of decaf and two large glasses of orange juice.

Anamae pulled a jar of peanut butter from her bottomless bag and put it in the center of the table. As far back as I could remember, we'd always put peanut butter on our pancakes. We asked for it once when we were at a restaurant, but they wouldn't give us their jar. After that, Anamae always brought one from home.

"What was up with Victor?" I asked, turning the mug between my hands to warm them.

"He was worried about you. We both were." Her tone was defensive.

"I'm sorry. I should've called, but I didn't have any service. And no matter what, Victor shouldn't have done that. I mean, he totally lost it."

"Really?" Anamae asked, feigning ignorance. "Hmm, I wonder why."

"Shut up." I rolled my eyes. "Seriously, what happened?"

"Victor stopped by to see if we wanted to get

something to eat. I guess it was around eight o'clock when he started getting worried. We both tried to call you and only got your voice mail. A couple of hours later, he wanted to go looking for you, but I made him wait with me. I didn't want him behind the wheel when he was so worried. The fact that he's in love with you combined with your neck art is what caused him to lose his mind. James is lucky he was able to walk away."

My stomach rolled as I remembered the sound of Victor's fist connecting with James's face.

"Although James might not have been so mangled if he'd only decked Victor once. Why didn't he fight back?"

The waitress appeared with our orders of silver-dollar pancakes, saving me from answering Anamae's rhetorical question. She put our checks alongside several tubs of warm maple syrup. The delicious smell kicked my appetite into high gear. After slathering peanut butter on the pancakes, I drenched them in the syrup. I felt my strength returning after a few bites.

"What are you going to do about Victor?" Anamae asked, spreading a layer of peanut butter on her own pancakes.

"Nothing." Victor had crossed the line. Our reconciliation would be up to him since it was entirely his fault. "I tried talking to him before he left. He wasn't interested."

"Give him a few days. He was just super worried. He doesn't trust James at all." She drizzled syrup on her pancakes. "No, it's more than that. I'm not supposed to tell you this, but Victor thinks James is dangerous. He's got it in his head that James is trying to take you away from us, away from Woodvine." She laughed lightly while looking at me for a reaction.

"That's silly," I spluttered.

*Get a grip.*

There was no way Victor could know that, and no way I could tell Anamae or Victor or anyone about what James had told me. I forced a laugh. "I'm not going anywhere. How can I? I'm only a junior in high school."

"I tried to tell Victor that, but he wouldn't listen. Victor swears James is hiding the real reason he's in Woodvine. When you didn't show up, he was convinced something had happened. He thought James had run off with you somewhere." She cut her eyes at me and grinned wickedly. "Then again, if James is up to no good, I'd like to hear the details. How did it go tonight?"

I should have been prepared for this. Of course Anamae wanted to know all about it, but telling the truth wasn't an option. I quickly made up a story. "We just drove around for a while. I actually thought he was going to break up with me."

"Apparently, you were way off." She pointed to my neck. "Do continue. What happened next?" she asked, giggling.

"Sorry to disappoint, but by the time we'd worked things out, it was late. I had to go home, take care of Sam, and get my butt over to your house. Which reminds me, where are your parents?"

"Some party at my dad's office. They won't be home for hours."

I glanced at the fried egg-shaped clock on the wall. It was midnight. I stretched and yawned. "Are you about finished?" I asked.

Anamae downed the last of her orange juice and wiped her mouth on her napkin. "I'm ready."

We gathered our checks and paid at the cash register. Anamae left a fat tip. The waitress stammered her thanks, clearly taken aback by the generosity of a teenager.

We climbed into the Camry, and Anamae pulled onto the two-lane highway to Woodvine. She put on an old CD we used to listen to when we were in middle school. We sang loudly and off-key as the Camry sped down the highway.

It was really too late the moment we entered the stretch through Crooked Dance Gorge. I wasn't sure if Anamae was over tired, her reactions slow, or if there was simply no way to avoid the deer on the curvy mountain road. She hit the animal doing fifty. Its body flew into the car, buckling the windshield. The airbags deployed and I screamed when they momentarily blocked my view. When Anamae slammed on the brakes, they squealed in response, and the car skidded onto the shoulder of the road. I silently willed us to stay on the mountain.

I had a few seconds of clarity amid the terror as the car slid off the edge of the road. James's face flashed to the front of my mind. My heart was ripped by deep regret. Regret for time we'd already lost, and for the little time we had left. Regret for the future, a time that would never be for us. And Victor. The last words I said to him were so full of hate. How could everything end this way?

The car crashed through the guardrail and skipped over the edge of the mountain. We plunged through overgrown bushes and tangled vines. The car landed with a thud, nose down on the tops of densely packed trees, settling on the massive limbs of one of the ancient oaks. As the car continued to sway, the dead deer fell off the hood. Its carcass tumbled into the ravine at the foot of the mountain that looked miles below us.

"Anamae!" I screamed. I stretched my left arm out, trying to find her. When I did, she wasn't moving. I screamed her name repeatedly until I was hoarse. Her cell phone was on the floor beside my foot. I was too afraid to unbuckle my seat belt to try to reach it. Terrified that even the slightest movement would cause the car to shift and send us over the edge.

There was a deathly silence all around except for my breathing, which approached hyperventilation every time I looked into the gorge below. I tried to eliminate the sounds of my breathing, straining to hear any from Anamae. Hearing nothing, I finally broke into quiet sobs, each hitch causing my heart to race, fearing we were going to fall. I jumped when I heard movement above.

"Is everyone all right?" called a man's voice.

After all of my screaming, I was now too afraid to speak. When a large branch snapped and the car lurched forward, I screamed reflexively.

"Can you hear me?" the man asked. This time, his voice was more urgent.

"Yes. But my friend isn't moving. She won't answer me," I said through my sobs.

"Just sit tight." The man seemed closer to the car. "My name is John. I'm a volunteer fireman. I was heading home when I saw your car go off the road. I already called for an ambulance. I'm coming down to hook a winch to your car's frame. That'll keep your car from falling until help gets here. You try to relax, okay? Take slow deep breaths."

"Okay." My voice was weak with fear, barely carrying my answer. I heard a low hum and tried to visualize an image of the man, dragging a heavy cable down the side of the mountain. A thud made me jump again, and new hysteria started at my sudden movement. I shrank against my seat and stared down the hood of the car that pointed the way to the end of my life. An engine started, and I felt another snap. This time, it was the cable as it stretched securely into place. I sat there frozen for a good ten minutes, barely breathing, until finally I heard sirens wailing in the distance. I prayed they would reach us in time. Anamae needed help. And I didn't know how much longer the car would cling to the trees.

The rescue team arrived a few minutes later and secured the car with another winch. Men in climbing harnesses edged around the driver's side of the Camry. A beam of light flashed, and I briefly saw Anamae. Her beautiful face was covered in blood, her long hair matted in wet tangles.

"Help her, help her!" I screamed. "Please!" A pinging sound caused Anamae's window to shatter into pebbles of glass. A man's hand reached inside and quickly checked her pulse.

"She's alive," he said, relief tangible in his voice. He peered around Anamae, looking at me. "Do you have any injuries?"

"I don't think so." I shifted and winced. The seat belt had definitely done its job. "Is she going to be all right?"

"We won't know until we get you both out of here and to the hospital. But her pulse is steady."

Anamae moaned.

I clutched her hand in mine. "We're okay, Anamae. We're okay." I couldn't think of anything else to say to her. I kept repeating the phrase until they pulled her out of the car, saying it to myself as they loaded me into an ambulance.

Somehow, Anamae's parents beat us to the hospital. They ran behind the stretcher as the paramedics wheeled her down a corridor on the left. Mine was pushed further down the hall, coming to a stop in a cubicle surrounded by a thin beige curtain. I guessed Anamae's parents had called Victor's parents because Victor and his stepfather, Will, arrived ten minutes later. Will intercepted my doctor as Victor rushed to me and collapsed by my side. He buried his face in the sheets on my bed and wept openly. I stroked his hair, trying to comfort him.

"We're okay," I said for the thousandth time. I curled my fingers around my father's wedding band, certain my father had somehow had a hand in my protection that night, and then I passed out.

I woke up a few hours later to a low rumble, still in the same cubicle. I felt the cuff on my right arm tighten as my blood pressure was automatically taken. Victor was sleeping in a recliner beside my bed, his hand resting beside my arm. I felt loopy and disoriented. I turned onto my side and groaned involuntarily.

Victor sat up immediately. He leaned over me and stroked my face. "Good morning," he whispered.

"Anamae?" I asked, holding my breath as I waited for his answer.

"She's going to be fine. She banged her head against the doorframe and had to get six stitches. They're keeping her overnight for observation."

"Can I see her?" I asked, trying to sit up.

"Not now, she's sleeping." He bent his head and lightly kissed the back of my hand. He looked at me, his eyes full of sorrow. "When Dad told me you were in an accident, I thought I'd lost you for good. I'm sorry for what I did last night. It was stupid. I'll do better if you think you can forgive me."

I was thankful Victor and I would have more time together. "Of course. We'll get through this," I said with a weak smile.

"Hey, sweetie," Will said as he pulled back the curtain. "They just released you into my care. Can you believe it? They'll turn you kids over to anyone." He said all this in a joking tone while checking me out through his doctor's eyes.

"Great, I'm ready to go." I rose too quickly and swayed.

"Take it easy," Victor said. He sat on the bed and put his arm around my shoulder.

"I called your mom," Will said.

I looked at him in distress.

"She's fine, she's fine," he said. "It took a while, but I convinced her to stay put until morning. The last thing we needed is a panic-stricken mother speeding home in the middle of the night. But since Anamae's parents are going to stay at the hospital, you'll be coming to our house."

A nurse appeared in the tiny cubicle with a wheelchair. "Ready to go for a ride?" she asked in a voice that was too cheerful for this early in the morning.

I nodded in response.

"I'll bring the car around," Will said.

The nurse removed the blood pressure cuff, and then helped me move from the stretcher to the wheelchair. She reached into a skinny closet for my bag and handed it to Victor. He took it, his eyes never leaving my face.

"I'm okay, Victor. Really," I said. "I just want to get out of here."

As soon as we were outside, Victor's cell phone rang. He looked down at the caller ID. "It's your mom. Might as well get it over with." He smiled and handed me the phone.

"Hey, Mom," I said.

"Leath." She sounded worried, but at the same time, relieved to hear my voice. "How are you, babe?"

"I'm fine. I don't even have a scratch. Why are you calling Victor's phone?"

"I haven't been able to get through on yours. I knew he'd be with you."

I smiled at Victor. "Yeah, sorry, my cell's dead. I'll charge it when I get to Victor's."

"Listen, I'm checking out of the hotel in an hour and then I'll pick you up at his house."

"No, Mom. Please stay there. I'm fine. Stay and enjoy the reunion." I was not going to be the reason my mother cut her first trip in three years short. "I'll be fine at Victor's." I hoped she knew my staying at a doctor's house was almost as good as her taking care of me herself. The line was silent for a moment. Mom was thinking it over.

"Okay," she consented, sighing loudly. "As long as you're feeling better. But call me if you change your mind, and I'll come straight home, okay?"

"I will," I promised. "I love you, Mom."

"I love you too, honey. I'll see you Sunday night."

When Will pulled up, the nurse allowed me to stand on my own. Victor insisted on keeping one hand on me as I got out of the wheelchair and we walked the three steps to the car together. He helped me into the backseat, fastened my seat belt, and then climbed in beside me. Victor raised his arm and I slid under it, resting my head on his chest. Exhaustion overtook me. I fell asleep as Will drove us back to Woodvine.

The rest of the morning was a blur. I barely remembered getting to Victor's house just as the sun was coming up, Marisol saying she'd already called the school, telling them I would be out until at least Monday. Victor helped me upstairs to the guest room. I felt someone beside me as I climbed into the bed. Sam. He nuzzled my face and then curled up behind me, whining softly.

"Shh," I said sleepily. I rolled over and woke up almost ten hours later. I was sore, especially across my right shoulder and left hip where the seat belt had kept me from being thrown from the car. I sat up carefully and swung my feet over the side of the bed. The first image I saw was of the blush-colored rose on the bedside table. James. He must have come while I was asleep. I bent to breathe in the beautiful fragrance, cringing from the pain in my hip. I decided a hot shower might help. Afterward, I made my way downstairs.

"Good evening," Marisol said, pouring me a cup of herbal tea. "Sit down and I'll fix you something to eat." She was dressed in a peach-colored dress that highlighted the golden tones of her skin. She pulled two eggs from the refrigerator and quickly scrambled them. While they cooked, she dropped a bagel into the toaster.

I blew across the top of the teacup before taking a careful sip. Sam bounced over to me and put his head on my lap. I scratched him behind his ears; his tail thudded loudly against the table leg. "Thanks for letting me and Sam stay over, Marisol."

"I'd have it no other way," she said. "Will and Victor went over to get Sam last night after we got you settled. I'm glad I remembered where I kept your spare house key. It's a good thing you guys never bothered to change the alarm code." Marisol slid the eggs on a bright blue plate and added the bagel. She set the plate in front of me, then poured a tall glass of orange juice. I ate quickly, tasting a hint of cinnamon in the eggs.

Will walked into the room, adjusting his tie. He bent to kiss Marisol, who moved his hands away from his neck, choosing to straighten the tie herself. "How's the patient?" he asked.

"I think she's going to make it," Marisol said, giving me a wink.

"Well, my work's done then. Think I'll hit the links," said Will.

"Too late today, mister," Marisol said, playfully scolding him. "We've got the fundraiser in an hour."

"Yes, ma'am."

"Dr. Kavanagh, how's Anamae?" I asked nervously.

"She's fine," he said, putting on his best reassuring doctor expression. "Not as lucky as you, though. Anamae has a mild concussion. She was released from the hospital this morning. We're going by her house to

216

check on her. And no, you may not come with us. You need to rest." He pointed at Victor, who had joined us in the kitchen. "You make sure she does."

Victor gave Will a mock salute.

"Would you please tell her I'll call later?" I asked.

Will nodded and smiled at me.

"Victor, would you please move your dad's car?" Marisol asked as she dried her hands on a yellow dishtowel. We're taking mine tonight."

Victor grabbed keys off the counter and headed out the door.

"We need to get going. The shop closes at seven," Marisol said, shooing her husband toward the kitchen door. "I'll have my phone on, call or text if you need anything. And take it easy." She smiled at me before closing the door behind them.

I carried my dishes to the sink and rinsed them before putting them into the dishwasher. A moment later, I sensed Victor behind me. He stepped closer and wrapped his arms around my waist. I leaned against him, resting my head on his chest. It was comfortable being in his arms. But that was all it was. Comforting. As much as I wanted to, I just didn't feel any real passion for Victor, no desire. We stood together silently until my thoughts strayed to James. I sighed guiltily.

"It's okay," Victor said, tossing his dad's car keys onto the counter.

"Do you know that I love you?" I asked, turning to face him.

"I do indeed. Do you know I love you more?"

"Yes." He had to for all he tolerated from me.

"No you don't, but you will."

I looked at him, puzzled by his prediction. His cell buzzed, and I jumped in his arms.

Victor chuckled, "I will show you how much I

love *you*," he said, determination punctuating his Spanish accent. He released me and checked his cell. "Marisol," he said. He turned away to answer the call, but remembering something, he turned back to me, handing me my cell phone. "Try to keep this charged, okay?" He swiped the screen on his phone, "Hey Mom. Yeah, she's fine," he said, walking out of the kitchen.

I absentmindedly scrolled through my text messages and was stunned to find one I'd sent a few hours earlier. Only, I hadn't written it. I followed Victor into the living room.

"What's this?" I demanded.

"Okay, Mom. See you soon," Victor said, ending the call.

"Well?" I asked.

"I was trying to be nice and tell James what happened."

"This doesn't sound nice," I said, holding the cell up so he could read the message. Get over to my house now a-hole.

"Before you get angry, I think you should read the other messages," Victor said.

There were two others I didn't recognize. The first was a text to James sent early this morning, not long after we'd gotten to Victor's house.

This is Victor. Leath's been in an accident. She's okay and at my house if you want to see her.

Okay, I felt bad about being angry with Victor. He had tried to do the right thing. I read James's reply, which had been sent just a few minutes before Victor's last message. I wondered why James had taken so long to respond.

Can't come. Have to take care of something at home

Disappointment must have been evident in my expression.

"And now you understand my text," Victor said.

"Really? What could have been so important that he didn't come over here right away, or call? Or at least text? What a jerk."

But James had come. He'd left the beautiful rose beside my bed. I read James's message again.

Have to take care of something at home

My heart pounded.

At home

Oh.

No.

Suddenly, the floor beneath my feet seemed uneven. I wasn't sure how, but I had to get out of here. I had to find James, immediately.

"Are you okay?" Victor asked.

"I'm fine," I said, trying to think of a way to get Victor out of the house. "I'm feeling a little off schedule, what with sleeping all day. A latte would help clear my head."

"Well, let's go get one," Victor said, taking his keys from his pocket.

I yawned loudly. "Better idea. How about you pick up a couple to go?" I asked. "I think it's the least you owe me for making my boyfriend think I called him an a-hole."

"Totally worth it." Victor laughed and headed into the living room. "Caramel?"

"Sounds perfect." I followed him into the living room and plopped on the couch. When I curled up, Victor covered me with a thick quilt from the recliner. He tucked me in, pressing a kiss to my forehead.

"Be back in a few."

Laying rigid under the quilt, I listened for Victor's car to pull away from the house. I forced myself to stay there for another five minutes before I bolted to the kitchen and grabbed my bag and Will's car keys from the counter. My fingers closed around the keys, and I slammed the back door shut. I held my breath as I drove down Victor's street, hoping he and I wouldn't cross paths. I breathed again when I finally turned out of his neighborhood and onto the road that would take me to Judaculla.

# 14

## Impasse

THE RELIEF I FELT AT FINDING THE BLACK ROVER IN the Judaculla Rock parking lot was short-lived. Just because his car was there didn't mean James still was. The fading sunlight squeezed through thick green leaves, making patterns on the ground as I walked the path to Judaculla Rock. My mind raced as I walked quickly and quietly to the boulder, hoping to get a handle on the scene before I made my presence known.

As I neared the clearing, I heard snatches of a conversation and made out phrases, "went off the highway," "concussion," and "was nearly killed." I crept silently along the fringe of the path, only moving when James spoke, using his voice to cover the sounds of my footsteps. I carefully approached the platform that surrounded the massive stone during the few seconds between when the sun switched off its light and the moon switched on from its perch behind me.

"I don't know what to do," James said, his voice ragged. "I love Leath. There's no way I can bring her to Judaculla. Leaving her in Woodvine was supposed to keep her safe, but look what happened. She could have been killed."

My first thought, or fear actually, was that James was speaking to Ever. *Who else knew about this place? I* became keenly aware of my movements, forcing myself to be completely still, breathing as silently as possible as I listened.

"I understand, son," said a man's voice.

*Son?*

I peeked over the edge of the platform to get a glimpse of a man I immediately recognized as James's father. He was handsome, tall, and lanky, just like James. Silver hair covered the man's head and accented his soft gray eyes. Behind him, bushes heavy with blush-colored roses swayed in an eerie pink sky. I remembered James's explanation for the beautiful roses he'd so often given me. *My house has a rose garden.*

I stared up at the moon. Wait. How could I be staring ahead at the moon when the moon was behind me? I turned around as silent as the grave to confirm the moon's position. Yes, there it was. Behind me. A little higher in the sky than the moon in front of me.

*Than the moon in front of me? Was I staring into Judaculla?*

"Come on home," James's father said. "We'll work it out."

I panicked when James stepped closer to the boulder. He couldn't leave me here. But James merely sat down at the edge of the stone, his father directly across from him as if they were about to share a meal at an oversized table.

"How can we work it out? It's impossible. It's a mess, and it's all my fault," James said, holding his head in his hands.

"Nothing's..." said his father.

"Impossible," James finished. He sighed. "We're not talking about Mom coming back to us Dad."

"You know she's there, right? I mean, can't you feel

her?"

*Has he seen me?* I froze, not even daring to breathe.

"Who?" James asked.

"Your mother."

"Mom's here? In North Carolina?"

"I think so. At least, that's where I told her to go."

"What?" James asked, sounding bewildered.

"I never wanted to have to tell you this, but I think you need to hear it now. I couldn't tell you before because I was trying to protect you. If you didn't know where your mom was, you couldn't tell anyone," his father said in a voice as old as the stone between them. "I loved your mom from the moment I first dreamed about her. And when we finally met, I knew right away that we were meant to be together. But when I brought her to Judaculla, I couldn't treat her the way I was supposed to. It broke my heart to even raise my voice to her.

"When you were born, I started making plans for her escape. I convinced her that the match between you and Leath didn't take. I pretended to be furious about her failure." He paused. "I ordered her to return to North Carolina and to do it right this time. I'm ashamed at how I shouted at her that day, but I had to make her leave. As soon as she was gone, I sealed her out of Judaculla. Your mother hasn't returned to us because she can't." He smiled at James, a sad, rueful smile. "You were her whole world. I didn't mean to deprive you of a mother, but I couldn't keep her in Judaculla. It just wasn't right.

"I tried the fading, but I have my doubts it worked. I don't think it took with your mom. I'm certain she never gave up trying to get back to us. I haven't given up either. Somehow, I know we'll be together again." He looked at James sternly, "So don't you go saying something is impossible, just because you don't know the way to make it happen. Nothing is impossible. Not when you love someone as much as I love your mom." He wiped his eyes. "Don't tell *me* about impossible."

"I'm sorry, Dad. And I do know how much you love Mom. I have something of yours." James took a slip of paper from his wallet. "I found this years ago. Maybe I shouldn't have kept it, but I just had to have something to remind me about how it was before Mom left."

James placed the paper on the stone and pressed down on it with his index finger. He slid the paper to the center of the table. His father pulled the paper toward him. It was hard to see, but a golden seam appeared in a translucent wall that was thin as a sheet of plastic wrap when the note crossed into Judaculla. James's father opened the paper, read it, and then smiled.

"And now you have found your love," James's father said. "I really think you have no other choice. You must stay there. Stay with Leath."

"How can I?" James asked. "I can't be the one who causes your judgment. I'm not going to let you suffer because I couldn't accomplish the one thing I was born to do."

His father smiled tenderly. "They won't hurt me. That sort of thing hasn't happened for at least a hundred years."

"If by that thing, you mean torture and then murder, it hasn't happened for a hundred years because that's when the last man didn't return. I'm not willing to take that chance."

The sky changed, and James's father's image became blurry.

"It's time for me to go, son," his father said. His voice seemed already far away. "I love you. No matter what you decide, please know I love you more than my own life. I won't blame you if you choose to stay there."

"I love you, Dad," called James. "I..."

His words seemed to bounce against the invisible veil between Judaculla and our world. The pink faded from the sky, taking the mutant moon with it. I leaned forward, straining to see James's father, and jumped when a twig snapped under my foot.

"You can come out now, Leath," James said, turning to look in my direction.

"How did you know I was here?" I asked, leaving my hiding place.

"You're about as silent as a sawmill," he said. James smiled as he walked toward me, stopping just a few inches away. "Should you even be up and about?" he asked, all signs of playfulness absent from his voice. "I saw Anamae's car. That was a pretty bad wreck. Are you all right?"

"I'm fine." I smiled at him, inviting him closer.

He silently inventoried every inch of me with cautious eyes.

I breathed his essence, waiting impatiently for him to move closer and take me into his arms. The seconds passed. No longer able to restrain myself, I stretched my arms up to embrace him.

James caught my wrists and slowly lowered my hands to my sides. His brow furrowed as he released me, seemingly lost in an internal battle. He raked his fingers through his hair and backed away from me, stopping a few feet from Judaculla Rock.

"What's wrong?" I asked.

His voice was strong and determined. "I know you heard me talking to my dad. No matter what he says, this..." He motioned between us. "Is impossible."

"I don't understand," I said.

He continued as if I hadn't said a word. "I tried to do the right thing, but then you went and almost got yourself killed on that stupid mountain."

225

"It was just an accident," I said, trying to reason with him.

He looked at me, an agonized expression aging his beautiful face. "There are no such things as accidents. If I hadn't come to Woodvine, we would have never met. If it wasn't for me, you never would have been on that road." He seemed to come to a decision then. "But if I leave you here and lose you anyway, what difference does it make if..."

"If what?" I asked, fear snaking up my back. "You're scaring me."

"For once, you should be for what I'm even considering. For even thinking of bringing you to Judaculla." His eyes locked onto mine. For a moment, I felt I didn't know him at all. Seconds later, he seemed to think otherwise and shook his head. "No, I won't do that."

"Don't I get a say in any of this?" I asked.

"Not this time." He sat on the edge of the rock and stared out over the trees.

I sat down and rested my hand lightly on his back. "We'll figure it out," I said. "There has to be a way."

We sat silently for a few minutes, as if we were waiting for something. For what, I didn't know. Maybe the answer would come to us, if we were patient. James wrapped his arm around my shoulder. I held him close as we watched thousands of stars put on their lights. I sighed, opened my mouth, but then closed it again.

"Don't hold back now." James sighed. "You must have a lot of questions. After everything I've put you through, it seems only fair that you get your answers."

I took a deep breath and sorted my questions, asking what I thought was the easiest first. "Why did the connection with your dad close?"

"Because there isn't a full moon," he said. "Unless

there's a full moon, the connection is unreliable. It's weird that way, more stable on a full moon, and even stronger on a blue moon."

*What was the saying? Once in a blue moon?* How many times had I heard that phrase and wondered what it meant? "Okay. Let's come back during the next full moon, blue moon, whatever, and get your dad out."

"It would take more than us. And, I'd need more than my one gun," James said darkly. "Besides, my dad won't leave Judaculla. Not when he thinks Mom is trying to get back to him. And I can't leave him there to fend for himself."

"But he said he wasn't in danger."

"Leath, he was only saying that to make me feel better."

I didn't want to argue the point, not now.

James stood and knocked loose pebbles from his palm. "We need to get back to Victor's house, so he doesn't get his panties in a wad. He really has a short temper, doesn't he?"

"About that," I said. "Why didn't you fight back when Victor attacked you?"

"There are rules for my being here." James helped me to my feet, and we made our way down the path to the parking lot.

"Such as?" I prodded.

"I can't draw blood." James saw my puzzled expression and continued. "I'm not supposed to call attention to myself. If I get into a fight, or into any kind of trouble, there would be too many questions I can't answer. I have no birth certificate, no driver's license, no identity."

"Any other rules?"

"My first contact with a girl had to be with you."

I remembered James's first day at Martin High and

Talia Morris' frustration with him for ignoring her. How she was further slighted when she watched James and I bump into each other, *"Like he did it on purpose somehow."*

"How did you register for school? I mean, if you couldn't speak to Ms. Wakely."

"I found the documents online and mailed them in."

I sensed he was hiding something else. Worried he would soon put an end to this Q&A, I quickly moved on to my next question. "What did your dad mean when he said the fading didn't take with your mom?"

James took so long to respond, I thought he wasn't going to answer me at all. He sighed. "Fading is something we do when we go back to Judaculla. We fade away from the minds of everyone we've met here. They have no memory of us whatsoever. It's as if we never existed." He hesitated, and then continued in a strained voice.

"Sometimes, the fading spills over into their lives, changing things to construct a different path, a new reality, one that hides the truth of our having been in this world. We do whatever it takes to leave this world unnoticed, especially since we're usually bringing our mate back. Those who are left behind subconsciously adjust their memories so the new reality makes sense to them. It's seamless, fascinating really, how well the fading works."

A feeling of suffocation constricted my throat. "Do you mean it would be as if *I* never existed? My mom, my friends, they would just go on as if they never knew me?"

James's voice was quieter, offering an apology inside of his explanation. "We don't want people coming around Judaculla Rock, trying to figure it all out."

*This was the reason for my initial uneasiness with James. The reason my intuition flared up when we were alone in those first few weeks.*

"I guess my dad used the fading on my mom when he

sealed her out of Judaculla, but I don't think the fading works that way. In my experience, the fading only works when you leave some place in this world, not when someone leaves Judaculla."

"In your experience?" I asked.

"I've had some success with the fading. I used it on the people I met when I was looking for you in Columbia and Charlotte. I had one really good friend in Columbia. We used to hang out all the time. But after I left, I never heard from him again. Not one call, not even a text." James glanced at me. "We were on the relay team together."

I remembered Victor's proof that James had been lying to me. Victor had said his cousin was on the AC Flora relay team. His cousin had said he'd never met James. "Sergio?" I asked incredulously.

"The very same," he said. "I heard it on good authority that Sergio has no idea who I am. Has in fact never met me, so I think the fading worked when I left Columbia."

I took his face in both of my hands. "Promise you will not do that to me," I said, struggling to keep my voice even.

James looked away, breaking my hold on him. "It's too late for that promise."

"What have you done?" I asked. "Tell me the truth."

"The truth doesn't matter."

"The truth is all that matters," I countered. "If you love me like you say you do, you owe me that much."

"I do love you, Leath. More than you will ever know."

"Tell me then."

"I already tried the fading with you," he whispered.

Anger flashed through me, tainting my vision with streaks of red. I managed to choke out one word. "What?"

"Relax, Leath," he said, taking my hand. "I tried, but it didn't work. I guess I didn't do it right." We continued walking to the parking lot.

"When?" I demanded. "When did you do it?"

"Our last night in Columbia when I first told you about our shared dreams."

I remembered the strange sensation I'd experienced before James left my hotel room. His touch on my face, telling me to "Forget this for now." I remembered how my mind was hazy, numb, trying to remember what we'd just been talking about.

"It was wrong, but I was testing you. I wanted to see if you could handle knowing everything about me. I thought if you could, it would be easy for me to justify bringing you back to Judaculla. When I told you about our dreams, you seemed open to the idea. But I knew I had to keep everything a secret until I was sure I could go through with taking you back with me. I used the fading on you that night. Somehow, you remembered through it. So, I'm not sure the fading will work on you."

"Promise me you won't do that again," I demanded.

"I can't make that promise. When I go back to Judaculla, the fading will be automatic," he said flatly. "It's not something I can control. I'll fade from the memory of everyone I leave behind." He looked at me with sadness in his eyes.

I stopped walking and stared at him in horror as my mind raced ahead to where this was leading. James had said he would not bring me to Judaculla. "So, just don't leave," I insisted.

James chuckled lightly. "I have to go back, eventually. And not just because of my father. There's a limit to how much time I'm given here."

"I don't understand." My stomach churned, and I felt dizzy.

"The time we're allowed to be in your world is based on the number of dreams we've shared. You and I have had enough dreams to give me about one year. When I first arrived, I moved to Columbia and enrolled in the final quarter of the last school year. My clock started ticking started then." Seeing the expression on my face, he added. "I have less than two months left."

*Two months?*

"You said you'd stay as long as I wanted you to," I said accusingly.

"That's true. And I will. But when I fade, you won't want me here because you won't remember me." We'd reached the lot and stood by the Rover. James brushed a stray hair from my cheek. "I have to leave when my time's up. My people are protective of Judaculla. And even if there was some way around the time limit and I stayed here, my dad would pay the price."

One terrifying notion after another assailed me. His father tortured, maybe killed, if James didn't go home. Losing James forever when he did return to Judaculla. Losing even the memory of him. And what would happen to him when he returned home? James would be an outcast, just like Ever. Would he and Ever? No. I would not allow my thoughts to go there. I wasn't sure how long we stood there, clinging to each other alone in a place that only ever had us as visitors.

"Give me the keys," he said.

His request shook me from my thoughts. "Why?"

"It's late. It's dark. I'm pretty sure you shouldn't be driving yet. I'll text Ever and have her drive Will's car back."

Jealousy pricked at the back of my neck at the mention of her name. Ever. The girl who gets to live in Judaculla with my James. Still, I hadn't looked forward to driving back alone. It was always hard to be away from James, but right now, I felt especially anxious about being separated from him. I gave James the keys, and he

231

tucked them above the window visor of Will's car.

"Come on," he said. "I'll take you back to Victor's."

The ride was silent. When we pulled onto Victor's street, anxiety filled me as I wondered how many more nights we'd have together. Our time was running thin. I wanted to delay getting out of the car, stay with James every second we had left.

"What was the paper you gave your dad?" I asked.

"That was a love letter he wrote to my mother before I was born. I found it in her things years after she'd left us. I always wondered why she left because I was one of the lucky ones. My parents actually loved each other."

"He still does," I said. I smiled, thinking about his father's dedication. "I wonder if you'll ever write a love letter to me," I said, immediately regretting I'd said this aloud.

James parked the car and cut the engine. Turning to me, his took my face in his hands gently. "Yes. I will. But first, I want to whisper it to you."

"I love you, James," I blurted.

"And I love you." He kissed me so sweetly I nearly forgot our dire situation. He released me, and we climbed out of the car. James held my hand as we walked to the front door of Victor's house.

"Grinds tomorrow morning?" I asked, wanting to put a time and place on our next time together.

"Sounds good," he said.

I was stunned to see Victor rocking silently on the porch swing. "Thanks for bringing her back, jerk," he said.

James ignored him. "Goodnight, Leath." He bent and kissed my cheek.

"I will see you again, right?" I asked as a feeling of abandonment swept over me.

"Of course," he whispered. "Remember, not even in

death." James smiled and stroked the length of my jaw line. He kissed me on my forehead, smiled, and then returned to his car.

I collapsed beside Victor on the swing, watching James drive away.

"Leathal," he said.

"Don't start," I said, irritated.

"I was going to say it's nice to have you home. Where's my dad's car?"

"A friend..." The word seemed to taste bad as I thought of Ever. "Someone's bringing it back later." We rocked in silence for several minutes, me fighting a battle between my worry about James and my sudden feeling of exhaustion.

"What's wrong?"

I smiled. That would be an interesting conversation. Probably the only one I'd never be able to have with Victor or anyone else.

"I'm just tired," I lied.

"Come on, let's go inside."

"No. We need to talk first."

"Not the..." He paused, making air quotes. "We need to talk, talk. I hate those."

Victor smiled, but his eyes were filled with disappointment. The swing wobbled as he stood up. "Save it, Leathal. I get it. You're in love with James. But that doesn't change my feelings for you."

The look in his eyes told me I was going to have to be firm. I had to draw the line. "I love you, too, but not in that way, Victor. You and I will never be a couple. Please, for all of our sakes, promise me you will try to accept that."

He took my hand and pulled me to my feet. "I can't," he said, softly wrapping his arms around me. "The only thing I can promise is that I will always love you."

Unfortunately, I believed him. Hadn't I always known as much? The day had been a long one. I was too tired to continue analyzing my relationship with James, or wonder why I felt such peace in being in Victor's arms. As selfish as it was, I loved them both. Somehow, I'd have to find a balance between these two.

"Come on, Leathal, you need to get some rest."

I followed Victor into the house, where he held me close for a moment. "I don't think I'll ever be able to hold you again without remembering the day I almost lost you. I love you, Leath."

"I love you, too." I added my goodnights and walked upstairs. Minutes later, a hot shower calmed my nerves, relaxing my muscles and my mind. I lathered with sweet-smelling soap and felt the stress slide off my body along with the suds that washed down the drain. I finally knew the truth about James, including the fading. Knowing about this secret and that it hadn't worked on me made me feel I was immune to its power. This gave me hope that everything would work out.

I dressed and climbed into bed next to Sam. The dog stirred, gave me an impatient look, and stood up. He walked in a circle three times before settling back down, his back to me. I scratched behind his ears. "Sorry, boy."

In the quiet darkness of the room, my thoughts turned to James. I hated being apart from him, especially when I knew our days together were limited. But not our nights. Never our nights. I thought of the dreams we'd shared, and I wondered if there would be more. I remembered all those nights I'd fallen asleep hoping, willing myself to dream about the boy in the hoodie. That night, I fell asleep while calling out to James with my mind.

# 15

## Sleeping Like the Dead

I AWOKE THE NEXT MORNING TO A FEELING OF IMMENSE peace. My worries from the night before seemed crumbs too small for even a mouse to bother. I stretched, reliving the delicious dream in my head.

We were walking hand-in-hand on the shore of a white sand beach. It was late summer and a light breeze danced around me, swirling my long hair around my face. The afternoon sun had heated the sand. I remembered how I'd laughed, hopping over the scorching dunes, racing him to the cool ocean tide. He'd caught me, lifting me off the ground and teasing that he'd toss me into the sea. He spun me around before setting me down gently, kissing me as the waves lapped around our knees. We'd walked for some time, watching kites soar over the ocean and chase the low fluffy clouds. The smell of a barbeque drifted over a privacy fence and my stomach roared in response.

He laughed. "Let's head back and grab some dinner."

We circled around, our interlocked fingers still tethering us together. I looked down, amazed as always by the deep contrast of his bronzed skin against the alabaster shade of my own. Another couple passed by, walking in the opposite direction. He raised his free hand in greeting and the wind gusted, lifting his white T-shirt, briefly exposing his smooth flat stomach. I smiled, happy in the knowledge he was all mine. In that moment, everything felt perfect, and I knew no matter what the future held, we'd face it the same way we'd tackled other challenges.

Together.

How many times had I dreamed about this boy over the years? How many nights had I lain awake, trying to figure out who he was? It seemed silly now. I stretched again and rolled lazily to the edge of the bed. Wincing, I rubbed my shoulder, wondering how long the pain of the accident would linger. It would be good to sleep in my own room tonight. I packed my things and headed down to breakfast.

All three Kavanaghs greeted me with smiling faces.

"Good morning, love," Victor said. He took the suitcase from my hand and kissed my check.

I wondered why he'd done that. I rubbed my face, puzzled by the warmth of his kiss.

"We were beginning to think you were going to miss lunch, too," Will said.

"Lunch? What time is it?"

"It's 12:30, sleeping beauty," Victor said. He opened the door, and Sam bounded in. He wagged and danced as Will tossed him a dog biscuit.

*12:30?* A sense of urgency shuddered through me. I was late for something, but I couldn't figure out what. My hand found the pendant hanging around my neck. My dad's wedding band. I felt the it, thankful for the comfort of the ring, but was surprised by its shape. Not a ring at all. A silver heart-shaped locket hung from the delicate chain.

*Victor's Christmas present.*

This didn't seem right. The desire to leave was suddenly overwhelming. I came up with a story to get away. "I better get going. I'm sure I've got a ton of schoolwork to get through, and I want to start cleaning the house to surprise Mom when she gets home." It was a thin lie. One that Marisol saw through.

"Lunch first," she said in her best mom voice. I knew there was no arguing with Marisol. My stomach grumbled, and I wondered if hunger had awakened me from my dream earlier. Marisol ladled tomato soup into a porcelain bowl, and then handed it to me. The hint of sweet basil told me she'd made this from scratch. "I'm really going to miss your cooking."

They all laughed at my slip of the tongue. The Kavanaghs were our closest family friends. My mom's cooking ability, or the lack thereof, was an inside joke. I finished my soup, enjoying every drop. "Seriously, thanks for everything."

"As always, it is our pleasure," Marisol said.

In that moment, I experienced a strong sense of déjà vu. There was a disconcerting dreamlike quality to this warm family scene. I tried to shake it off. Of course everything felt familiar. I'd been to this house thousands of times, had eaten more home-cooked meals here than in my own kitchen. I gently rubbed my forehead just above my right eye.

"Are you all right?" Victor asked.

"What?" I asked. "Oh, yeah. Fine. Just still feeling a bit groggy from the accident, I guess."

Victor flinched and looked away.

"It's okay, mijo," Marisol said, patting Victor's arm. "Everything will go back to normal in no time. Just wait and see."

*Déjà vu or not, something's off*, I thought.

"I have tried to tell him the accident wasn't his fault,"

Marisol said sympathetically.

*His fault?*

"Come along, dear," Will said. "These two will have to sort things out on their own." He turned to me. "I know you want to get things settled for your mom, but take it easy today, okay? Doctor's orders." Will winked as he led Marisol out of the kitchen.

Victor sat beside me, pulling his chair close. He wrapped his arms around me, sliding me off my chair and onto his lap. "I am so sorry," he said. "I don't know how it will be possible, but I hope you will forgive me. It was stupid. I should have been the one to tell you, not Anamae." His next words were hard as steel. "But it was stupid of her to tell you the way she did. That was not a conversation to have in the middle of the night on a dark mountain road. She could have killed you both with her careless poor timing."

I squeezed my eyes shut, trying desperately to make sense of his words.

Victor tucked a stray hair behind my ear, and his warm lips kissed my cheek again. "Don't worry, love. Dad says you'll remember everything in time. When you do, I hope you'll remember how much I love you. I always have and I always will."

His words pulled me under. I felt like I was swimming upstream in a river, drowning in a current of confusion. My thoughts were scattered as I tried to piece the puzzle together. Some things made sense. I knew Victor loved me, had always loved me, and I had always loved him. I knew this to my very core, to the deepest levels of my subconscious. Hadn't my own dreams confirmed he was *the one*?

I found some memories of the accident as well. Anamae had been behind the wheel. We were coming home from... breakfast? No, it was dinner. The cobwebs cleared a bit. We'd had breakfast *for* dinner. The thoughts lined up obediently in my head.

I'd been staying at Anamae's house while Mom was at her high school reunion. Anamae's parents had gone to a party and wouldn't be home for a while. It was late, and Anamae and I were in the mood for... pan bottoms. We'd driven to a restaurant in Asheville.

"You're remembering something, aren't you?" Victor asked.

I nodded, eyes still closed, trying not to break the flow of memories.

"Dad, come in here," Victor shouted.

I struggled, trying to get it all back. Anamae and I singing in her car. Then, just my voice with the music.

"I don't sound that bad, do I?" I'd turned to look at Anamae and saw a single tear flow down her cheek.

"What's wrong?" I'd asked, startled by her emotion.

"Victor is going to positively kill me," she'd said. "But I don't care. He's had enough time to tell you, and he's too chicken to do it."

I remembered the sense of dread. The feeling that my world was about to be knocked off its axis. "What are you talking about?"

"Victor was angry, and I was... well, I was just being me. It meant nothing, Leath," Anamae said, wiping her cheek. "Nothing. Do you hear me?"

*Nothing.*

Then there *was* nothing. I opened my eyes and glanced at Victor. His expression was worried.

"Remember I love you," he whispered.

"Let me take a look," Will said, easing me back onto my own chair. He shone a tiny light into each of my eyes. "How are you feeling?"

"I'm not sure how to describe it," I said. "I know this sounds weird, but I feel a little less muddle-headed."

239

Will laughed. "Excellent news. Less muddle-headed means we're on the right track."

"Like I said, everything will go back to normal," Marisol said, giving my shoulder a gentle squeeze.

"But don't try to force things," Will urged. "I know it's hard, but everything in due time." He took my hand. "And don't be alarmed if some of your memories are a bit jumbled at first. You had a serious concussion. That, plus the trauma of the accident... well, it may be a while before everything makes sense. But this is a great first step."

I smiled half-heartedly, but not because I was happy. I found I had no feelings about the matter either way. I smiled because it seemed that was what he'd expected, what they'd all expected.

I had hoped I would be allowed to go home after lunch, but no such luck. "Your mom is on the way back," Marisol said. "She wants you to wait here until she gets home."

Victor convinced me to watch a movie with him in the family room. We propped our feet up on the coffee table and settled back to share a faded quilt. It was odd how insignificant things seemed to trigger memories. I recognized the quilt as the same one Victor and I had used to build a fort in this very room a dozen years before. This and other memories popped into my head as if announcing themselves before they drifted back to where they belonged in their designated place in my mind.

Victor slipped his arm around me, and I rested my head on his chest. I dozed off and on, finally falling asleep halfway through the movie. When I woke up, I was alone on the couch. Fear rippled through my body as if I'd been deserted.

"I'm right here," Victor said softly. He sat in a chair

on the far side of the room. He moved to join me on the couch, curling me close to him. "Feel better?"

At his touch, my heart slowed. Victor had always been able to calm me. "Yes," I answered. We sat together as the room darkened, signaling the end of the day. "Where are your parents?" I asked.

"Running errands."

I looked at the grandfather clock in the hallway. "Mom's going to be home soon," I said.

"Yeah, Dad gave me the go ahead to take you home whenever you're ready."

At that moment, all I wanted to do was go home, but something nagged at me. A memory from earlier. Disappointment grew into frustration by how slowly things returned to me, and then I realized I didn't have to wait at all. I looked at Victor. "I need you to tell me what's going on."

"I don't think that's a good idea, Leathal. Dad says you have to remember on your own time."

My cell buzzed. I picked it up from the coffee table. "It's Anamae." I read her message.

Are you ukay?

Clearly, she was on heavy pain meds.

I'm fine. Go back to sleep. I'll call you tomorrow.

Live you, Beath.

I shook my head. I'd have to show her these later. She'd get a kick out of them. I laughed and showed the text to Victor.

A look of disgust marred his handsome face as he looked away.

My earlier memory haunted me. Anamae and I just before the car accident. She had been on the verge of telling me something.

*It meant nothing.*

My mind worked overtime as I tried to remember.

241

Something snapped into place, and my eyes found Victor's. He and Anamae had been together. I didn't know where or to what extent, but I knew for sure something had happened between them. I shook my head. "You said she had been stupid. What was she trying to tell me right before we crashed?"

"Can't we skip that part?" he asked, a desperate plea in his words.

"I don't think so," I said. "Your dad said some things won't make sense to me. He said I couldn't trust all the memories. But I trust you. If you tell me, I'll know it's the truth."

Victor sighed heavily and leaned back. "I don't think this is a good idea, but I'll try. If I get a hint that it's too much for you, I'm going to stop," he warned.

"I'll be fine," I said. "It's a lot worse not knowing, not being able to rely on my own memory."

"I guess it is," he agreed. "I don't know where to start." The minutes stretched out before us, and I thought he'd changed his mind. "First, no matter how this sounds, I am not trying to make excuses. I accept responsibility for what I did. I'm sorry I hurt you, and if I have to spend the rest of my life proving that, I will."

I nodded, too afraid he would stop if I spoke aloud.

"It started when your mom's friend Beth came for a visit. Do you remember that?"

Something floated to the surface. Beth and her... *son.* What was his name? I stopped myself from being sidetracked with trying to remember that detail. Beth had come to visit and brought her son. He was older, a senior in high school. We spent the first night shut apart in separate rooms. He was brooding about being stuck there; I was on my cell...trying to placate Victor.

"You were mad because Beth's son came with her," I said. I suddenly remembered the boy's name. Quinn.

Even as the details filled in, something felt very wrong about this memory. *Wait. Didn't Beth have a daughter?*

"Yeah. I was pretty ticked off."

I struggled to clear my head. "But you had to know nothing would happen between us," I said.

"The logical part of my brain knew that," he said. "But I lost it when you texted me the next morning to say you were on your way to the range with him."

Another memory resurfaced, competing with this one. Years ago, Victor asking me if I wanted to go to the gun range. Saying he'd learn to shoot and we could go together. It was too soon after Dad had died. I wasn't ready to share that part of my life with anyone else. I had overreacted, screaming, crying, transferring my anger over Dad's death to Victor, as if he were trying to take away the last piece of my father I had.

"I'm sorry. I shouldn't have taken him there," I said.

Victor chuckled darkly. "You have nothing to be sorry about. I, on the other hand, have plenty." He took a deep breath. "You must have called Anamae, asked her to check on me. She texted, asking if I wanted to get a coffee. I knew if I didn't go with her, I'd end up driving to the range, and that wouldn't have been a good thing. I told Anamae I meet her at Grinds."

*But Grinds was our place.*

I shook this random thought from my mind. "Go on."

"I went on a ten-minute rant and then Anamae put me in my place. She told me I was behaving like a child and should be treated as one. She went to the counter to get our coffees and came back with my coffee in a sippy cup."

I couldn't help but laugh.

Victor's tone turned serious. He gauged me for a reaction as he continued. "I don't know how it happened, Leath. Never in a million years would I..."

My heart skipped a beat. Where was he headed with this?

"We stayed at Grinds for about an hour. Anamae said she needed to go, that she was meeting Matt for dinner. I walked her to her car. The next thing I knew, I was kissing her."

I held my breath.

"I am so sorry, Leath. Even at the time, I knew I shouldn't have done that, but I still did it. It felt wrong, and Anamae knew that, too."

"Is there anything else?" I held my breath, waiting for the final blow.

"What? No. No way," Victor said. "I'm sorry, Leath. I was angry. I was hurt, and she was there. It was a stupid mistake."

"Why didn't you tell me?" I asked.

"I was selfish. I wanted to tell you, but at the same time, I was afraid you'd leave me. I'd planned to tell you when we went out of town on that College Cruise to Columbia. I thought if I told you while we were out of town, we'd have time alone together to work through it. Do you remember that trip?"

I nodded. "Yes, Anamae and I shared a room."

"That's right," Victor said. "Your mom had told me about a coffeehouse, Goatfeathers, and I thought you'd like to go there. But the night before..." He stopped and looked at me cautiously.

"The night before, some jerk tried to attack me," I said angrily.

"He did. Something else I'll never forgive myself for. I got there just in time. I nearly killed him."

I remembered the fight. Victor knocking the boy to the ground with one punch. Screaming at him to get up and fight like a man. Anamae and I both dragging Victor from the frat house.

"That wasn't your fault," I said.

"Yes, it was. I should have stayed by your side at all times. I won't make that mistake again. I didn't think it was a good idea to tell you about Anamae after what happened at that party. You seemed so fragile. And then, you were in the accident." Victor took my hand. "I'll never forgive myself for hurting you. I understand if you don't want to see me anymore."

We sat in silence as I processed this. One thing that struck me was my non-reaction to Victor's confession about Anamae. I loved Victor, he was everything to me, yet it didn't seem to bother me that he'd kissed another girl. No, it was more than that. It didn't bother me that he'd kissed my best friend. And Anamae... Why didn't I feel the slightest anger toward her? Hadn't she broken the girlfriend's code?

Adding to my confusion was the fact I felt guilty for going to the range with Beth's son. I didn't remember why that was. Had something happened between Quinn and me? Uncertainty about that day with Quinn made me think that to be angry, jealous, or even disappointed in Victor and Anamae would make me a hypocrite. Of course I would forgive him and Anamae. My inexplicable guilt would have it no other way.

I reached out, caressing his cheek. "How could I live if you weren't in my life?" I asked.

Victor smiled and slowly leaned forward. His kiss, warm and comforting, worked at the numbness inside me.

*Just go with it, Leath.*

Something sparked within me. Hadn't I wondered, fantasized for years, about kissing Victor? Curiosity gave way to desire as I pulled him closer. I let go of all doubt, pressing myself against his warm body.

"Whoa," he said. "Are you feeling all right? Not that

245

I'm complaining, but this is a little unlike you."

"I guess that bump on the head knocked some sense into me."

He laughed. "Yay for me."

I hit him playfully on his upper arm and grinned.

"It's good to see your smile," he said. "Since the accident, you've been walking around here like a zombie."

That seemed a fair way to describe how I'd been feeling. I'd definitely been in some kind of funk. Looking into his dark eyes, I found some clarity. I felt light as even more of the haze dissipated. The pressure to remember everything seemed unimportant. I mentally squashed the feeling something was missing and set aside the warning in my head that said all was not right. I could trust Victor to tell me what I needed to know. He would help me remember. Impulsively, I hugged Victor close, feeling hopeful about what lay ahead.

"I love you," he murmured.

"I love you, too."

The grandfather clock sounded, causing me to jump.

"I think we'd better get going. Penny's going to be back anytime now," Victor said. "I'm sure she's eager to see you. It was all Dad could do to keep her from coming back right after your accident." Again, he reacted to the word, a tortured expression on his face.

"You have to stop doing that," I said. "I don't blame you."

"But I still feel responsible. If I hadn't kissed Anamae..."

Something flashed in his eyes. This time, I had a reaction to his confession. *Pain*? Yes, pain. And another feeling. Fear. The fear of being left behind, abandoned. I smiled at Victor. "That was an accident, too. Okay? Let's agree to let both go."

"I don't deserve that, but I'll take it," Victor said as

he took me into his arms and kissed me. "Everything always works out the way it's supposed to."

# 16

## Destiny

VICTOR HELPED ME LOAD SAM AND MY SUITCASE INTO his car. He then drove us home. He insisted on waiting with me until Mom got back, which was all of five minutes after we arrived. Sam jumped up from my feet and took off, skidding over the hardwood floors. He met Mom at the door and bounced around her as she tried to get by him without dropping a large pizza box. Then Sam did his special welcome home greeting. His "mad minute" when he ran excitedly in a circuit from the kitchen to the living room and upstairs. When he made his second pass, it sounded like he knocked something over in my room.

"Mom," I said. The word felt so good on my lips.

She set the pizza on the table and scooped me into her arms. "Are you okay?" There were tears in her eyes as she searched my face, my whole body, checking to be sure that I was all right.

"I'm fine, Mom. Really."

"Think I'll head out now," Victor said. He kissed my cheek.

"Thanks for staying with her," Mom said, giving him a quick hug.

"Anytime," Victor said. "Oh and here's her medicine. Dad says she's supposed to start taking it tonight."

I hated standing there like a child, sent to stay with the other parent for the weekend. It was as if Victor was passing off his responsibility for my care. Mom read the label. "This is the same stuff we give some of our patients. One tablet at bedtime. Got it." She set the bottle on the table. "Thanks again, Victor. And thank your parents for me."

"Will do." Victor gave me a wink before closing the door behind him.

Mom hugged me again. "Well, I learned my lesson, that's for sure. The one time I go out of town, and you nearly get killed in a car accident."

"Stop it, Mom. You're being silly. You know one thing has nothing to do with the other."

"That doesn't help with mommy guilt. You sure you're all right?"

"I am completely fine. I only have a few bruises from the seat belt." For once, my memory loss was a blessing. I remembered nothing about the accident, and I was thankful I could spare Mom the details. I eyed the pizza box, hoping to change the subject. She took the hint.

"Let's eat while it's hot." Mom reached for two plates out of the cabinet and put them on the table with the pizza.

"And you can tell me all about the reunion." I pulled two sodas out of the fridge and sat down beside her.

Mom smiled. She grinned, actually.

"I'm guessing you saw Desmond?"

She opened her mouth, closed it, and looked at me.

"Come on, Mom. Spill." I smiled at her encouragingly.

She took a deep breath. "Yes, I saw Desmond. He hasn't changed one bit," she said wistfully. "Except he's single." The more she talked about him, the more at ease she became. "He was only married for one year. He said they both realized it was a mistake, and they parted as friends. Desmond focused on building his own software company. He's spent the last twenty years traveling the world because he can do his job from any location."

"See, it's a good thing you decided to go to the reunion."

"There's more." She paused.

I smiled at her again, proving I could handle this.

"Desmond said he thought about looking me up after his divorce, but he'd heard I'd gotten married, so he didn't want to interfere. He said he hadn't had another serious relationship because he never stopped loving me."

"Whoa." I was amazed and impressed by Desmond's devotion to my mother. He'd waited his whole life for someone he might not ever have. I wondered if I could do the same.

"I know it sounds crazy, but I invited Desmond up on Friday. If that's okay."

I smiled at her. My experiences this weekend, the accident, my time with Victor, it had taught me valuable lessons—be honest with and cherish the time given with loved ones. I wanted Mom to be happy. She deserved to be happy. "He sounds like a great guy. I mean, he's loved you all these years. That's really something."

"I hope you'll like him, Leath. That's the most important thing to me. That you like him."

"I'm sure I will."

Mom told me all about the reunion. Who had children, who was still married, who still had hair. Hearing about the people and seeing them through my mother's eyes made me feel as if I knew them. I listened as she told me every detail of her weekend. We talked for an hour before Sam interrupted us, demanding to be let out. I put him outside while Mom cleared the dishes. Once the kitchen was cleaned, I helped Mom unload her bags from the car, and then brought Sam back inside. Mom was exhausted, telling me she was going to take a shower and go straight to bed.

"Here, take your pill," she said, holding the bottle out to me.

I frowned.

"I know you don't like taking medicine, but this will help you rest. You won't have to be on it very long, okay?"

I took the bottle, shook out a single pill, and swallowed it with the last of my soda. After I hugged her goodnight, I made my way to my bedroom where I noticed right away that my nightstand was askew. Sam must have ran into it during his mad minute. I straightened the nightstand and climbed into bed, falling into a dreamless sleep.

What seemed like five minutes later, my alarm sounded. Sneaking a peek at the time, I groaned loudly. I must have hit the snooze button several times because I was running late. I threw on my clothes, gulped down some orange juice, and tossed a protein bar into my book bag. As I dashed outside, I hoped I hadn't kept Victor waiting too long.

He laughed when he saw me running down the steps. "Slow down, Leathal. We have plenty of time."

"Sorry," I said, climbing into the car. "Overslept."

"It's okay. Take it easy. You're still recovering, remember?"

I nodded as I caught my breath, smiling when he handed me a latte.

He grinned at me. "I figured we wouldn't have time to stop at Grinds. How was Penny's trip?"

"She had fun. She ran into her old boyfriend. It was pretty cool." I told him all about Desmond's devotion to my mother.

"Good for her," Victor said.

When we arrived at school, and after much arguing, Victor carried my book bag to my locker. In the end, I was glad he'd done so. Everyone had undoubtedly heard about the accident. Many of the kids put on misty eyes and wished me well as we passed in the hallways. The teachers were a little better, many saying how glad they were to hear my injuries weren't serious. I'd guessed Mr. Miller had given them a heads-up about my memory problem because even Mrs. Green gave me a break for not having my homework finished.

She'd clucked her tongue. "Poor thing. Just get it turned in to me as soon as you feel up to it."

I was relieved when I finally entered the guidance office, glad to be away from prying eyes. I nearly collapsed on the pew, weak from exhaustion. I was grateful Victor had made me promise to wait here for him. If we waited a few minutes after school, the hallways would be clear when we left.

"Are you feeling all right?" Mrs. Wakely asked.

Her voice seemed to travel from far away inside a bubble, one of hundreds vying for my undivided attention.

*No, I am not.*

I gave her a faint smile. "I'm fine. Just tired. It's been a long day."

"Well, it's almost over," she said. "Hold down the fort. I've got to make some copies and run some errands." She closed the door behind her on the way to what I was sure would be a rest-of-the-afternoon smoke break.

My teachers hadn't given me any make-up work, not that I had the focus to complete an assignment if they had. I checked my cell; there were no texts. Anamae must still be out of it, and Victor busy in class. I curled up on the pew and fell asleep.

After what felt like only seconds, Victor gently shook my arm.

"Hey, Leathal," he said. "You ready to go home?"

I yawned and sat up, feeling disoriented.

"Did you manage to make it through your classes?" he asked in a joking tone.

"Very funny," I said, still groggy.

We collected our things from our lockers and made our way to the student lot. Victor drove home, keeping the conversation light. I was sure he'd been told by his dad to keep my stress level low. I was surprised to see Mom's car parked in the driveway when Victor pulled in.

"Everything all right?" I asked as I opened the front door.

"Everything's fine," Mom said, hugging me. "Will and I think it's best that someone stay close to you for a while. I've got loads of unused sick days, so I'm taking some time off until you get back to being yourself."

"Mom..." I groaned.

She looked at me with mock sincerity. "Are you really going to argue with medical advice given to you by a doctor and a nurse? Especially when one of those people is your mother?"

I laughed. "Guess that would be an argument I'd lose."

"Severely," Mom said, laughing with me.

"Okay, okay," I yawned. "I don't know why I feel so tired."

"You feel tired because you're worn out from being at school all day."

"Maybe." I yawned again. "Mom, can I quit taking the medicine? I think it makes it hard for me to remember things."

"It probably does," Mom said patiently.

"I don't like the way it makes me feel, like I'm completely out of it," I complained.

"That's a side effect," she said. "But the medicine also helps you heal. You won't have to be on it long. Tell you what. Let's have an early dinner, and then you take a nice long soak in the tub. Okay?"

"Okay," I grumbled.

The next two weeks passed in this manner. Victor drove me straight to school and straight home where Mom waited for me every afternoon. It seemed the most trivial of memories returned effortlessly. I could remember my locker combination, my class schedule, where I kept my toothbrush. But the more significant events, like exactly when did Victor and I start dating? Those memories eluded me. I became depressed by how long it was taking me to heal, but I continued taking my mind-numbing medication, counting down the pills as their numbers dwindled.

"Not much longer," Victor said. "I can feel something's going to happen any time now and bring you all the way back to me."

It was Friday afternoon. We sat at our regular table at Grinds. The coffee shop was packed with people. A couple who sat at the table next to ours distracted me. The boy had brown hair with golden highlights. The girl was blonde with crystal-blue eyes. One word could describe both of them. Stunning. The girl was speaking animatedly, engaging the boy in some a conversation that was punctuated by the boy's rapt attention and smile. They looked like they belonged together. I wondered about my relationship with Victor. Did we belong together? If so, why couldn't I remember our first date? Our first kiss? Did we ever look as in love as the couple next to us did?

"Were we different before the accident?" I asked.

"What do you mean?" Victor asked.

"Did we go out? Did we go dancing? Did we kiss? Did we..." I let the last part trail off, but I was sure he understood my question.

Victor smiled and pulled me to my feet. "Yes, we went out." He began leading me in a slow dance beside our table, oblivious to the stares of others around us.

"Yes, we went dancing." He leaned down and gently kissed me.

"Yes, we kissed." He chuckled. "We kissed a lot." And to prove his point, he kissed me again, this time more intensely.

"And no, we have not been together."

Something stirred inside of me. "Why not?"

Victor stopped dancing and looked at me, seemingly perplexed. We returned to the table and sat down.

"What is it?" I asked.

"Leath, we'd only been dating a few weeks when you were in the accident. Are you asking me about this because you remembered something?" He swallowed hard. "Something with someone else?"

The sadness in his eyes nearly crushed me. "No," I said quickly. "Of course not. I was just wondering how serious our relationship had been before the accident."

Victor took my hand in his. "Our relationship has been serious since the first time I met you. I will say this to you as much as you need to hear it. I love you. I always have, and I always will."

"I'm sorry," I said. "I'm just trying to remember."

"And you will. I promise," Victor said. He saw that my cup was empty. "Would you like a refill?"

"That'd be great, thanks," I said.

I watched Victor as he ordered the coffees, so thankful to have him in my life. The kindness of him, the love inside him. Victor was an amazing person. Great sense of humor, intelligent, and definitely good looking. If he was so right for me, why did I feel something was wrong?

*It has to be the accident*, I thought.

The boy sitting at the next table over glanced my way and smiled. The blonde-haired girl quickly scooped his hand up in hers as if laying claim to him. For the briefest moment, I felt like an intruder and looked away. A few minutes later, the couple gathered their things to leave. The boy's keys fell out of his jacket and landed on the floor next to my foot.

"Excuse me," he said. A heavenly scent wafted to me as he bent to retrieve his keys. I stared at him curiously. I recognized the fragrance, but could not place it. The boy looked at me with his beautiful gray eyes and smiled.

"So that's the final test then. Can we go back home now?" asked the blonde impatiently.

"You really need to brush up on your acting skills," the boy replied.

The girl took his hand. "Stop tormenting yourself about it."

The boy looked disappointed, yet relieved at the same time. "You're right. There's no reason to stay here any longer," he said. He helped her with her coat, and they walked away.

I felt a stab of longing and a strange grief I could not understand as I watched the boy leave Grinds. I blamed the unexplained emotions on my medication, but I could not shake the sadness I felt at watching the gorgeous boy walk away. My eyes drifted back to their table, and I noticed a perfect salmon-colored rose. The image did nothing for the odd depression that settled over me.

"Did you know them?" Victor asked when he returned to our table.

"Yeah," I said.

"How?" Victor asked.

"How what?"

"How do you know them?" Victor nodded at the retreating forms of the boy and girl.

"I don't know them. How would I?"

"I think you've had a long day. Let's head home," Victor said. He took my hand and pulled me to my feet.

He was right. Fatigue washed over me as I followed Victor outside. I hated the feeling of being constantly sedated. I was tired of banging my head against the surface of wakefulness and desperate to break free.

I made my decision that night as I stared at the bottle of pills on my nightstand. I'd had enough. I knew the medicine was supposed to help, but all it ever made me feel was lost and alone. Besides, Anamae was returning to school tomorrow, and I refused to greet her in my zombie state. I took one of the pills out of the bottle, carried it to the bathroom, and unceremoniously flushed it down the commode. This simple act of defiance made me feel in control of my life again. I fell asleep, feeling hopeful for the first time since the accident.

I woke up in the middle of the night, awakened by the strangest sensation. It was as if someone were in my room, standing over me while I slept. At first, I thought maybe Mom had come in during the night to check on me. But I could hear her soft snores down the hall. Her rhythmic breathing eased me back to sleep and into the first dream I'd had in weeks.

My heart soared when I saw him. The boy was wearing a hoodie, sitting on the edge of a dock with his feet dangling over the side. I walked swiftly to him, calling out, "I'm here."

The boy was lost in his thoughts and didn't respond. It seemed to take days to cover the short distance between us. When I was close enough, I bent to pull the hoodie off. I begged him to look at me. The hood fell away, exposing the wavy blonde hair of a beautiful girl whose face twisted into cruel laughter.

*Ever?*

*James?*

*James!*

His name was on my lips the moment the alarm clock woke me up.

I kicked the covers away and sprang from my bed, hopping on one foot while I pulled on yesterday's blue jeans. I flung my nightgown off and grabbed a sweatshirt from the back of my desk chair.

Picking up my cell, I called James. I was sent straight to a robotic voice mail message. I hung up and tried again, getting the same result. For a split second, I froze in fear. But I refused to allow insecurity to creep inside my head. James had said he still had two months here. I had to believe we'd spend every minute of that time together. We'd have even more time, once I convinced him to take me to Judaculla and bring his father to Woodvine.

I slipped on shoes and ran down the stairs.

"Good morning, Leath," Mom said.

I stopped in my tracks. Why was she awake? Mom usually slept while I got ready for school.

"Don't worry. I'm headed back to work in a few days," she said.

"Hmmm?" I asked distractedly. I looked out the window, but was disappointed. The black Rover was not in the driveway.

"Victor called to say he was running a few minutes late," Mom said.

"Victor? Why is Victor coming?" I asked.

Mom looked at me with concern. "Are you all right, honey?"

"What?" I asked. "Yes. Just thought I'd gotten up too

late."

"Want something to eat before you go?"

I forced myself to calm down, breathing in slowly before responding. "No, thanks." I doubted I'd be able to keep anything down, but I knew she wouldn't let me off so easily. "I've got a protein bar in my bag."

I heard a car in the drive and grabbed my things. "See you later, Mom." I ran out the door before she had a chance to respond.

I climbed into Victor's car and was surprised when he pulled me close. When I realized what he was about to do, I pulled away. He hadn't gotten the message last night.

"I'm really trying here, Victor," I said, buckling my seat belt. He gave me a wounded look. "Can we please just get to school? James must be waiting for me."

"James who?" he asked, perplexed.

So that was how he was going to deal with it? Pretend that James didn't exist? Worked for me. I wasn't in the mood for diplomacy. I'd rather not discuss James with Victor anyway.

"Are you feeling all right?" he asked.

Why was everyone asking me that? "Yes, I'm fine," I said impatiently. My mind was preoccupied with trying to figure out where James was. I thought we were going to Grinds this morning. Once I caught up with James, I'd text Victor to remind him I wouldn't need a ride home. Or maybe I shouldn't. Just let Victor wait after school and find I'd already gone. Maybe it was time for some tough love.

Victor didn't say another word, but watched me from the corner of his eye the entire way to school. When we finally arrived, I thanked him for the ride and headed to first period. On the way, I checked my cell phone. There were no texts, not even a voice mail from James.

It didn't surprise me that James was absent in English class. By this time, I'd figured out why he hadn't picked me up, why he wasn't in school. If I only had two months left in Woodvine, two months left in this world, I would have dropped out of high school, too. At the same time, I felt cheated out of the time we could have had together on the ride to and from school, time in English class, and at lunch. He could have at least called or texted. My mood changed from miffed to agitated.

A manila envelope sat in my usual seat in Mrs. Wakely's office. "Sorry about that," she said. "Here, let me have it. I was holding it out for a parent who's stopping by to enroll their daughter."

I gave her the envelope and sat down.

"I can't believe we've grown to 816 students," she said wistfully.

"817," I corrected.

"No, this one makes 816. Mark Thomas Polder was number 815."

Either she was joking, or she needed to retire. Or maybe as I'd already guessed that James had officially withdrawn. I decided not to split hairs over it. In another hour, I'd be riding home with him. I worked industriously to finish all of my homework before the end of last period. That way when I got home, I'd be free the whole night to be with James.

As soon as the bell rang, I bolted to my locker and then headed for the student lot. James's Rover wasn't there yet. I sat down on one of the blue metal benches and waited. The car line had reduced to a handful of cars when I heard my name. It was Victor.

"Hey, Leathal, what's the hold up?" he asked in a friendly tone. He crossed the road, coming to sit beside me on the bench.

"James must be running late," I said. "You go ahead.

He should be here in a few minutes."

He looked at me with concern in his eyes. "Who are you talking about?"

Victor was taking this avoidance thing too far. "Okay, that was funny this morning, but now it's just annoying," I said.

"I'm not trying to be funny or annoying," Victor said. "I have no idea who you're talking about."

If this was what it took for Victor and me to remain friends, it was a small price to pay. He and James would never be buds. There were worse things. If Victor wanted to live in denial, so be it. I looked at him, wondering why he was still there. When my eyes met his, I saw there was nothing but good old-fashioned worry behind them.

"Maybe you hit your head harder than we thought." Victor raised his hand and tucked a lock of hair behind my ear. "I think I should take you to my dad's office."

"Why? I'm perfectly fine," I said.

"I'm not going to argue with you about it. I'm not the only one who's worried. Anamae said you'd sent a message to her about James. Leath, Anamae doesn't know anyone named James."

I stared at him in disbelief.

"Look, I thought about calling your mom when we got to school this morning, but I didn't. I'm starting to think that was a bad idea. If you don't come with me to my dad's office right now, I'm going to have to call her." He stood and put his hand out.

I took it and rose from the bench. I knew if I didn't give in, Victor would tell his father, who would call my mother. I didn't know what game Victor was playing, but I really didn't need to have that conversation with Mom. I'd go see Dr. Kavanagh and let him examine me. Then Victor wouldn't be able to threaten me about it again. And I wouldn't bring James up around Victor. I just wouldn't. I glanced around the near empty lot again, wondering where James was.

I decided it was best to get this matter with Victor resolved and out of the way. I followed Victor to his car and allowed him to drive me to his dad's office in Asheville without argument.

When we arrived, Lucy, the receptionist, greeted us warmly. She ushered us straight back to Victor's dad's office. "Dr. Kavanagh will be right with you," Lucy said, closing the door behind us.

We sat down and waited in silence. Victor avoided my gaze by absentmindedly flipping through a golf magazine.

"Hey, guys," Will said in a booming voice. "To what do I owe this unexpected honor?" He sat behind his imposing desk and gave us a grin.

"Dad," began Victor, "I'm worried about Leath."

Will's grin slid off his face as his eyes darted to me.

"He's being ridiculous. Childish. He made me come here to see you, and I'm sorry we've wasted your time," I said.

"What's going on?" Will asked.

"She's been talking about someone who doesn't exist," Victor said.

"And here's where he's being childish. He refuses to acknowledge James." I felt like a tattling twelve-year-old. I continued, struggling to keep the edge from my voice. "Seriously, Victor, I thought we'd gotten past this. I am dating James. I'm sorry if that hurts you, but that's the way it is. You really need to get over it."

Will rose from his chair and perched on the corner of the desk, looking into my eyes. "Who did you say you were dating?"

"James. Of course it's James." I sighed. I was frustrated he was indulging Victor in this way.

Will moved closer to me. "May I?"

I smirked. "Why not?"

Will helped me to my feet, and I felt beyond silly as he put me through the paces of a brief neurological exam. I had to take off my shoes and walk forward on my toes, and then on my heels. Will told me to put my hands out in front of me. He told me to resist as he tried to push my hands together. Next, he tried to pull my hands apart. He had me close my eyes and try to touch my index fingers together. After a few other tests, he used a silver flashlight to look into my eyes before finally telling me I could sit back down.

Will pulled a pad from the top drawer and wrote out a prescription. "I don't feel any bumps, you don't seem tender, and your physical exam is normal."

I gave Victor an I-told-you-so look.

Will looked at me with a gentle expression. "But sometimes after a trauma, there are psychological problems. How are you resting?"

"I haven't been sleeping well, but it's not because of the accident. It's because of the medicine you gave me. I didn't take it last night, and I slept a lot better."

"That happens sometimes. There are many other medications we can try. We just need to find the right one," Will said. He tore the page off the pad and handed it to me.

I took the prescription slip from him unwillingly.

Will turned to a locked cabinet behind him. He handed me a bubble pack with two tablets. "Here's a sample until you get the prescription filled. Take one of these before bedtime. It will help you relax, so you can sleep better. If this doesn't help..." He paused and looked at me for a long moment. "I might refer you to a therapist just to talk things through about the accident."

I laughed before I realized he wasn't joking.

"I'm going to call Penny later and let her know you stopped by." He locked the cabinet and stood. Victor and I rose as well. Apparently, this office visit had come to an end.

"Thanks, Dad," Victor said.

"No problem. Let me know how it goes, Leath. See you at home, son." He smiled and left us sitting in his office.

Five minutes later, we were speeding down the same highway I'd thought would kill me just two weeks before. A gaping hole marked the place where Anamae's car had lost the road. I shuddered at the sight of the broken treetops where the car had finally come to rest. Two turkey vultures perched on one of the lower branches. I guessed they were debating a trip to the deer carcass at the bottom. Victor reached over and took my hand.

Struggling to understand what was going on, I thought about possible explanations for everyone's sudden ignorance of James. Maybe I'd somehow slipped into a parallel world, met James, and then slipped back. Maybe I'd dreamed him up and, for some reason, the dreams bled into my reality. Maybe Will was right, and the stress of the accident was just too much for me to process. Or maybe I was losing my mind altogether.

Wait.

*What was I thinking?*

James was real. I'd touched him. Kissed him. Loved him. My entire being longed to be near him. Whenever we were apart, it felt as if a piece of me was missing. These were not emotions one could conjure, fake, or would feel about an imaginary friend, a dream, a ghost. Something was definitely wrong. Just not with me. Why was everyone around me acting as if James didn't exist? The only explanation was the world had gone crazy. Even as I thought this, my memories of James were riddled with holes. I had a hard time remembering exactly when we'd met. Where we'd met. Was it at school? And where was he now?

Victor pulled into my driveway and killed the engine. "Take the pill tonight and get the prescription filled, Leath."

I nodded, anxious to be away from him. I felt trapped, as if I were in some backward, bizarre world. A world in which I no longer belonged.

"Do it, Leath. Please." He pulled me toward him and kissed me.

I figured it would be best if I just played along. "Yeah, you're right. I've really been feeling exhausted these past few days. I'm sure I'll feel better after I get a little sleep." I gave him a weak smile and climbed out of the car. After I unlocked the front door, I turned back and gave him a wave and another smile. He waved before he slowly backed down the driveway.

I stepped inside and closed the door. I only made it two steps before I sat down in slow motion. Sam stood in front of me, curious as to why I was in his domain on the floor. He sat next to me, squirming on his hind legs, nervously wagging his tail. I stroked the dog's head, remembering how he had become a part of our family. My father had found Sam on the side of a busy road three years ago. He'd dropped the puppy at home, left to buy dog food, and a drunk driver had made sure he never came back. It was a harsh reality for a fourteen-year-old girl.

I stroked Sam's neck absentmindedly as I came to terms with another harsh reality.

James wasn't coming back either.

Moreover, I was the only one who believed James ever existed. Victor, his father, Anamae, none of them acted as if they had ever heard of James. Maybe this was

sort of James intervention. Maybe they had all
agreed he was no good for me and planned this as some
sort of united front. Then I remembered Mrs. Wakely.
She wasn't linked to the others at all. The fact that she
didn't remember James crushed my conspiracy theory.

I analyzed the days and nights I'd spent with James.
True, we were alone most of our time together. But there
were many times Victor, Anamae, and everyone else had
been with James and me. It hit me. I had no photos of
James. No proof of his existence whatsoever. Frantically,
I quickly called him. Again, I was sent straight to voice
mail. I scrolled through my text messages, looking for
the string of texts James had sent the other night. There
were none. Panic overwhelmed me as I realized I could
not remember where he lived. Yet, none of this shook
my resolve.

James was real.

I would not be swayed from this even though my
memories were muddled.

Sam whined and put his head in my lap. I had no
idea how long we sat there in the hallway, but the light
from the living room window was fading, casting eerie
shadows in the room.

"It's okay, boy." I scratched behind his ears, and he
lifted his head. "Come on. It's time for you to eat." I
stood and stretched. My legs were stiff from sitting on
the hardwood floor for so long. I fed Sam before putting
him outside. I wandered around the house in a daze,
going from one room to the next, trying to remember
something, anything. I tried to find any physical
evidence from my time with James. All the while, I was
edgy, nervous, beside myself with worry that I would
never see him again. I wondered if I was losing James, or
losing my mind.

Mom came home armed with questions about my

visit to Dr. Kavanagh's office. She wanted to rehash the details of the accident, my injuries, and most of all, she wanted to know why I hadn't told her I hadn't been sleeping. It was a long and circular conversation. She must have asked me a half a dozen variations of the same question. An hour later, I finally convinced her I was completely okay. She insisted on staying home with me that night and watched me take one of the medication samples with my dinner.

After my shower, I staggered to my bedroom in a groggy sleepwalk. I collapsed on the bed, wincing when I sat on something hard. I groped under the blankets until I found a large rawhide bone. Ugh, it was soggy with dog drool. I tossed it to the floor and laid down. I was so sleepy, so tired, I barely noticed when Sam bounced onto the bed and settled beside me.

The light of the moon shone through the window. I watched golden specks dance in the shaft of moonlight, stretching my hand out to touch the dust motes. When my fingers made contact, the particles froze in place, and then poured to the floor like grains of sand. I leaned over the edge of my bed, certain I'd find a pile of dust on the carpet. There was nothing on the floor but a flicker of light reflected in the darkness. I climbed out of bed. Crawling on all fours, I found a tiny glass bottle. I got back into bed and studied the bottle in the moonlight. It was a vial with a yellow crystal stopper. Curious, I removed the stopper and inhaled the fragrance within.

Thoughts of James broke through my haze. My heart and mind burned to see him. I fought to remain conscious as the sedative overtook me. I was pulled into a restless and fitful sleep. I woke myself, moaning loudly in my sleep.

"Shh, Leath, I'm here," James murmured. He sat on the side of my bed.

_A_y body reacted, immediately alerted by his voice. _A_t up and threw my arms around him as tears streaked my face. "Where have you been?"

"We don't have much time." He rocked me slowly as he held me.

"What? Why not? You don't have to go back yet."

"I've already gone."

I gripped him tighter. "That's impossible. I can feel you."

"No, you don't."

He made no sense, but I didn't care. I lifted my face to his and kissed him while moving closer to him. James seemed to search every corner of my heart with that one kiss. He was lost in me, and I was lost in him. Nothing mattered except we were together again. This time, it was forever. I just knew it. We had to be together because we would never survive apart.

My bed creaked as I pulled him beside me. I wondered if my mom heard the noise, but I didn't care. Let her come in. I _wanted_ her to come in. Then she would see James and would have to acknowledge him.

"No, Leath." James sat up and moved away from my bed. "I only came here to say goodbye."

I drew in a deep breath. "What?" I croaked.

He turned to face me. "I love you, Leath. I always have. I always will. But I have to go back." His expression was agony. He combed his fingers through his hair as his eyes lit up for a brief second. "Just know I won't ever leave you completely."

Then the cruel dream shifted. We were no longer in my bedroom. We strolled down a path surrounded by thick woods to a black boulder in the middle of a clearing. James stepped ahead of me toward the large stone. I didn't know why, but it terrified me as I watched him walk to the other side.

268

"Things will be different now. You will remember our dreams, but forget our waking hours, just as it was before I came here. I won't be far away, but I'll never be with you in this world again." He spoke to me from across the boulder, his voice faint and growing distant. "I will never stop loving you," he said. "Not even in death."

My eyes flew open. I was alone in my room, my breathing shallow and a light sweat covering my forehead. James's words repeated in my mind.

*Things will be different now.*

The hell they would.

A quick glance at my clock told me it was 3:42 in the morning. It didn't matter. I had to get to James before it was too late. After dressing quickly, I forced myself to calm down and breathe for just one second. As I scanned my bedroom, my eyes came to rest on my closet door. Without hesitation, I retrieved my pistol and made my way downstairs silently. I keyed in the code for the alarm system and started to leave when I thought better of it. Motherly guilt caught up to me for a moment; I ran to the kitchen where I scrawled a note for Mom, telling her I couldn't sleep and I had borrowed the car. I knew there would be trouble when I got home, but at the time, it was of no consequence to me. I rushed outside, cranked the engine, and headed to Judaculla Rock.

The radio blared, too loud for the dead of night. "That's right, folks," the announcer said. "Look up at the sky. It's a blue moon tonight, the second full moon of the month." I turned the radio down. As I drove, every beautiful treasured memory of James returned to me, and I knew what I had to do.

It was obvious. There was only ever one choice.

I understood and even appreciated the fading. Once I passed into Judaculla, my family and friends would melt together, blotting me out of their reality.

remembered a spray foam Dad had once used to a small hole in the foundation of our house. As he sprayed the foam into the hole, I was amazed by how it expanded, completing sealing all gaps. I was the hole, my friends and family the foam. There would be no memory of me, and it would protect them from missing me.

Victor was my proof the fading worked. Hate was an emotion as powerful as love. As much as Victor hated James, he had absolutely no memory of him now.

And while both boys had said they had always loved me, I could tell the difference between these declarations now. Victor's claim extended back to the day we first met. I could remember that exact point in my life.

James, however, had loved me since before I could remember. James and I had connected while we were both new souls and his, "I love you. I always have," seemed more powerful than I could have ever imagined.

I knew Victor would be all right. He and Anamae had dated when James was in our world and had kissed when James wasn't in our world. Maybe they were meant to be together after all. Maybe they would be together, if they were in a world without me. And now that Mom had Desmond, I knew she'd be okay when I faded from her life. They could travel the world and build a new life together.

They would all be just fine without me.

*What would you give?*

I smiled and answered Anamae's question one last time.

"Everything. I'd give it all."

I drove into the parking lot too fast. The tires slid over the loose gravel, spraying rock on the road. The car came to rest in the middle of the eternally empty lot, and I left it there, not taking the time to park it properly. Why bother? No one ever came here. In my haste, I stumbled down the path. I fell twice, once scraping the heels of my hands. They burned like a jagged flame as I finally made my way to the clearing.

I ran to the boulder where a single blush-colored rose waited for me. Wrapped around the stem was a gold chain with the wedding token from James's key ring. I slipped the chain over my head, the token making a tinkling sound when it brushed against Victor's silver locket. I bent to pick up a note, held in place under a handful of pebbles.

The note read: For the only one who matters. – James

The sky was clear, and the full moon lit up the carvings on Judaculla Rock. I gathered the pebbles and placed one on each of the tips of the seven fingers of Judaculla, letting the remaining pebbles fall back to the ground. The sky changed, pink clouds swirled, and a new sky opened up in front of me. I stared at the duplicitous moon, daring it to stop me. I tucked the note into the back pocket of my jeans, picked up the rose, and put one toe inside Judaculla.

THE END

# Acknowledgements

I THANK MY CREATOR. WITHOUT WHOM, I WOULD have nothing and be nothing.

To my husband Andrew, thank you for making my heart still flutter after all this time. Thank you for making me laugh, especially at myself. And, for somehow making this whole thing feel as if it's just the beginning for us.

I love you.

"Even in death."

I'll hold you to that.

To Connor and Stephanie: One by birth, the other by marriage both by the Grace of God. I love you so much that my heart grows larger each time I see your beautiful faces. What wonderful inspirations and blessings you are to all who know you. I'm humbled to call you son and daughter-in-law.

To the middle one and the baby, Charles and AnnMarie, how blessed I am that you are my siblings and I love you both. How blessed are we to have such wonderful kids? So proud of my nieces and nephews, Kristin, Mary, Trey, Preston, Sarah, Karen, Hannah, Harry, Emily, Megan, and bonus kids Nick and Sunny. Thanks for tolerating my many Aunt hugs.

...anks to fellow writers and critique coaches for ...help while Fading was still Amāberis, Lynn Chandler Villis, Demetria Gray, Sandra Rathbone, Susie Boles, Mark Fleming and Tom Hardin. Additional thanks to Donna Shelton giving Amāberis a read. So who was it? Victor? Or, James?

Hey, Lynn. How many days before that deadline? Yeah. We got time.

Special thanks to the folks at Clean Teen Publishing for giving the Fading Series a home. I'm so thankful to be working with such talented people. Melanie Newton, Rebecca Gober and Courtney Knight, thank you for believing in Fading. Big thanks to my amazing editor Cynthia Shepp for keeping me straight. Oh, and have you seen the cover? A huge thanks to Marya Heidel for the stunning artwork. To my agent, Michelle Johnson and Amanda Jain at Inklings, thank you for loving Fading almost as much as I do.

# About the Author

CINDY CIPRIANO LIVES IN NORTH CAROLINA WITH her husband, son, and their twenty-seven pets.

Not really.

Just three dogs who think they are children and three cats who think they are raccoons. It only seems as if they make twenty-seven. When Cindy isn't writing, she enjoys spending time with her family and the avoidance of cooking.

Fading, The Fading Series Book One, (Clean Teen Publishing) releases in 2018. This is the first in a three-four book series in which seventeen-year-old Leath Elliott wonders if the new boy in town is literally the boy of her dreams.

.dy's Miller's Island Mysteries series is described .novative in blending science and fantasy. Eighth .aders, Grace and Jack, travel through time solving mysterious science events. Miller's Island Mysteries #1 The Case of the Toxic River (Vulpine Press) released in August 2017. MIMS #1 is the first in an eleven-book series.

Cindy's first novel, The Circle, Book One of The Sidhe (2013), won the 2014 Moonbeam Children's Book Silver Award for Pre-Teen Fiction – Fantasy. Other titles in the series include The Choice, Book Two of The Sidhe (2015), and The Lost, Book Three of The Sidhe (2017). Look for The Secret, Book Four of The Sidhe to release in May 2018. The series follows Calum, Laurel, and Hagen from middle through high school as they first rescue Calum's kidnapped cousin, and then save the Otherworld from dark Sidhe. This series is published by Odyssey Books.

Cindy's article, Level Up Intrinsic Motivation, was published in the JOURNAL OF INTERDISCIPLINARY LEADERSHIP in 2016 and two of her short stories were published in the Children's anthology, Doorway to Adventure (2010).